Palette Knife

A Novel of Love, Intrigue, and Nazi Terror

By R. Manolakas

To Otto Dix and Max Beckmann, German Expressionists who

braved tyranny.

To Millie . . .

"Hear it not, Duncan, for it is a knell. That summons thee to heaven

or to hell."

–   William Shakespeare, *Macbeth*

FOREWORD

Palette Knife: A Novel of Love, Intrigue, and Nazi Terror is historical fiction inspired by true events and real people, during the twenty-two-month period from May 1937 to March 1939. The *fictional* characters, including its main characters, Max and Frieda Bauer, are mixtures of historical personalities, mostly German Expressionists, and high-ranking Nazis. No one *fictional* character is based upon one actual human being—past or present—and any similarities are purely coincidental and unintended.

This period is arguably the most important in history. It set up the international problems we face today. The dozen true-to-life, landmark Nazi events woven into this book were condensed in time, in order to serve the dramatic needs of the novel. That doesn't alter their horror or significance. This story is studded with anecdotes, which are accurate. For example, Adolf Hitler was truly fascinated by the movie *King Kong.* The spine of the story—creative freedom colliding with tyranny— resonates today, with assaults on free speech all over the globe. The Nazis spread their terror, as certain groups do today, and most of us must decide how much we will sacrifice to stop it.

This book also highlights German Expressionism, a vastly underrated genre of art that easily rivals French Impressionism. The story, although set in the worst of times, exemplifies the best of human instincts: courage, exemplified through strong male and female roles; and love—Romantic love, artistic love, love of artistic freedom, and the love for the people who died to preserve it.

— R.M., September 2016

Prologue

Battle of Cambrai, November 1918:

Max Bauer, filthy and reeking from the mud and excrement that filled his smoldering Great War foxhole, sketched the bright cardinal resting in the birch tree not thirty meters away. The vibrant, red feathers rescued him from the misery of war.

Hearing the sniper from the enemy line, he ducked, stuffing the drawing pad back into his torn, grey tunic next to his silver palette knife, which he kept for good luck. Being a sniper too, Max knew that he must keep his head down or get picked off.

The perimeter of the parapet was lined with barbed wire and heaped with sandbags and decomposing bodies, which added to the syrupy stench. Nauseated, he lost his breakfast of haricot beans and bacon. He then grabbed the rifle lying in the mud next to him.

The distant silhouettes of charging British soldiers—against the sunset's burnt-orange background—provided easy targets. Max aimed the 7.92 mm, Mauser 98 sniper rifle through his telescopic sight. The chest of a dark figure—about five hundred meters away—expanded into his field of vision.

He pulled the trigger gently, and the target aerosolized into a pinkish mist. The next figure advanced, and Max pulled the trigger again. Another chest exploded as the man's helmet flew into the air. Twice decorated for marksmanship over the past three years, he seemed to never miss.

He had inserted his last magazine, which held five rounds. The heat from the barrel warmed his face as the scent of the gunpowder mixed with his sweat. He pulled the trigger again; nothing happened. His ammo gone, he threw down the rifle and pulled his revolver. Max heard the whines of the enemy casualties as they thrashed on the fences, tearing their flesh upon the sharp metal. They just hung there as the German machine guns, positioned to the right of Max and down the line of the embankment, riddled them with holes.

The British soldiers stormed the German trench, only to be met, this time, by the Kaiser's flamethrowers. The wall of fire roasted the charging soldiers. One man had made it through, storming Max's trench. He charged Max with his bayonetted rifle. Max emptied his service revolver in the Englishman's chest, dropping him two meters short of the precipice.

Another charged. He leaped down into the trench, attacking Max with his bayonet. Their bodies collided. Max spun around as he shoved his hand into his tunic, grasping the handle of his palette knife. He drove the weapon though the soldier's neck. He placed the knife back into his tunic.

The strange shape of a monster approached the line, gripping Max with terror. Clanking and hissing, the rectangular, metal contraption glided on tracks through the mud. Its turret-mounted machine gun spit bullets as it rolled over the barbed wire. The British "tanks" had arrived.

Three German flamethrowers buried the tanks in fire, the flames shooting through the ventilation holes below the gun turret. Scorched and smoking, the behemoth at last halted, exploding into an orange ball of fire.

At the top of the metal beast, soldiers popped out of the hatch, with the German snipers handily picking them off.

A gentle breeze then blew Max's way. It signaled more death, enemy gas hitching a lethal ride. Mustard gas exploded around him. It coated the ground and his uniform, and poisoned the air. His lungs and skin burned.

The German high command hadn't issued gas masks that day. Often they did little good, anyway. The deadly chemical seeped into the uniforms and through the skin, quickly penetrating the mucous membranes of the eyes. With no gas mask and no ammo, Max looked desperately down the mile-long trench, observing his fellows scurrying aimlessly about, struggling to get to high ground to escape the worst of the gas.

Max remembered the birch tree and the cardinal. They had rested on a small hill. He scanned the terrain in front of him, noticing that the tree and the bird had been destroyed. Only the hill remained.

He crawled to it, inching over hundreds of bodies—almost too late. His neck bled from the welts caused by the gas. Hot pokers pierced his eyes while his legs turned to rubber.

Finally reaching the hill, Max just lay there, in the muck, turning his head from side to sided, choking. He decided to give up. That was when he noticed the vibrant red of the cardinal's feathers—all that was left of the bird.

The dwindling rays hit the plumage at just the right angle, electrifying Max with nature's palette. The firelight from the weapons—dampened by the sickness in his eyes—created a strange halo effect.

Fire enveloped his left hand, burning his fingers. Max, mesmerized by the fading, yellow color of the inferno, felt at peace. The crimson feathers disappeared into the flames. His eyes crashed into blackness as the gas spread.

As he passed out, his last thoughts clung to the beautiful cardinal—and his art.

I'm through killing. Maybe I'll paint you in heaven—if there is one.

* * *

"*SOLDATEN KRANKHAUS.*"

As Max came to, his eyes slowly focused upon the sign hanging on the drab, grey wall: "SOLDIER'S HOSPITAL."

Grateful that he could distinguish shapes and color again—indeed to be still alive—his gaze wandered from his cramped hospital bed down the long and dimly lit hall, which reeked of urine and feces. Countless patients lay on bloodstained cots. The white-gowned, wounded soldiers screamed for their girlfriends, wives, and mothers, but none came.

Max noticed that many of the casualties didn't budge, but just rotted there in misery—paralyzed, suffocating, or mortally burned. Some still coughed up their lungs through their singed, bloodstained lips. Others moved with the aimless, flailing actions of the blind. Max shifted his long body under the harsh wool covers, scratching the welt on his neck, and cursing the itch under the heavy dressing covering his left hand—not his painting hand, thank goodness.

The crosses over the beds marked this as a Catholic hospital. The soldiers knew that Catholic infirmaries slopped out better food and doled out better care. A nurse, a petite brunette, approached Max, striding down the hall with a small gold box under her arm. She accompanied an elderly man wearing the red and blue insignia of a Prussian colonel.

"Hello, blond warrior," she said to Max. "We have something for you."

"I'm no warrior."

The nurse and the officer had stopped at the head of his cot. Max looked away, across the narrow corridor to another wounded soldier. He wore a blood-crusted bandage around his forehead. He thrashed restlessly in his bed. His piercing, milky blue eyes drilled through Max. The man sported a toothbrush mustache, common among the enlisted men, who needed their facial hair to fit inside their gas masks.

The colonel's tired eyes rested on Max. "You're Private Max Bauer, of the List Regiment?"

Max nodded. He saw the colonel fiddling with a small metal object that he had taken out of the gold box. He then glanced across the hallway again, to a small table next to the strange soldier. A sketching pad and pencil lay upon it. Next to the table, a few drawings decorated the wall.

The colonel cleared his throat and shouted in a deep, guttural tone, "Sons of the Fatherland. Today we decorate two of our bravest men." He read from a piece of paper. "Private Max Bauer receives the Iron Cross *Second* Class."

The colonel turned toward the mustached soldier across the hallway. Looking down at the list, he shook his head. "And the Iron Cross, *First* Class, to—this *corporal* here." He pointed to the unknown artist.

The colonel pinned the medal to Max's gown. He then strode to the corporal, pinning the cross on him, too. The angry young artist remained silent, glaring at the floor. No one applauded or paid any notice to the ceremony.

"It's my heavy duty to inform all of you," said the colonel, "that the German High Command ordered an armistice today, November eleventh. The war's over; Germany has lost." His voice broke with emotion. "The Kaiser abdicated. He fled to Holland."

The room exploded in cheers. Plates and food flew through the air. The colonel stood ramrod still, stunned by the unexpected jubilance. Max looked around the ward and sensed the ugly mood. A few soldiers waved red flags.

The corporal—his luminous blue eyes catching fire—screamed, "Profiteers, Socialists, filthy scum! Traitors stabbed us in the back. November criminals—that's what they are!"

Jumping from his covers, he planted his bare feet solidly on the cold, cement floor, his hands on his hips, his forehead dripping with sweat. "Heads will roll!"

Somehow, Max believed him.

Then, Max observed the whole room explode in cheers for the young firebrand. Two orderlies sprinted down the hall and rushed into the room. They restrained the wild corporal, pushing him back into his cot. He fell silent, staring at the ceiling.

Max observed the old colonel as he strode toward the exit. One orderly escorted him while the other remained near Max.

Max asked the orderly, "Who's this crazy corporal?"

"His name wasn't on the list. He claims to be an artist."

"He's a brave soldier, though," said Max. "I think he's been in the trenches too long."

"Yes. The other orderly knows him well. I believe his name is Adolf Hitler."

Chapter 1

Berlin, Nazi Germany, May 1937:

Max Bauer sat at his easel in the oval-shaped studio, part of the avant-garde Bauhaus—the mecca of Germany's Expressionist art movement.

He dipped his brush into the pile of burnt umber paint resting on his palette. Taking the measure of the model posing on the pedestal ten meters away, he constructed the small breasts, the outline of her lithe figure, and the round contours of her buttocks.

He heard the screech of distant tires. He looked away from the model to the source of the noise—an open window. Gunshots crackled. He dashed past rows of shabbily attired artists.

Squinting from the glare of the afternoon sun, Max glanced through the glass from the third floor of the building, to the front parking lot.

Six army staff cars blocked the entry.

Jackbooted SS soldiers fanned out over its perimeter. Max recognized the young and slender officer climbing out of the back seat of the long Mercedes, hopping down from its running board, scoping the premises. His fastidious black uniform, high cheekbones with the slicked-back, white-blond hair, and the white rose pinned to his lapel matched a photo Max had seen in the newspaper, the *Volkischer Beobachter.*

Max realized that the infamous SS Colonel Siegfried Hock—also known as "Hitler's Executioner"—had led the raid on the premises.

Max bolted over to the model and draped her with a smock. "It's the Gestapo." More gunshots rang out from below. "Get out through the stairwell."

Throngs of terrified students crammed the stairs, desperately clawing each other to push ahead. As Max descended the crowded steps, he glanced out the porthole windows. He saw soldiers in the yard, firing their rifles through the shattering glass—the fleeing students like targets in a shooting gallery.

Reaching the first floor, Max sprinted to the back door. The SS men had blocked the way, just as they had the front. Brandishing clubs and Walther PPK pistols, the soldiers flooded the entire main floor.

Max saw the SS looting the gemology laboratory, fighting over the choicest pieces. Jewelry hung out of their pockets. His way barred, he backtracked, running back up the stairs to the top floor, where, if necessary, he'd risk climbing down from the roof to the tree-lined courtyard below.

As he frantically ascended the stairs, Max glanced back and saw the black tunics gaining on him, attempting to secure the roof. He climbed faster, ducking and weaving to dodge the increasingly more frequent—and accurate—rifle shots crashing through the windows of the staircase, sending shards of glass flying everywhere.

Reaching the top floor, he kicked open the emergency exit and dashed to the edge of the sundeck. He looked down onto the courtyard. He smelled smoke.

Max observed the soldiers below, equipped with flamethrowers, torching the faculty quarters situated behind the Bauhaus. One of his old professors—who had caught fire—screamed and thrashed on the front lawn.

Only three days before, Max recalled, this same man publicly insulted Heinrich Himmler—the chief of the SS-Gestapo.

Terrified students crashed through the door to the roof, quickly followed by many others. The Gestapo poured onto the roof as well, beating the exhausted and wounded students with clubs. Two of Max's colleagues approached one of the soldiers—a hulking brute with menacing eyes. The trooper drew his pistol and shot both of them in the neck at point-blank range. He then stole a gulp of liquor from a small flask that he had fished out of his uniform pocket. Max noticed that a string of pearls hung from his belt.

The bedlam reached a chaotic pitch until the sound of three pistol shots— exploding from the direction of the door—froze everyone in their tracks. Soldiers and artists alike stood silent, staring at the intruder who had fired them.

Max saw the imposing figure of the man with the pistol, carefully stepping to the center of the roof. On the way, his buzzard like eyes pummeled the students, as if smashing cockroaches. Colonel Hock glared at his troops. "Order!"

He pointed at the terrified SS brute with the flask and pearls. "*You*, come over here."

Chapter 2

"You there, Private, I said come over here," commanded Colonel Hock softly as he pointed to the heavyset soldier with the pearls. The unshaven man approached the colonel, the tail of his black shirt hanging out, the string of pearls dangling from his belt. The reprimanded soldier's eyes vibrated with fear. He halted in front of Hock, snapping to attention.

"Disorder's never tolerated. What's that hanging around your waist?" Hock eyed the soldier as he would a worm invading his garden.

"I—found it—on the ground," uttered the recruit.

"You're lying. I smell liquor on your breath."

"—Yes, Herr Colonel."

Hock smiled. His smooth, calm voice underscored his menace. "Brandy, I'd say—*cheap* brandy, too."

He walked in a circle around the private, his leather riding crop jammed under his arm. Hock looked around at the other men as he paced, slowly removing his white glove.

Max noticed the smooth fingers and manicured nails.

"The SS man is the Aryan ideal," lectured the colonel, "his motives are pure, his conduct beyond reproach."

"Colonel—"

Hock struck him across the face with his crop, then continued to circle. He unbuttoned the catch on the pistol hanging from his waist, stopping in front of the soldier. "These artists are vermin. *We* are the elite. We do what's correct."

"Sir—"

Hock swatted him across the face again, jamming the crop under his belt. He walked over to the edge of the roof, looking over the side. "Private, stand over here."

The soldier stepped over the low railing and stood at attention. All the SS men on the roof stood silently—also at attention—watching the punishment. The terrified artists and students looked on in frozen silence.

"Throw down the flask, the jewelry too—over the side," commanded Hock as he pointed to the roof's precipice.

The soldier hesitated. Hock pointed the pistol at him. He then complied, tossing the articles over the side.

"This roof is five stories high," Hock said.

The condemned man stood with his back to the men, looking down over the side of the building, to the pavement below. His knees shook.

"Now dive off," said the colonel coolly. "Fetch your treats, head first."

The hapless recruit dove to his death.

The colonel spoke solemnly to his men, as a minister would address his congregation. "He didn't scream. At least he died with dignity. Let his dissolute conduct be a warning to you. There *will* be order."

The colonel strode back to the center of the roof and inspected the prisoners. He selected certain artists by tapping their shoulder with his crop. Max stood there in silence, wondering his fate.

"*Du*," the colonel said to Max as he tapped him. "You. You're Max Bauer, the war hero, aren't you? Winner of the Iron Cross?"

Max nodded. Hock's eyes scanned the faces of the crowd on the roof. "Those I've chosen, go over there." He pointed near the exit. He then barked orders to the officer standing at attention next to him. "Round up the others. Take them down to the wooded courtyard immediately. This smaller group—with Max Bauer—goes right after them."

Chapter 3

The SS men herded Max, with a half-dozen others, down the stairwell in one group, and the mass of students, visiting artists, and professors down in another. Max had pegged the SS colonel—on the face of it—harsh, but correct, in his conduct. Rough justice had been dispensed, but, so far, almost all the captives had been spared.

Maybe this fellow isn't so bad.

Max saw one of his good friends standing within the larger group. It was young Hans Beckman, the Expressionist portraitist moonlighting as a railroad mechanic. His tall and skinny frame shot above the heads of the others.

This gifted twenty-two-year-old—perpetually garbed in black leather and sporting a shaggy mop of red hair—suggested to Max a human lamppost with a crimson bulb. Max waved to him from across the courtyard. Beckman jauntily winked back.

Colonel Hock clapped his hands, and a dozen SS men opened their satchels and removed coils of rope. Each rope had a hangman's knot. The men quickly threw them over the thick, sturdy branches of the giant poplar trees dotting the courtyard. Soon, dozens of nooses hung down, flapping in the breeze.

Max looked on with shock. As the ropes went up, some SS men drew their machine guns, training them on the prisoners, who were alarmed by the sight of the impending executions.

"By the order of the Fuhrer," intoned Hock, "this tribunal— lawfully and properly constituted—sentences the accused to death by hanging, for crimes against the Reich. The Bauhaus, the focal point of infectious filth and madness, is now officially closed, forever."

The prisoners pushed and shouted, but the beatings and machine guns kept them at bay. Max felt he had been duped. Hock's polite veneer had hidden the beast lurking within. "Hitler's Executioner" had been an apt title after all.

The colonel speedily moved over to the smaller group of prisoners, taking Max aside. "As a decorated veteran, you're given clemency—along with the others in your group. The Fuhrer admires your paintings, Herr Bauer. The propaganda minister—Dr. Goebbels—does too. Someday, they may request a service of you. Live, and prosper."

The large group of condemned men, ignoring the guns and vicious dogs, rioted, attacking guards and making a run for it. The guards mowed them down. The survivors raised their hands in surrender, as the vicious dogs chewed on their legs.

The hangings proceeded, and even the wounded were readily strung up. Max carefully approached the enigmatic, SS colonel.

"They've done nothing," Max said desperately.

"To the contrary, Herr Bauer, their language is subversive."

"Language?"

"The tongue of the artist, who paints Bolshevik madness, infecting our culture just as undesirable sperm is infecting our people . . . "

With an artist's eye, Max noticed the colonel's features in finer detail, even as he listened, stunned, to his insanity. Most notable were the pale-grey eyes, which, although of flawless proportion, color, and composition, lacked empathy.

Hock thought a moment and pursed his delicate lips. "Tell you what, Bauer, you may choose *one* person to save. Only one."

Max, speechless, felt nauseated with disgust.

"You'd better get going," said the colonel blandly, "or they'll all be gone."

Not wasting any time, Max dashed over to Hans. He grabbed his friend by the arm and yanked him over to his small group. Usually a longwinded blowhard, Hans stood silently, his scraggly head lowered.

The mass hangings proceeded with chilling efficiency.

Hock cornered Max. "Get out of here. Take the other trash with you." He grabbed Max by the collar for emphasis. "You see, artist, I'm a sporting sort. Count yourself lucky. I'll be watching you."

Chapter 4

Berlin, June 1937:

"Mr. Bauer, do you have trouble sleeping? Poor appetite? Self-destructive ideation?" Dr. Frieda Holtz, a young neurologist who'd been recommended by Hans Beckman, sat across from Max, taking notes as she obtained his medical history.

"Didn't we go through this last time?" Max asked.

"You have a new problem. Your left hand."

"Then let's talk about the hand." He looked down at her from the examination table. "I'm not nuts, Doctor."

Frieda rolled her eyes. "You damaged the ulnar nerve in your hand during the war. You reinjured it. It *can* cause depression. Does it affect your functioning?"

"Sometimes it's hard to hold things."

"You're right-handed, aren't you?"

"Yes. I hold my palette in the left hand. I brush with the right."

"I'll give you some exercises to do—with a ball of putty—you squeeze it."

Frieda rose from her stool and examined him with her stethoscope. She listened to his lungs and heart, then observed the fundi at the back of his eyes, with her ophthalmoscope.

"Everything's fine." As Frieda tended to him, Max studied her, sneaking glances as she worked. The look of her engaged his artistic sense—and more.

"From my angle too," said Max.

She ignored the impertinent remark.

Max admired the work of the American painter Norman Rockwell, and he wanted to paint Frieda in that style. Her honey-colored hair wound tightly in a bun, with her black-rimmed eyeglasses, warm, umber brown eyes—evident even through the lenses—and her trim figure under the white lab coat all suggested an appealing portrait.

"Do you like Modernist art, doctor?"

Frieda palpated his thyroid. "Some."

"Expressionist art?"

"Please, Max, I'm tying to work."

Well, she used my first name—not a bad sign, Max thought. "I received my anatomical training from a doctor."

"Who?"

"My father."

"Does he still practice?"

"He's dead."

"I'm sorry."

"He and my mother almost starved during the war—then got sick." Max's dour tone betrayed his latent sorrow concerning the horrendous event. "British blockade. Then the Spanish influenza finished them."

"That's an awful story. I can relate . . . "

He wondered why she stopped in midsentence. Telling him to recline, she palpated his liver. Her reflex hammer fell to the floor.

"I'm not making you nervous, am I, Doctor?"

She retrieved her hammer. "Your art is what makes me nervous."

"I had no idea you knew anything about my art."

"Sit up."

She checked his reflexes with the hammer. "You got that scar on your neck in the war, didn't you?"

"Yes."

Max eyed the diploma on the yellow wall, next to the Japanese prints: "FRIEDA RUTH HOLTZ; DOCTOR OF MEDICINE; DRESDEN UNIVERSITY MEDICAL SCHOOL, HONORS CLASS 1935."

"Have you seen my recent paintings?"

Frieda put her instruments down on the elevated tray. She took a seat on the stool, again burying her nose in the medical chart. "I haven't. Is this information correct: one hundred seventy-five pounds, six-foot-one, thirty-seven years old? My nurse forgot to weigh you."

"Correct. Don't you like it?"

"Your weight's perfect—"

"I mean my art."

"Sometimes people don't want to explore what's underneath a painting—especially if they recognize themselves in those dark places." Frieda pursed her lips. "Did you recover from the war?"

"Well, my hand—"

"No, I mean *mentally*. You had trouble waking up in the middle of the night—sweating. That's from a note in the chart, from about three months ago."

"I don't recall that."

"I take it the sleep is better."

"Yes, better."

"Why?"

"Simple. I've been painting more flowers. Cherry blossoms heal a lot of madness. *Bad* madness—made by people."

"Is there a good kind?" she asked.

"I think so," Max said.

"You seem to have an interesting perspective."

"What are they?"

"What?"

"Your dark places."

"Can we get back to medical matters? I'm the one supposed to be asking those questions." Frieda shrugged. "All right, then. Sometimes I think I'll have a tragic life."

Max's eyes fastened on hers. As she reflected, he noted a sad note in her voice.

"My parents left Germany a year ago—after the Berlin Olympics," Frieda explained. "They live in Poland now."

Max felt that he he'd better change the subject. He hadn't intended to upset her.

"I'll bet Monet's your favorite artist."

"How did you know I like Monet?"

"The color of your walls." Max pointed around the room. "The Japanese prints. Monet's dining room had the same design. And you have one of his reproductions hanging over there," he said as he pointed at the opposite wall.

"Actually, Max, despite its strangeness, I like *your* art better, believe it or not." She smiled.

Max, stunned, realized that this might be his opening. "How about a lesson?"

"Back to your medical problem . . . "

She smiled—a very good sign, thought Max.

"I'll set you up with an occupational therapist for the hand exercises. By the way, I noticed the small cut on your forehead." Frieda frowned. "I heard about what the SS did at the Bauhaus. It sickened me. It's a wonder you survived."

"It's impossible to described what happened. I could only paint it. But then, I'd be arrested."

Her voice became very businesslike. "I'll leave the room now." She walked towards the door, stopping next to him. "Get dressed."

Max, who had removed his shirt before the examination, but not his pants, threw off his patient gown, and donned his rumpled purple shirt.

Frieda ran her eyes over his nicely defined chest and abdomen. "How long have you had that shirt?"

Embarrassed to answer, he did so anyway. "Five years."

"Very bohemian."

"Thank you, Doctor."

"I want to see you back in two weeks," she said firmly.

"I want to see you in one week," he said, "sooner if you like, but not here."

Their eyes met, the alchemy between them now bubbling. Max jumped down from the exam table.

She handed him the prescription. "Medicine and exercises— look, Max, I told you a year ago, getting involved personally with a patient is unprofessional."

Max felt her thawing. "The Berlin Library has a great series on Monet—one of the few Impressionists the Nazis haven't banned. The picture books are extraordinary—"

"No, I'd better not."

"Let me show you the exhibit. I'll fill in the details."

She nodded and then left the room, throwing out her answer as she closed the door. "All right then. We'll go."

Max felt a head rush, as if finishing a great painting. He had an odd feeling about her parents, though, and what might have actually happened to them.

Something in that story was missing.

Chapter 5

"First, consider using the complementary color to shade an object. The apple's red, so try to mix that with viridian. Do you see what I mean, Paul?"

"I'm trying to, Herr Bauer. I'm not sure I should be doing this."

"Doing what?"

Paul didn't answer.

Max stood over his husky pupil, as Paul sat at his easel.

He took the brush out of the young man's hand and applied paint strokes, the sharp scent of turpentine irritating his nostrils. "The paint's still wet on the canvas, so you can mix the colors on the support if you want to. Make sure you load enough paint on the tip of your brush. That's the number one mistake with most beginners, besides not knowing the true color wheel."

"What do you mean, 'true'?" Paul asked.

"There are no pure colors, —they're all mixtures, —so know what's in them, and mix them accordingly. Yellow and blue don't make green, but variations."

"I don't understand."

Max noticed that Paul sported one of those ugly, close-cropped haircuts, cleanly shaven around the ears, commonly seen with Brown Shirt recruits. He had seen them marching along the street, shouting vitriolic songs as they went.

He considered this art student a mediocre prospect at best. The boy's famous grandmother didn't agree. She sat painting at another easel across the studio. He glanced over at the heavyset, matronly doyen of anti-war Expressionism, and thought, *There's Lena Krebs painting another masterpiece.*

Max refocused his attention on the struggling grandson. "Sometimes I apply the colors in small dots next to each other, to give the piece more energy. It's called 'pointillism' and works by optically mixing the paint in the retinas of your eyes—instead of on the canvas, or the palette."

"Why?"

"Because it's so."

Max handed the brush to Paul and then strode to the window, jerking it open, expelling the biting fumes. He looked down at the vast expanse of the grand boulevard of Under Den Linden, a tony but hectic street, whose huge trees offered passers-by shade from the intense afternoon sun.

The weather, like the political climate, had been unusually hot.

His apartment—which doubled as his art studio, and where he also taught— occupied a busy corner on the fifth floor of one of the many Teutonic-looking, steep-roofed, Neoclassical high-rises.

Like most painters, Max desperately needed to make more money. Already a respected artist throughout Germany, he hungered for more fame and commissions, so he could build a spacious studio in a quieter, more artsy section of Berlin.

"Max, get your butt over here!" shouted Lena.

Max looked at her from the window. She stood with her hands on her wide hips, scowling at him. Even her huge muumuu, splashed with loud complementary colors, strangled her ample girth. Lena loved the Polynesian attire, which had been all the rage before the Nazi takeover, much as it had been with Impressionists in the 1860s.

Max made his way over to Lena's easel, studying her latest creation.

"How's *he* doing?" Lena asked in a grating voice, nodding toward her grandson.

"Trying; he has to leave for a meeting soon."

Lena turned to her easel, with a worried face, applying her paint delicately. She worked in a red monotone. Max stared at the twelve-by-sixteen-inch, stretched-linen canvas, feeling queasy from the harrowing image.

A Great War trench, lined with filthy, wounded soldiers, plunged Max back into the depths of human viciousness. The hollow stare of a German soldier, the grimacing of other recruits, the distorted human skeletons, and missing body parts—all the horror of the war—pummeled him relentlessly.

"It's powerful, Lena."

Still, thought Max, the painting illustrated valor of sorts, and maybe even glorified war, in its own way. Perhaps that explained—in addition to it being technically apolitical—why the authorities had not yet confiscated Lena's work.

"Well, don't just stand there like a dummy, tell me what you really think of it. I'm almost done."

Max looked into her brown eyes, the color of a pitcher of dark tea soaking up the bright sun. Her disheveled, grey bangs, escaping over her forehead from a kaleidoscopic scarf wrapped around her head, partially covered one of her painted, black eyebrows.

"I like it, Lena. One word comes to mind when I look at it."

"Well?"

"'Lost.'"

Lena smiled, wrapping her bulky arms around Max's broad shoulders. "One thing about you Max—" She pushed him away. "—You understand everything. That's why you can paint everything."

"Get back to work," he said.

"Show me yours, first. Everyone's wondering."

Max wondered too. This one might shake things up a little with his Expressionist friends.

Chapter 6

Max led her over to his canvas, displayed on his easel in the middle of the room. Beside it rested a photograph—perched upon a tall stool—of a pastoral scene of the shallow hills and dales that dotted the Prussian countryside. In it, a sturdy farmer, blond and tanned, toiled over his crops with his family, in the bright sun.

Max's pastoral landscape represented the photo accurately, but with a vibrant—somewhat Fauvist—color harmony, a slight distortion of form, and a strange perspective lending a Modernist hint to the homespun image.

Lena picked up Max's special palette knife off his easel—the foot-long, silver implement that he had carried around with him since the beginning of the war, and that his father had given him. She held it up to his painting horizontally, checking the dimensions.

"I love your painting, and I hate it. Rather, I'm *wary* of it, like this wicked palette knife of yours." She threw the utensil back on the easel's shelf.

"Explain," said Max.

"The colors, the composition, the tradition are powerful. It's a cross between Pissarro's work and van Gogh's *The Red Vineyard*, the only painting he sold when he was alive."

"Van Gogh? That's praise indeed. What don't you like?"

"I'm not sure I like the *feel* of it."

Max crinkled up his freckled nose, his eyes narrowing. "I hope I captured the feeling of the soil, the community, the peasantry, the honest toil of the countryside, a simple life. Not like the Prussian warmongers or slimy politicians."

"Yes, I know," said Lena, "that's what bothers me . . . "

Paul's plaintive tones rang out. "I need help over here."

Max had forgotten all about his hapless pupil. As he ambled back over, he admired the remodeling of his studio. He had displayed his best art on the burgundy-colored walls in three parallel, horizontal rows. What light didn't come through the windows shone from recessed fixtures. Black leather chairs and couches filled the middle of the room and led to a bed, a partially retracted partition in the corner, and the bathroom door.

When Max reached Paul's easel, he heard loud singing through the open window.

"What's that noise?" screamed Lena.

"Probably schoolboys playing on the street," said Max.

"Hell it is," blurted Paul, "that's 'The Horst Wessel Song.' The SA is marching down Unter Den Linden!"

Paul sprang up from his stool. He rushed to the window, looking out onto the street. "There they are, hundreds of them!"

Lena strode over to Paul, pushing him away from the window. "Don't mind that trash." She scanned his clothing. "Why are you wearing that brown shirt—and those hokey shorts?"

Max, not having noticed what the boy had been wearing, now recognized the style. He had seen the SA—or Nazi Stormtroopers—wearing something similar.

Lena grabbed her grandson by the arm. "Let's go home."

Max stepped closer, wondering whether the grandson would make a scene. "Paul, do as your grandmother says."

The boy turned red. His eyes glowed with menace. He dug his hand into his leather shorts and pulled out a Nazi armband, winding it around his arm just above his elbow. "I joined up this morning. I'm going down there. No one's going to stop me."

Lena slapped him across the face.

Paul was at first stunned, then shook with rage, his eyes blazing. "I'm still going."

Lena put her hands to her mouth. Max confronted Paul. Quite surprised at his protective, knee-jerk response to Paul's aggressive behavior, Max instinctively felt that Lena's safety trumped his own pacifist leanings.

"Get out of my studio, Paul."

Paul clicked his heels in defiance. "Heil Hitler!" He rushed out the door.

"Hitler's a maniac. He'll plunge us into another war," Lena said as she started to tremble. "My grandfather died fighting in a war; so did my father, and one of my sons, too." She cupped her face in her hands and then sobbed.

Max wrapped his arms around her, telling her softly, "He's young. He'll learn."

Like many avant-garde painters in Germany, Lena had built her career upon the subtle theme of war's madness. Consequently, she and her fellow Expressionists faced suspicion of treason—even insanity—by the authorities. Many colleagues had already been closed down or deported—or had emigrated. Others had committed suicide or mysteriously disappeared.

He guided Lena back to her easel, noticing that the singing had gotten fainter. "Lena, try to paint. Things will work themselves out."

But, deep down, Max wasn't so sure: the savage war; then the bloody, Bolshevik takeover of Munich and other German cities; inflation; and the Great Depression. The endless party feuds and political backstabbing of the Weimar Republic followed, and then Hitler, who had all but extinguished democracy, not without some positive results—full employment, order and national pride restored—but all at a cost . . .

Lena had regained her composure, wiping her eyes. "Of course they'll get better." She quietly resumed her painting.

Max returned to his easel. He had reason to have great hope. Germans now had money to buy art, and Max felt—overall—that it was a good time to be a painter, if one could only find the right niche and not run afoul of the authorities.

He would bury himself in his work and his growing reputation. Maybe the Nazis were like a troubling medicine, whose temporary side effects would be offset by restored health. "Yes, things will work themselves out," he repeated under his breath.

They had to.

Chapter 7

Berlin, July 1937:

Something had unsettled Max as he tossed and turned in twilight consciousness, a place where suppressed fears and dark passions trespassed. He glanced over to the window across the room, noticing a strange orange glow, accenting the ultramarine blue of night.

The mounting whine of fire engines intruded as the scent of smoke aroused him, forcing him to get up and look out the window. He saw a red halo around the Reichstag's spired dome, about a quarter mile away, near the Brandenburg Gate.

Max threw on his clothes and ran outside, rushing off in the direction of the fire.

On the sidewalk, he passed kiosks with government posters wrapped around them: "BEWARE OF COMMUNISTS!" Past the pillared Brandenburg Gate, crowned with the chariot and horses that symbolized victory, Max turned the corner into a clearing just in front of the Reichstag.

A towering inferno enveloped the huge Gothic structure, making the silhouetted statues rimming its roof appear like dancing caricatures. On top rested a giant slab of marble, with the deeply carved words *"DEM DEUTSCHEN VOLK"*—"to the German people."

Scores of white firetrucks, laden with huge cisterns of water connected to hoses, lined the sizzling perimeter of the building. As the firemen battled the flames, the iconic monument to the will of the people—and of a defunct Weimar Republic—crumbled into charred ruin.

A throng of people had assembled around Max, gawking at the fiery spectacle. SS men scurried about, searching out the nooks and crannies of the burning edifice with police dogs. Max, about fifty meters away, recognized the grey, trench-coat-wearing apparition emerging from its smoking entrance.

The intense, milky blue eyes catapulted him back nineteen years, when he lay rotting in a stinking army hospital. Since then, he had seen that same face in newspapers and on billboards.

There stood Adolf Hitler—now Reich Fuhrer—shouting orders at his henchmen.

Max pushed through the bystanders, carefully advancing, observing the Fuhrer talking to a tall, thin, SS officer. The officer's sleek black tunic—and the white rose pinned to his lapel—provided the unmistakable markers of Colonel Siegfried Hock.

Max heard Hitler shout, "The Communists did this! Shoot them all down *on sight*! Like dogs—no trials!"

"Yes, my Fuhrer," said Hock.

A squad of SS dragged a young woman by her hair to where Hock stood. She thrashed and screamed. One soldier hit her across the head with the butt of his rifle, knocking her out.

Max rushed over to help her. A trooper punched him in the stomach, doubling him over. He looked on, as the hapless woman, garbed in pajamas and slippers, lay there unconscious. Max moved away from his attacker, burying himself in the crowd, his eyes still fixed upon the colonel.

Hock strode up to the woman. He unholstered his service revolver, and then aimed at her head. Glancing back at Hitler, to make sure that his boss was watching, he pulled the trigger. The savage violence of that deed shook Max to his core. Hock marched back to Hitler, who met the colonel with a Nazi salute.

"My Fuhrer, the Communist whore is dead," Hock shouted.

Max had had enough and left for home.

On his way back, he recognized Hans Beckman walking across the street—his shock of red hair blowing in the wind. The headstrong artist was headed in the opposite direction, toward the fire. Hans kept his head down as he walked, his hands jammed into his pockets.

"Hans!" Bauer waved him over.

"What's the fracas about?" asked Hans, stopping in front of Max, looking over toward the fire.

"Reichstag's burning—SS men rounding up suspects. They say it's the Communists."

"You really believe that?"

"I don't know," said Max.

"The *Nazis* started the fire, stupid."

"You don't know that they did."

"You don't know they *didn't*. They stand to benefit, not the Communists—long live the Red Front!"

"Be careful, Hans—best go back home." Max's stomach ached from the punch he had received. "I'm going back to bed."

"That's it. Just turn your back, and run."

"What the hell do you expect me to do?"

"Fight."

"Fight who? With what?"

"Asshole."

"All right. I'm an asshole." Max marched off, leaving his friend to shout after him.

"They hate degenerate scum like us! You'll find out the hard way!"

Chapter 8

The unusual summer heat had given way to the cool fog of morning, and that, with the blue smoke billowing from the roaring engines of a half-dozen locomotives, made the glass-enclosed Berlin Central Station look like a surrealistic cloud. This created an artistic effect that the Impressionist Monet—and, before him, the Pre-Impressionist Turner—had cherished.

Max strode down the passenger loading area and across scores of greasy, intersecting tracks, finding Train 63. Its locomotive sat idle and empty in the maintenance dock.

Hans Beckman, chief mechanic of the railroad yard, fussed with a locomotive's clogged oil line. As Max approached him, carrying his backpack and folded easel, his friend waved. Hans grabbed his bagged lunch off the chair beside him. "Well, if it isn't the ambitious artist."

"Shut up, Hans. I see you're still alive."

Max assembled his easel and paints. He placed his silver palette knife on its shelf.

"You know," said Beckman, "those SS swine killed hundreds of Communists. Others too." He stuffed his mouth with cheese. "The Nazis are passing more laws that take our rights away." He plopped the Muenster cheese, rolls, and a can of beer on the chair. "Want some?"

Max shook his head. "Frieda's meeting me here for lunch." He positioned his portable easel, which held a half-finished painting. "I'll have to work fast. "

Max picked up a filbert brush and covered the white linen support with a thin film of yellow ochre, giving it a few minutes to dry. "This man Hitler considers himself an artist. There may be opportunities," added Max.

He took his silver palette knife and dipped it into the burnt umber paint, slathering it on the canvas in rich, thick impastos. "He's a rough customer, though, I'll say that."

"Opportunities? You're crazy. We're next for the chopping block. Musicians, actors, writers, artists, we're all screwed; unless your art pleases them, of course."

Hans grabbed another greasy chair, and sat down next to Max's easel, wolfing down his food. "All the Communists they didn't murder the other night went underground. We're not finished yet, though, just wait."

"Very brave of you." Max used a fan brush to paint the billowing smoke, creating an ethereal effect. "I saw young Hitler in the war," he continued, "he seemed a passionate fellow. A bit mad, too, but he had just been gassed."

"He's a goddamn monster," Hans said.

"Politics bores me. Nothing's worth killing for."

Hans fell silent, munching his roll.

Max stood back about ten feet from his painting, admiring his creation. "What do you think?"

"I see a young man in it," commented Hans, "he's lost in pink clouds—"

"Screw yourself."

Hans laughed. He spread the soft cheese on the roll and took a huge bite, chatting with his mouth wide open, as usual.

"How'd you get that easel in here?" Hans wiped his cheesy hands on his dirty overalls, then stood up to stretch. "I'm a yard foreman, goddammit. Even *I* have trouble getting mine in here."

"Easy. I told the supervisor that I'm the famous Max Bauer, and the competition—Berlin Main Station—wanted me to paint there instead. I said I preferred the most beautiful station—*this one.*"

"Monet's old trick," said Hans.

"Right. You're just not as famous as I am, Hans."

Max lost himself in the swirling clouds of smoke that he painted, applying light, crisscrossed strokes of greyish paint.

Beckman cleaned up his mess, throwing his trash away. "This doctor woman—Frieda. You owe me. Quite a looker; you gone on her?"

"We had fun on our first date. This is the fourth." Max worked quietly for a moment, then looked at Hans. "I think she's grand, actually."

"Where did you take her on the first date?"

"The—library."

"Oh, for Christ's sake! You cheap bastard."

Max laughed, putting down his brush, and moving closer to Hans. He took a seat on another stool, eyeballing his friend closely as he pointedly changed the subject, his voice more serious. "You've got to be careful, Hans. Do you hear me?"

"All right. I'm sorry I called you cheap—"

"You know what I'm talking about. This Communist nonsense needs to end. Muzzle your big mouth."

Hans, donning his oily gloves, looked over to the shiny new train pulling into the track next to them. On its lavishly decorated caboose flew a giant swastika flag.

"Fancy," said Max, noticing the train coming to a sooty stop. "Must be somebody important."

Hans spat on the ground. "That's Fatso Goering's train, the air minister. He's supposed to be quite the art connoisseur. He's a thief, too."

Out of the rear door of the caboose waddled a very rotund man, dressed in the light blue uniform of the Luftwaffe. The medals, ribbons, and epaulets shouted high rank. His florid, round face looked as smooth and powdery as a baby's butt.

"Well, well; look at the dandy," Max said.

Goering descended the steps of the car carefully, his pudgy right hand playing with the huge diamond rings on his left. Max saw other uniformed men descending the stairs of the caboose behind him, carrying large chests.

Goering barked at his minions, his gruff, loud voice audible from even that distance, "Be careful! These are delicate objects. Some are for the Fuhrer."

"What's that stuff in the chests?" asked Max.

"Paintings. I'm talking van Gogh and Picasso here, OK? Goya and Rembrandt, too—the cheap stuff's in the boxcars. He's looting art all over Germany and salting it away in Switzerland—or in his grand estate just outside Berlin."

"How do you know?" asked Max.

"Easy. Bills of lading and the chaps here that spy—they're old union members and Communists. Trainloads of the less valuable pieces are sent to junkyards or burned in some kind of work camp."

A portly railroad official, with a dirty conductor's hat many sizes too small, approached one of the Luftwaffe men near Goering.

"See that guy over there with the conductor hat?" Hans asked. "He runs the place. His name is Victor, and he hates Nazis. He knows all about the stolen art."

Hans waved his colleague over. Finishing his conversation with the air force recruit, Victor ambled over to Hans and Max.

"Aren't you done with the oil line yet?" Victor asked. "Who's this?"

"Victor, this is my good friend Max Bauer."

Max shook Victor's hand. The railroad manager had a sympathetic look in his eyes and a gentlemanly, but direct, manner that suggested integrity.

"I admire your work," said Victor to Max.

Hans put his hand on the railroad man's shoulder. "I told Max about these art shipments."

Victor lowered his voice. "Not here." He shook his shaggy, messy head of black hair. "Ears are everywhere." His prudent eyes crawled over Max, sizing him up.

Max felt acceptance, but not trust—not yet anyway.

"Bring Max around again sometime for lunch. Now, it's back to work for all of us."

Victor walked off, crossing the gangplank, heading toward some offices.

"A great guy," said Hans. "His wife disappeared late one night, after a prohibited union meeting—*Nacht und Nebel*."

"Night and Fog?" Max shook his head. "That's awful. The Gestapo, most likely."

Hans nodded.

Max walked back over to his easel and packed up his art supplies. He glanced at his watch. "I'm joining Frieda in the station cafe."

"She's a headstrong girl," Hans said, "too smart for you."

"Sure. I'm holding a salon next week. Lena Krebs will be there, so will others—Expressionists mostly. Tell you more about it later."

Ready to leave, Max placed his hand gently upon Hans's shoulder, his eyes intense.

"Think about what I said."

"Of course," Hans said.

"Work hard and forget politics."

Hans picked up his oil funnel. "But will *it* forget *us*?"

Chapter 9

"WELCOME TO WANNSEE BEACH."

Max and Frieda strolled under the sign hanging over the green and white striped, public beach house, located just west of Berlin, welcoming bathers to one of the longest beaches in Europe. Hardly a bare spot on the hot sand could be seen, with the unseasonably hot Sunday afternoon attracting record crowds to the huge lake.

Max pointed to an empty place just beyond the lifeguard station. They raced to it, spreading their towels. Frieda tossed down her straw pocketbook, and they sat down next to each other in their street clothes.

"My God, you're mad," said Frieda. She laughed. "Look at the way you're dressed."

"How about you, country girl?"

"What's wrong with it?" Frieda said, feigning anger.

"Anyway, to an artist, madness is the ultimate compliment."

"Where are my glasses?" she said, rummaging through her purse. "Oh well, I only need them for reading, anyway."

"You know, your eyes are too pretty to hide behind lenses."

"I'm surprised they let that happen," said Frieda.

"What, your eyes being too pretty?"

"Look at the sign, silly."

Max, aware of the German obsession with signs, spied the one near the shoreline:

"NUDE BATHERS *ACROSS* LAKE ONLY . . . "

"Oh, Nazis don't mind nudity, I can attest to that. Look at their art," commented Max.

He removed his stylish tan fedora, and the white bush shirt with the wide pockets. Next his olive tall pants came off, and then his brown oxfords and socks. His red bathing suit lit up in the bright sun. Max piled the clothing in a bundle at one corner of his towel.

He looked at what Frieda wore. *And she's a* city *girl?* Max tried hard to suppress a laugh and nudged her with his elbow. "Your turn, *Heidi*."

"I'm going to the tent," Frieda said firmly. "Don't think I'm a prude."

"Why would I think that?"

"I'm not."

"Prove it."

Frieda, to Max's surprise, jumped up from her towel. She looked around at the people lying around them, couples and families enjoying the sand and the water.

She successively peeled off her *trachtendirndl*—a traditional country dress, with a tight cotton bodice and a full skirt. The white silk blouse, with puffed and gathered sleeves—and the heavily embroidered collar—came off too.

As she removed the pieces of clothing, Max realized that Frieda, being a medical genius, probably wasn't used to many things ordinary people did, including holiday beach trips. "You know, Frieda, you surprised me wearing something like that."

"Well, I try not to stand out too much," she said—as far as Max could gather—in all earnestness.

"You wouldn't in the Tyrol . . . "

She twirled around in her blue one-piece bathing suit, her arms extended from her side as if modeling in a fashion show. "There, happy now?" She picked up the pieces of clothing and threw them on her towel.

"But you're too fat to wear that—"

"Fat! At five-seven, and one hundred and ten pounds—"

"Too *old* then."

Frieda plopped down on the towel, scooping two fists of sand, and threw them at her tormentor. "I'm seven years younger than you!" She started laughing.

Max grabbed Frieda's elbow and playfully drew her to him, rolling with her in the sand, pouring some over her head. He put a handful down her back.

Max felt that she had been having a good time. Good thing too, because something gnawed at her from the inside, but what, he couldn't tell.

He turned toward the blanket a few feet away, noticing a frail woman with grey hair. She sat with a man, a younger woman, and a little boy. Apparently, a grandmother out with her family—Max surmised. The woman then smiled knowingly at him, as if she remembered what it was like to be young and in love—and full of life.

Frieda sprang up from her towel and pointed to the water. "Let's go, Bauer."

Max considered Frieda a fun puzzle. He had expected her to be dressed in one of those fancy, expensive summer getups, but he had been wrong. This buttoned-up neurologist, from snooty Dresden, definitely had a zany side to her.

He liked that. "I'll race you down there."

They tore off to the shoreline between the tightly packed bodies, kicking up sand and trampling deserted towels. At the water's edge, Max picked up Frieda and stepped in deeper, to his thighs, tossing her in. He dove in after her.

They wrestled in the lake, trying to dunk each other. He held her tight.

They embraced and then kissed . . .

Frieda glanced to the shore and the onlookers and then pushed him gently away. "Let's get something to eat."

"There's a grill at the tent," Max said, "do you like knockwurst?"

"Naturally. Can't you tell by my outfit?"

Max loved that answer. In fact, he was beginning to love *her*.

As she climbed out of the water in front of him, Max appreciated her appealing lines and the slight apricot hue of her fair skin—how it played with the light. Her honey hair sparkled. Her agile figure allured him, and her quick mind closed the deal.

As they approached their towels, Max noticed the black tunics and jackboots on the sand. SS soldiers had formed a circle around the family next to their towel.

The grandmother cried as the soldiers pushed the father of the little boy off the blanket. One Nazi officer pointed over to a sign by the lifeguard station.

The mother picked up the boy, her eyes wild with fear. The soldiers herded the family off the beach.

Max and Frieda looked on with disgust. They dressed silently, picking up their towels, heading for the tent. Max detoured close to the sign.

As they passed it, he read the words: "NON-ARYANS FORBIDDEN."

Max looked into Frieda's sensitive eyes, recognizing the revulsion that he also felt.

"I'm not hungry," said Frieda.

"I know," he agreed. "Let's get out of here."

Chapter 10

Max and Frieda hopped off the *S-Bahn*, the electric trolley that connected West Wannsee Station to central Berlin, via the Kurfurstendamm Station. They walked south along the tony boulevard's shops and restaurants. The huge glockenspiel next to the war monument struck six—the night still young.

Max had planned to walk Frieda to her apartment just a few blocks up. Ashamed that he couldn't yet afford to take her to nice restaurants, every one they passed rubbed in his poverty. All his money had gone into his painting and rent—and his new gallery, which would soon open.

The elegant Cafe Heck, a favorite *bierstube* of the Nazi elite, sounded of lively conversation and flowing spirits. A charming, ivy-covered fence and strings of colored lights stretched out in front of the hardwood trees, beckoning him almost as much as the aroma of the roasted pork and fresh-baked strudel.

As they ambled down the spacious sidewalk, they enjoyed the neon signs and art deco lanterns that had just been installed throughout the city—the creation of Minister Speer, Hitler's architect. They passed the venerable Vox nightclub, an avant-garde cabaret before the Nazi takeover, now a respectable supper club that featured Wagner and marching tunes.

Max noticed that the crowds were light and the autos few. As they approached a major cross street, he noted that policemen had blocked off the traffic. Huge parade floats, lit up like Christmas trees, glided above the sea of heads that had lined up along the festival route.

The booming music from Richard Wagner's "The Ride of the Valkyries," from the opera *Die Walküre*, rang out into the full-mooned sky.

"I think I know about this parade," Max said to Frieda, "it comes from Munich."

His guess confirmed by the Roman togas and powdered wigs of the actors perched upon the floats, he took Frieda's hand and led her in the opposite direction.

Like a fish fighting a hook, she resisted. She yanked him toward the spectacle. "It looks interesting."

Frieda had high spirits and a mind of her own, and that appealed to Max, but he had his doubts about this parade.

"Oh, it's interesting all right."

Max's artist friends, hardly shocked by anything, had warned him about the ribald pageantry, imaginative decorations, and risqué "costumes." He plowed through the crowd lining the street, securing them a place up close.

"Let me know when you want to go," he said.

"What's the theme?" she asked.

"Skin—"

"What!"

"The parade's called 'The Night of the Amazons,'" said Max, "and the theme is *skin*."

"All right, let's try it," she said softly, as a loving wife would prod a recalcitrant husband.

Max looked sideways down the parade route and saw the approaching float, a rolling stage with sets, props, and young men and women—mostly women—which glided by them with the impact of a Freudian dream. The extraordinary range of Wagner's musical piece synergized with the strangely erotic images.

Oceans of white silk strands intersected in the mounted spotlights, enveloping the floats with a cloudlike aura. Tall young women, at least six foot by Max's estimate, posed on different levels of the cloud, holding long, shining swords, their points resting on the set's cottony base.

Barefoot, the women wore their hair up on their heads, pinned up with diamond tiaras, sparkling in the lights. The perfectly toned, lean bodies sparkled too, for they stood completely nude, their muscles heavily oiled, the shadows contouring them to hint power, not just beauty. The women, many blonde, wore no makeup whatsoever, and no jewelry aside from what rested on their heads.

To Max's mind, a kitschy, erotic symbolism of national power—not just sex—provided the subtext for this bizarre peep show.

"I see what you were talking about," Frieda said.

Max looked around at the crowd. Most observers also looked stunned by the savage immodesty. Some were elated—mostly men—and a few drunks had started fights. SS guards, monitoring the parade route, singled out one young dissenter who had thrown raw eggs. They beat him savagely.

Max, having been distracted by the parade, noticed—distressingly—that Frieda had disappeared. He quickly broke away from the crowd. Frantic to find her, he desperately scanned the faces of oncoming strangers, rushing to view the parade.

He finally saw her standing next to a kiosk—one with a picture of Frederick the Great wrapped around it. The old warrior's dour stare burned into Max's eyes, the distant, Wagnerian music making them even more menacing.

"I was worried." Max gently cupped her elbow with his hand. "Why did you run off like that?"

"I'll continue home—you don't need to escort me."

"What's wrong?"

"What's *wrong*?"

He regretted the stupid question as soon as he had uttered it. "I know. I warned you, didn't I?"

"Yes, you did." She put her hand gently on his shoulder. "I'll see you soon."

"Can I call you later?" *Dash it all*, he thought, *there goes the evening—hopefully not more.*

She nodded and then took off down the street in the opposite direction of the parade. Max watched her, her loveliness pulling him with her. He thought it best, though, not to go after her.

Then she turned and waved at him—with a smile—and continued on her way.

That picked him up. He also felt that something was happening out there that night, a speeding train with no brakes.

And he still thought something else—deep down—nettled Frieda.

Chapter 11

"WILLKOMMEN IN SCHLACHTHOF 1"

The banner hung over the entrance of Max's new gallery, the thick yellow letters popping out of a purple background: "WELCOME TO SLAUGHTERHOUSE 1."

Slaughterhouse 1, a defunct and rotting structure that Max had leased and renovated with a small loan from Lena Krebs, had finally opened. Just past the entrance, he greeted his guests with a warm handshake and a table full of champagne. The drinks waited in sparkling goblets of Dresden crystal.

"Good evening, Minister Goebbels." Max swallowed hard when he recognized the face of the approaching guest. "I hope you and your lovely wife are well."

The minister's limp, often attributed to a childhood illness, had been very evident when he walked in. Max hadn't expected Adolf Hitler's minister of propaganda and enlightenment—Joseph Goebbels—to show up so early at the open house—or at all, for that matter. Although possibly a lucky break, his attendance could also harken disaster.

Moreover, knowing that the minister might be there, Frieda had declined to attend. Max understood, but her absence saddened him, and he wondered how much more there was to it than dislike.

Goebbels held up his glass to the host, oblivious to his empty-handed wife. "To Max Bauer, the war hero, the great artist." He took a small sip from his goblet. "I hesitated to come tonight. Not because of you, Herr Bauer. It's the other artists I'm not sure of."

Max let the comment pass. He allowed his trained artist's eye to quickly scan the famous guest from head to toe—a fascinating study in caricature. Small-gutted and rodent like in his tux, Goebbels trapped you behind the big, brown curtains of his fawnlike gaze, which simultaneously exuded both innocence and evil. Max thought that if he had to paint this strange man, he would do it as an allegory—using the body parts of several different, unsavory animals.

"Magda here told me all about your art," Goebbels said, deftly changing the subject, as he waved his small hand at his wife. "She's a fervent party member from way back."

Max bowed his head to the stately lady, hiding his irritation at the husband's lack of a formal introduction—and manners. "Thank you for coming, Madame."

Magda nodded, started to say something, then remained silent after glancing at her husband, who cast her a disapproving glance.

"I hope you like my gallery, Herr Minister."

Somewhat nervous, Max glanced around the vast, rectangular space, the walls painted in four shades of grey. He scanned the diagonal rows of paintings, with the largest pieces in the middle. Some pictures hung from meat hooks. Carving tables displayed prints. Cozy chairs lined the center of the enclosure, and sinks, which once held choice cuts of beef, now held sculptures. This working-class aura contrasted with the classical music playing from the phonograph: Bach's sugary Brandenburg Concerto no. 3 in G Major. He couldn't afford an orchestra.

"Why a slaughterhouse?" asked the minister pointedly.

"In most good paintings, it's what's below the surface that counts. Underneath, the skin, bones, and sinews tell the story," responded Max. "What could be more fitting?"

Goebbels chuckled, his eyes aggressive, not mirthful. "Bones, sinews? To me the atmosphere symbolizes the simple and honest work of our folk," added Goebbels.

"Actually, it's all I can afford. I hope the art pleases you and your lovely wife."

Max's remark produced a sharp look. "If I thought I'd loathe the paintings, Herr Bauer, there wouldn't be paintings to see."

Max caught the ominous implication. He considered how the Nazis distrusted Modernism in any fashion, except most weaponry. His business venture, risky at best due to the changing times, enjoyed an avant-garde location in the bohemian Kreutzberg section of Berlin, near the River Spree.

Up to his eyeballs in hock, he'd gambled everything.

"Herr Bauer, do you like flowers?" Magda asked.

"Of course. I refer you to my paintings, Frau Goebbels."

Magda Goebbels, a head taller than her husband—and unlike him, a poster-perfect, Nordic human—wore a flowing, pink-chiffon evening dress, with her golden pigtails hanging down past her ample shoulders. Considering her middle age, the oddness of the hairdo struck Max. Her dull, green eyes betrayed loneliness, reminding him of a caged monkey.

"I don't recognize your guests," said the minister, glancing around.

Other guests arrived, stacking up behind them. Max waved at them intermittently. They included local business people, artists, and a few civil servants.

Compared with his black slacks, turtleneck, and loafers—more in line with the clothing worn by most—Max considered the minister and his wife tastelessly overdressed for this strictly informal affair. Goebbels's suspicious eyes frisked the other guests as they ambled by and then refocused on Max.

"I've admired your work for a long time. Most of it, anyway."

"Oh?" Max longed to move on to the other guests and out of the danger zone. He could feel the change in the mercurial minister's mood, now more aggressive.

"You capture the heroic spirit of the German farmer, Herr Bauer." Goebbels glanced up at his wife with those liquid-chocolate eyes, she nodding in agreement with her husband "The surreal quality is hard to mix with traditional ideals," he added.

Surprised at the golden, deep tones from such a little man—and his perfect diction—Max saw in the propaganda minister a bundle of contradictions. One thing he knew for sure, the minister wasn't a man to disappoint. He enjoyed massive connections, not only with Hitler but also with the vast majority of successful artists who had thrived since the Nazi takeover. His dictates ruled in all matters cultural.

Max's route to international fame, he grudgingly realized, began in Germany. Either that, or flee abroad. Even if he wanted to emigrate at this point, he had—unlike some of his more internationally famous friends—no money, contacts, or papers to do that, since the Nazis loved to confiscate passports. Moreover, host countries were reluctant to accept you.

Max recalled that Goebbels—by all accounts—considered himself a progressive. He had attained graduate degrees and authored plays, albeit flops. Jesuit priests had educated him. If Max could work with any of the government honchos, he decided, it should be Goebbels.

"Well, Herr Minister, have a look around." Max nodded to Frau Goebbels and then made his move. "I think I'd better put more champagne on the table—it's running low."

Before Max could make a clean break, he saw the minister trip on the wooden floor, where the planks were slightly uneven. Magda Goebbels, coming to her husband's aid, grabbed his hand. Having regained his balance, he yanked her arm down violently, almost forcing her to her knees. His nails dug into her skin. "You're helping the *cripple*! Is that it? Don't touch me!"

Realizing that he might have been overheard, the minister pasted on a tight smile and relaxed. Max—his first reaction to come to the wife's aid—checked himself.

Max strode over to Hans Beckman, who was conversing with guests. The host glanced back at the unhappy couple. Goebbels and his wife had wandered over to one of Lena's paintings, near the refreshment table, the strange minister laughing as if nothing had happened.

As he stood next to Hans, Max wondered what landmines lay in store for him that evening. Now that he had met Goebbels, he realized that some of the paintings hanging in his gallery could be dynamite—and the unpredictable propaganda minister the match.

Chapter 12

"You've lost loved ones, Frau Krebs," said Joseph Goebbels. "Women, being more emotional, are naturally depressed by war. A war mother like you is sacred."

Goebbels, with his wife standing beside him, ogled the red-monochrome, twelve-by-sixteen-inch oil painting that Lena had recently created in Max's studio.

The title card hung on the wall beside it: "*THE BONE FACTORY,* LENA KREBS, 1937."

The hollow stare of the German soldiers, the grimaces reflecting terror, the distorted human skeletons hanging on the barbed wire along the trenches—all plunged the viewer into an emotional inferno.

"I have seven children, Frau Krebs—four of them little girls—and one young boy from her previous marriage." He tilted his head sideways toward his wife, but his eyes never shifted from Lena, as if Frau Goebbels had nothing to do with it. "I only wish they were *all* sons. The Fatherland needs strong, young men."

"*War* mother?" Lena's wide, brown eyes flashed like lasers under the thin, painted eyebrows—complementing her irate tone. "I'm not sure what you mean by that, Herr Goebbels."

Frau Goebbels, lost in thought, said nothing, her long mouth slightly agape, her sad, green eyes fixed on the painting.

"By the way, it's *Dr.* Goebbels."

"Doctor of *what,* may I ask?"

Goebbels's face flushed, his teeth gritting. "I received my doctorate of philosophy from Heidelberg University."

Lena planted her hands on her wide hips, her billowy, black evening dress doing nothing to camouflage her largeness. "Well, *Doctor*, my son puked his lungs out on a French battlefield."

"I'm aware of that," Goebbels said softly.

Lena's eyes lost their fire, giving way to mist.

She looked over to the table of champagne, where Hans Beckman—slamming down glass after glass of bubbly—shifted his unbalanced weight to and fro. "I could use more of that champagne," she said.

Goebbels looked around at the other guests, seemingly weary of his current conversation. "Give my regards to your grandson, Paul. Considering his background, we'll take a special interest in him."

Lena's face froze. "*Paul*? What do you know about Paul?"

Herr Goebbels's mesmerizing stare reflected yet another mood, threatening Lena like pistols held at point-blank range. "*Everything*. That's our job, Frau Krebs."

From the growing crowd of guests, Max appeared, carrying two glasses. Goebbels drew him into the conversation with a wave of his hand. "Women *should* be temperamental; a man must accommodate that. It's their lot to exaggerate. That's why some of them make good painters. How about Mary Cassatt or Morisot, for instance? Right, Herr Bauer?"

"Well—" answered Max, being mercifully cut off by Lena.

"'*Exaggerate*,'" blurted Lena, regaining her feistiness.

Max handed glasses of champagne to Magda and her husband. "Well, Minister, I can tell you that Lena's painting is very accurate, when it comes to war."

Max glanced at Lena, his voice firm, as if instructing an obstreperous child. "On the other hand, I think the minister has genuine opinions"

Goebbels nodded uncertainly. Max filled in the pregnant silence generated by his non-opinion masquerading as an opinion. "So, Herr Goebbels, you're familiar with the work of Cassatt and Morisot, are you?"

"Not all of us Nazis fell off the hay wagon, Herr Bauer. A few men leading our movement seem rough and common. But some of us are different."

Goebbels shifted his weight, seemingly favoring one leg over the other. "The Fuhrer himself instructed me that to be a great leader, you must also be a great artist. Frankly, I'm not out to destroy German Expressionism, but to redefine it. We may have that in common."

"I need a drink," blurted Lena, who abruptly exited.

"Charming," said Goebbels as his eyes followed her departure. He clutched his wife and ushered her thither. Max dutifully, although reluctantly, followed.

As they wandered, they approached Max's display. With the minister in attendance that eventful evening, Max had worried about landmines. He had just avoided one. There promised to be others.

* * *

"Let's study this one first, Herr Bauer." Goebbels halted in front of Max's latest painting. Magda's eyes wandered.

"This pastoral's marvelous," said the minister, "the way it plays with the light. The poor little towheads clinging to their mother, the tanned, muscular father at the plow. They wear rags but proudly showcase Teutonic virtue. How did you paint the vibrant sun?"

"How?"

"What colors? What type of yellow? Naples?"

"No," answered Max, "lemon yellow, with some green in it. That and lead-white at the center—in faint spirals."

Goebbels moved toward the wall and read the label out loud: "*PEASANTS EARNING THEIR DAILY BREAD,* MAX BAUER, GERMAN EXPRESSIONIST PAINTER, 1937."

"Wonderful, Herr Bauer. The fields are blue; the dales, shades of purple. Features are slightly distorted—but I like it. The skin's somewhat dark; why is that?"

"Long, hard toil in the bright sun, Herr Minister, what would you expect?"

Goebbels turned and faced Max, his enthusiasm boiling over. "I'll buy this one. How much is it, Herr Bauer?"

"The price is *free*." Max smiled, removing the painting from the wall, and handed it to Frau Goebbels. "To Magda, with my compliments."

The minister snatched the painting from his wife, admiring it up close, and then handed it back to her. "I'll give this one to the Fuhrer," he said, as though his wife's gift had never existed. "Don't drop it."

Frau Goebbels, seemingly oblivious, gazed at the next painting hanging on the wall. "I think I like that one."

Clutching Max's landscape, she stepped over to the next piece, the rest of the party following her. Max noticed her husband's scowl. He had thought twice about including it in his gallery, but who could find fault, he had thought, with such an innocent bit of fluff?

But then, he hadn't yet met the minister.

Chapter 13

"I love the yellow pig in the purple straw," said Magda, the slight slur in her speech divulging the effect of the champagne. "Look at the green sky over the barn. It's *sooooo* green."

Goebbels, irritated by his wife's animation, studied the painting carefully as he viewed it from different angles and distances, his hands clasped behind his back and his spine extended, as if inspecting the troops, and not art. Max held his breath. This Modernist rendition of a farmer's pigsty had perhaps been too bold.

"This one, Herr Bauer," Goebbels said, pointing at the pig. "It's smiling."

"Excuse me?"

"I said, it's *smiling.*"

"What's smiling, Herr Minister?"

Goebbels walked up to the label on the wall, reading it out loud: "*THE SMILING PIG,* MAX BAUER, 1920."

"Tell me, why is a fat, dirty hog smiling, Herr Bauer? For that matter, why is it yellow?"

"It's a pig, not a hog, Herr Minister."

"All right. Why is the *pig* smiling?"

"Not because it's yellow," said Max.

"Very well, forget the color for now."

Max, lost for words, uttered the first thing that shot into his head. "Because it's happy."

"How can a pig be happy?"

"Well, it *can* be *un*happy—the opposite—can't it?"

"I suppose," agreed the minister.

"If it can be unhappy, then it can be happy."

"All right, how do we *know* when the *pig* is *un*happy?"

Max couldn't fathom the depth of absurdity of the conversation. "Well, I suppose when a naughty farmer kicks the poor pig, it's unhappy."

Goebbels's face turned red. His hands, resting on his hips, knotted into fists. "All right," he said with his smooth voice. "Does a pig *frown* when it's unhappy?"

"I don't know; it might."

"Have you ever seen one frown?"

Max didn't know what to say.

"I think I have," said Magda lightheartedly. "Or, maybe it was a rhino. In the zoo, I mean—"

"Shut up!" The minister's eyes burned into his wife.

"What about it, Bauer? Back to the point: Have you ever seen a pig smile—especially a pig that's yellow?"

"A *yellow* pig?" said Max. "No."

"*Any* damn color pig!" Goebbels, obviously exasperated, calmed down. "What's your reasoning here?"

"That's one of my early pieces, Herr Minister. I can't remember my reasoning."

Max, of course, knew that reason had nothing to do with it.

Then, unexpectedly, the minister's face slackened, and his mouth formed an O. Goebbels beheld the image of the pig like a monk savors a holy triptych. His eyes shifted to Max, the daggers melting into butter knives.

"I see," said Goebbels. "The Aryan laborer toils with joy; blissful Nordic farmers. The racial spirit even permeates the livestock. What wonderful symbolism!"

"That's it," agreed Max. *What the hell?* he thought. "The joyful, yellow, Aryan sow."

Frau Goebbels frowned. She ventured a comment to her husband. "No, you're right, dear. The pig scares me a little, too."

He rounded on her violently. "Scares? Who's scared? *Me—scared*! The painting's ingenious. I'll take that one too, Bauer. I like the gold frame. I'll hang it in my office. This time I insist on paying you."

"Very well, Herr Minister."

Goebbels, looking a bit unsure, moved on. "What's next?"

"Whatever you like . . . "

The minister, glancing across the room, pointed. "I see something over there."

Max realized—with trepidation—that Goebbels had indicated Hans Beckman's exhibit. That's exactly the place he *didn't* want to go.

"But Herr Minister—"

"I *said*, that one."

* * *

The wounded, uniformed young man—the subject in Hans's painting—who had posed with the perspective at his eye level, stared desperately into the future—that is, the eyes of viewers to come—clawing at their consciousness. To Max, he warned of war's incalculable horrors.

With one arm missing, and the stump pointing directly at the viewer, the hapless recruit rested on a rumpled bed. A nude young woman stood in the background. Pale, muddy-green strokes of paint, in close juxtaposition to dabs of yellow ochre, mixed with bone white, fashioned the uniform. The thick, blue hair of the soldier played with his vibrant, orange skin, his terror-injected eyes purple spirals. The woman flashed a toothless smile. Her disquieting eyes—blank, white ovals—startled the observer.

"*SOLDIER AND SLUT*, HANS BECKMAN, 1933."

Oh, wonderful, thought Max, as the minister read the label. The damn painting, of course, had to be vintage Beckman. The lanky, tall figure, dressed in black leather slacks and an Oriental-style smock—his large feet jammed into curled, Persian slippers—stood unsteadily, about ten meters away from Max and the Goebbels.

His calloused hands running through his unruly, red mop, Hans's high-pitched voice, in lively conversation with two untraditional young women, stabbed the air dissonantly. Glancing over in their direction, Hans tossed Max a jaunty wink, then frowned when he saw Goebbels.

He turned his back on the Nazi couple.

Max had warned Hans not to hang that painting, but he had sneaked it in anyway, at the last minute. He had also warned him—apparently in vain—not to drink too much.

He braced himself for the collision.

Chapter 14

Both of the women standing with Hans wore brown suits and paisley ties. The blonde one, her hair parted to the side, offered the brunette—her hair cropped short—a sip of her champagne and a light for her cigarette, held elegantly in a long, silver holder.

This togetherness attracted the attention of Doctor Goebbels. His startled gaze groped the trio—Hans and the two women—from head to toe, as if stumbling upon a dung heap.

"Who are the women?" asked Goebbels.

"I suppose visitors, Herr Minister," answered Max.

"I mean, *who* are they? Some names."

"Never seen them before," Max lied. "No idea."

The two young women walked away, leaving Hans alone near his provocative portrait. Goebbels eyed the young ladies with disgust as they exited. He then studied Beckman's painting again, only this time moving much closer. When finished, he approached Hans, as if stalking a rat.

"*You* there. Aren't you Beckman?"

"Herr Minister, shall we go look at the prints?" Max asked.

Goebbels ignored him. He repeated the question to Hans in a louder voice. "I *said,* aren't you Hans Beckman?"

Hans, the question too loud to ignore, turned his head from his painting and glared at the minister. His eyes intense from drink, he replied acidly, "You know I am."

Goebbels clasped his hands behind his back as he positioned himself in front of the insolent young artist. He then paced back and forth in front of Hans, eyeing him from different angles. Frau Goebbels, looking as though she'd stumbled upon a lion's cage with its door open, put her hand to her mouth, turning her head away from the altercation.

Max stepped forward between Goebbels and his friend.

"Dr. Goebbels, Hans is one of our best artists. He's a little tipsy, but—"

The minister halted, putting his finger to his mouth. "Shush!" He then continued his pacing, his limp more pronounced, halting again in front of Hans, staring him in the face.

"Do you know who I am?"

"Of course. Who could miss the clubfoot, Minister?"

"Hans!" Max rushed his friend, pushing him towards the door. "Go home!"

Goebbels's eyes blazed, his hand shot up in the air. "Stay out of this, Herr Bauer. He'll have his hearing—"

"Go ahead and threaten me. I don't give a damn," Hans blurted in a slurred voice.

The minister's tone turned soft and deliberate. "Young fellow, I never threaten." His eyes narrowing, he continued. "That painting of yours insults German womanhood. It degrades the sacrifice of our soldiers. It's filth. You're a madman. Degenerate scum—"

"Hans, keep quiet! Go away, please," Max shouted.

"A *'madman'*? Sir, considering the source, you just paid me the ultimate compliment. That's exactly why I paint."

Goebbels smiled and then looked over at his wife. "Home."

"But Joseph, I—"

"Home. Go home. Call a taxi. I have important things to do. The driver will take me later."

"But the other painting . . . "

"Herr Bauer will ship it to us. I *said*, home with you!"

Frau Goebbels, carrying Max's painting of the pig, obediently left the gallery, absently waving goodbye to Max. He thought that if she had worn a dog collar, she couldn't have been more humiliated by her husband.

Goebbels pulled a pocketknife out of his tux, and then unfolded the sharp blade. He held it up to Hans's face.

Max, alarmed, took a step forward to protect his friend. Instead of stabbing Hans with the knife, Goebbels walked over to the painting and cut it out of its frame. He rolled it up, tucking it under his arm. "I'll hold on to this for safekeeping."

Walking up to Max, he extended his hand. Max accepted it.

"I'll be in touch," said Goebbels. He reached into his coat pocket and pulled out a business card, handing it to Max. His eyes—now gentler—then shifted to Hans. "Herr Beckman. I'm sure our paths will cross again."

Goebbels walked away. After a few steps, he stopped and turned, glaring at Hans.

"Before I go, I'll tell you a short story. When I was very little, my father beat me because of my foot. It made me cry, but it made me hard, too. As a good Catholic then, I prayed. He just beat me more often."

Goebbels pointed to his mouth. "When I had a bad tooth, he would yank it out with pliers. That made me even harder."

His baleful stare took on a faraway quality. "He didn't want to do it, but he did it anyway. He told me that a bad tooth would rot the other teeth, and the best way to protect the healthy teeth is to tear the bad ones out by their roots—no matter what the cost. Good night, Herr Beckman."

He left.

Max held up the gold card. It read: "DR. J. GOEBBELS, PhD: MINISTER OF PROPOGANDA AND ENLIGHTENMENT. OFFICES: *REICHSKANZLEI.*"

He turned on Hans. "Well, you really stepped into it this time."

"Screw him, the little bastard. His teeth and his clubfoot, too—"

"Don't be silly. You're hurting yourself."

"I don't care."

"Others too."

"Who?"

"Who do you imagine?"

Hans's eyes fixed on Max. His voice softened. "I'm sorry, Max. I didn't mean to do that. You used to be with us."

"What do you mean?"

"The purity of your art was everything to you. I thought you were sincere."

"Poverty, Hans."

"Piss on poverty!"

"Prison."

"Screw prison!"

"Night and Fog, Hans. *Night and Fog!*"

Hans dropped his head, audibly exhaling, his tone subdued. "Yeah, Night and Fog."

* * *

Goebbels stood in the rain in front of the gallery—the night air balmy—hailing a long, SS staff car. It stopped. He got in. Beside him sat Colonel Siegfried Hock. The minister admired the fastidious nature of this SS officer but disliked him otherwise. The colonel—rather rudely—had a nasty habit of staring at his gimpy foot.

"Well, Herr Minister, what did you find?" asked Hock.

Goebbels nodded sideways toward the gallery. "There are some pretenders in there—vermin who degrade our culture. In due course, we'll deal with them."

Goebbels stared out the window as the car sped off. "We must be careful, though; the Fuhrer admires Max Bauer. To be clear, so do I. He's actually a genius. Those of us who truly appreciate art can recognize that."

Hock nodded. "That's important for me to know."

"And he may prove useful," offered Goebbels. His eyes shifted to the colonel. "At least for now."

Chapter 15

"Hide that, Max, don't let anyone see it."

Frieda, sitting on a bench beside Max at the Berlin Zoological Garden—just inside the Elephant Gate entrance, off Budapester Street—grabbed at the sketchpad, as Max playfully held it above her head.

"Give me that!" She put her hand to her mouth, stifling a laugh. "If they catch us—"

"Things aren't that bad."

Frieda stopped laughing. "That's one thing that bothers me about you, Max. How bad do they have to be? You understand everything—too much."

He continued sketching with his colored pencils, mulling over the mild rebuke, intermittently glancing across the footpath at his subject. Bobby the gorilla had been the zoo's sensation all year. With his hands clutching the bars of his cage, the famous ape seemed to be pleased about posing.

"What do you think now?" Max held up his sketch.

"I don't see how you can do it. It's so *true*."

Bobby's likeness covered the paper, his hairy body rippling with muscles. But instead of Bobby's face, the visage of Adolf Hitler frowned at the viewer.

"That's exactly how Hitler looks in the newsreels—wild," commented Frieda.

Winking at the bright afternoon sun, she sprung from the bench, straightening out the new cotton dress that she had bought for the summer. "Let me see Goebbels again."

Max, turning the page of his sketchbook, held up the drawing. The picture of a weasel, with the face of Joseph Goebbels, mesmerized Frieda. The dour, fawn stare, the tight, almost lipless mouth, the huge head on the small torso—all captured the minister's essence pretty well, Max thought.

"I didn't know you do cartoons."

"I don't. Tell me what you see."

"A weasel with an ugly face."

"I mean underneath."

Frieda, now thoughtful and serious, gave her answer. "*Devious.*"

Max quickly thumbed through the pages and held up his next piece. "Try this one."

"That's Goering." Her eyes narrowed. "With the body of a hog. Not an original thought, Max."

"Guilty as charged."

"Violent."

"You got it."

Frieda grabbed the sketchbook out of his hands. She opened it up to a new image and flashed it at Max. It had the body of a jaguar. "Who's this?"

"Very funny. Me."

"*Ambition*, perhaps?" she said.

Max closed the book, rising from the bench.

"Maybe." He dusted off his denim overalls. "I'm not ambitious, exactly. Determined, yes. I want everyone to appreciate the meaning of my art, from the most obtuse Nazi to the most smug bourgeois."

She drew him close to her, taking his hands in hers, staring into his eyes. She kissed him. Frieda led him to the picnic table across the pathway, just next to the panda exhibit. "Okay, no more gallery psychology."

"Deal. I'll sketch the big panda on the rock."

Frieda glanced over to the huge cage that held the bears. She sat down, and Max, taking his place beside her, reached into the pocket of his overalls for two candy bars. As he sketched, they munched on the chocolate.

"After the other night—at the parade—I wasn't sure you'd see me again," Max said as he wielded the brown watercolor pencil. "Thought I'd blown it."

"These are evil times," she said.

He dropped his pencil, retrieving it from the ground. "I know, beyond weird."

"It had nothing to do with you of course, but . . . " Then, again, she caught herself, her mind seemingly far away, riveted to something else.

If only she'd open up to me. . ., thought Max.

Max showed Frieda his quick sketch. "Guess who?" He held up an image of the panda with the head of a famous British politician.

"That's easy. Winston Churchill. I saw him puffing on a cigarette holder—just like that—yesterday on the front page of a newspaper. He's not happy."

Max looked at his watch. "Let's catch an early dinner—there should be specials on. Unless I sell more paintings, we may eat canned beans."

"I'll buy."

"No thanks."

After about thirty seconds, while walking toward the exit, Max answered his own unspoken question. "War."

"What do you mean?" asked Frieda.

"It's the meaning underneath the last sketch."

* * *

They left the restaurant about dusk, strolling down the sidewalk past the cafes and shops lining Unter Den Linden, and headed toward the Brandenburg Gate.

As Max passed the kiosks, he checked out the art and photographs displayed on their wide columns. He observed images of tanks, planes, soldiers, and famous Nazis.

"Max, look at the crowd over there." Frieda pointed across the street.

He saw about a hundred people milling about on the sidewalk, interspersed with Brown Shirts, and a couple of SS men. Curious, Max led Frieda across the street. As they approached the crowd, Max noticed that people had formed a circle around a couple—a tall woman and a short man.

A three-story apartment building stood in the background. Dressed in a crumpled business suit, the dark-haired young man— his eyes and his face bruised—stood close to a young woman, with tousled red hair. Tears streamed down her face.

A sign hung around her neck.

The passers-by and spectators jeered and taunted the couple. Stern-faced troopers stood by, scanning the crowd for do-gooder troublemakers. A few people in the crowd shook their heads, seemingly in sympathy with the victims.

Frieda read the sign out loud, her voice halting. "'In this place . . . '"

Max, his voice soft, reassured her. "That's all right, dear, let's go."

He led her away, glancing at the sign again, not sure that he had read it right the first time.

He had: "IN THIS PLACE, I'M THE GREATEST SWINE, I TAKE IN JEWBOYS AND MAKE THEM MINE."

Chapter 16

"Be still, Herr Roth. I'm almost done."

"My bladder won't hold out much longer."

"I've painted three portraits for your family. This one's—well, you'll see."

"My wife sends me. I'm not much for art. Sarah loves it."

Max stood back from his oil portrait of the middle-aged department store magnate, dressed in his dark, three-piece suit and other bourgeois finery. From the steady brushwork and the frequent turning of his head, the scar tissue on Max's neck smarted.

"Your wife has a keen eye," said Max.

Roth sat on a stool facing Max's easel, his balding head slightly turned in a three-quarter profile. Irritated by the paint fumes building up in his studio, Max went to open the window.

He saw that the cloud cover had softened the afternoon sunshine. Soldiers marched in formation along the side of the street, displaying their field-grey tunics and shiny helmets, as their polished jackboots thudded the pavement.

Coming back to his easel, Max glanced over at his fidgeting subject. "Right, just a few more seconds." Returning to the easel, he picked up his fine sable brush.

Roth's plaintive voice crackled in a rhythm similar to short bursts of gunfire. "Business is bad, can't get contracts—the damn government . . ."

Max sensed his customer's caution about commenting further on the regime.

"Just a touch on the eyes; all right, done!" As Roth climbed off the stool, Max pointed across the studio to the W.C. "Over there."

Max inspected his completed piece. He liked what the saw.

The sparse grey hair, much greyer and thinner than the actual subject, underscored its nonrepresentational feel. Shocked, red-spiral eyes, buried in a greenish complexion, popped out at the viewer.

Presently, Roth returned to inspect Max's product. His eyes widened. "I'm paying you five hundred marks for this?"

"It's not supposed to look like you exactly, Herr Roth." Max wiped his hands off with a towel. "It's what we call a 'psychological'—"

"Don't care what you call it. I'm not paying." Roth brushed off his finely tailored coat, then threw his hands up. "All right. Maybe Sarah will like it. She likes anything you paint. "

Max carefully placed the painting in a carry-box as the customer removed his wallet, thumbing through his cash.

"Here, Max." Joel Roth handed him the bills. "It doesn't much look like me, though."

"Well," Max said as he placed his hand gently upon his customer's shoulder, "in ten years it *will* look like you."

"I only hope I have ten years. But, after all," he chuckled, his eyes then mirthful, "why wouldn't I?"

* * *

The pounding on the front door startled Sarah Roth. She dropped her fork on her plate of stuffed cabbage—her husband's favorite dinner. She glanced at him anxiously. "Joel—at this hour—who could it be? Didn't you lock the front gate?"

He sat across the long, meticulously polished dining room table, his dark eyes darting about the room. Herr Roth looked at the grandfather clock, beside the string of vibrant oil paintings strung on the wall.

"I forgot."

Among the Modernist images hung his portrait, the one Max Bauer had recently painted.

"It's past nine," he said.

"They'll go away. Finish dinner before it gets cold."

The pounding harsher, Joel sprung up, throwing his napkin down on the table. "Better see who that is."

Frau Roth, a well-tended lady with a rosy complexion who pleasantly filled a black silk evening dress, fiddled nervously with her diamond necklace. The dim candlelight in the high-ceilinged room softly illuminated the Expressionist paintings—mixed with traditionalist fare—that surrounded them on all four walls.

Angry voices filtered in from the direction of the front entrance. Then, the door to the dining room crashed open. Six SS men, carrying large crates, strode to the paintings, snatching them from their anchoring and throwing them in the containers.

At first stunned, Sarah screamed, springing out of her chair.

"Run, Sarah!" shouted Herr Roth.

Two other uniformed men bolted into the room, attacking her husband, yanking him out of his chair. Throwing him to the ground, they kicked him repeatedly.

Another tall, lean soldier slowly entered, his chin slightly up, his cold, light-colored eyes scouring the room, as if exterminating mice. Sarah's eyes shot to the white rose pinned to his lapel, next to his medals, and frilly insignia.

She rushed to her husband, who lay helplessly on the floor. One of the troopers barred her way.

"No!" shouted the tall officer. "Leave her be. Help Herr Roth up from the floor."

Joel Roth got to his feet by himself. Sarah embraced her husband.

The officer stepped closer to the couple. "I'm Colonel Hock of the Gestapo."

He reached into his tunic and pulled out a piece of paper, handing it to Herr Roth, who breathed heavily, holding his side. "I'm here on behalf of Reich Minister Goering," announced Hock, "to collect your art—*all* of it." He pointed to the paper. "That's a bill of sale. The Reich minister purchased the paintings, and we're ensuring delivery."

"But—"

"Naturally," continued Hock, "Herr Roth, you're cancelling the charge, as a gift to the Fatherland."

Roth nodded. "Yes, of course, take them. They're yours."

He hugged his wife, and then guided her over to the couch. As Sarah walked past the colonel, she looked into his eyes. What she saw made her shake.

"That's right," said Hock, "relax on the sofa. I apologize for the inconvenience."

Sarah and Joel dutifully sat down on the couch, silently watching the proceedings.

Hock's eyes hooked onto something hanging a few meters away from him. He stepped over to it, pointing. "Tell me, Frau Roth. Who painted this trash? The initials are 'MB.' This depraved portrait looks like you, Herr Roth, and then it doesn't. "

Sarah looked at her husband. He looked up at Hock. "Not sure. The auctioneer didn't mention the artist."

Hock, staring dubiously at the portly husband, shifted his attention to his troops. "Be careful with this insane filth cluttering the walls. The Fuhrer has big plans for it. Get a move on!"

The SS men finished packing the goods. Hock rushed his men out of the room, stopping in front of the terrified couple. "Thank you for your kind cooperation."

Sarah, shaking and in tears, hung her head. Hock nodded and then left.

When the soldiers stepped outside the mansion, the colonel nailed a sign near the front door. Standing back to savor his efforts, the bright red letters warned in Old German script: "*KAUFT NICHT BEI DEN JUDEN*"—"don't buy from Jews."

Chapter 17

The recently completed Reich Chancellery stood on Voss Street.

Joseph Goebbels entered through the immense gates of the building's Court of Honor, flanked by two huge statues of ancient German warriors, sculpted by the renowned artist Arno Breker. When he reached the reception area, bronze sculptures of female nudes greeted him. He ambled through the room to an oak door, almost seventeen feet high.

This door opened onto a large hall, clad in mosaic. The propaganda minister then ascended marble steps, passing through a lofty, round room with a tall, domed ceiling. A wide, gilded door opened to reveal a gallery almost one hundred meters long. As he ambled along, the hardness of its burnt-orange, marble floor shot tongues of fire up the minister's gimpy foot.

Two very tall, uniformed SS sentries stood at attention on either side of huge bronze double doors. At the top of the door, two giant, gold letters welcomed the visitor: "AH."

The guards nodded to the dark-haired visitor as they pushed open the doors, allowing Joseph Goebbels into Adolf Hitler's hallowed, private office. Across the dimly lit room, the wary minister observed the Fuhrer standing near his marble-topped desk, his back turned to him. He recalled that Hitler usually received his guests with his back turned to them, and wondered whether this was some sort of psychological maneuver.

Beside Hitler stood an easel, upon which he was painting his latest landscape. Goebbels slowly approached his boss. Hitler paid him no heed until he stood inches from the easel. The minister, scrutinizing the image on the canvas, coughed nervously. He tried to never interrupt his master when painting.

"I know you're there, Herr Minister," said Hitler softly. "I heard you approaching."

Hitler, his tongue protruding, massaged his lips as he painted, like a child drawing with crayons. He stroked his support with a round brush, creating the sky and horizon of the image. "Your leg hurts more today."

Goebbels marveled at the Fuhrer's intuition and attention to detail. His amazing memory could recall the smallest incident or fact—even from years before. This unnerved not a few of his minions, who wondered which of their indiscretions would be recalled when one of his black moods beset him.

"Yes, my Fuhrer. Thank you for noticing. Your painting's very interesting."

"Take a seat, Herr Minister."

As he sat in front of Hitler's desk, Goebbels noticed that, as usual, there were no people in his paintings, and the foreground and the perspective of the mountains were slightly askew. Hitler glanced in his direction, his eyes—forbidding and untrusting —fastening upon him for only a split second. Goebbels, who considered himself very sensitive, shuddered at his own thought.

Does that glance betray a glint of paranoia? Would he like to murder me?

"I know what you're thinking, Herr Goebbels. You're wondering why I never draw people. The old Social Democrats—my enemies—used to dig up any dung they could find on me, going back even to my postcard-painting days in Vienna."

The Fuhrer loudly scoffed at his detractors, as if they stood in the room. "'You're nuts!' That's what they barked at me. Just because I didn't paint people!"

He waved his paintbrush at the minister, as if it were a weapon. "But why paint people, when you can paint something much more precious: nature, exactly the way she is? Do you see what I mean, Herr Minister?"

"Yes, yes, I believe I do."

Hitler's eyes—milky blue, dreamy beacons—shifted between his easel, and him. Or rather, somewhere close *behind* him, noted Goebbels, since the Fuhrer often looked *through* you, not *at* you. If there was true eye contact, you'd usually be in for trouble.

"I should retire and be a full-time artist," continued the Fuhrer. "That's what I wanted to be, until insane art professors stood in my way, not appreciating my talent."

As he painted, his stokes of paint became more uncontrolled. "Now, I'm forced to give myself to the people—to lead the masses—who in the end are like whiny children. I'm doomed to a life of sacrifice, Herr Minister."

"But we're all grateful, my Fuhrer. Never forget that for an instant."

Hitler's eyes lit up. Goebbels then heard an ominous growl.

Blondie—Hitler's beloved German shepherd—crawled out from under the desk, sniffing at the intruder. The minister chuckled, but underneath his pretense of amusement, he was terrified that the dog would lose control and chew off his clubfoot.

"Hello, Blondie," Goebbels said. "I hope you're well today."

The dog growled again—only louder—and Hitler reached over to the treats resting on his desk, tossing one to the beast. "Now, be nice to the minister. He's very afraid of you."

The dog, pacified, relaxed, carefully chewing on the morsel. Goebbels noticed that the mountains and the stream in Hitler's landscape looked exactly like mountains and streams anywhere. The elk grazing in the meadow looked up, except one eye that strangely shot sideways, toward the viewer. It had a human quality.

In fact, thought Goebbels, it shared a remarkable likeness to the paranoid look that Hitler often threw his way.

"This picture's wonderful, my Fuhrer. I enjoy the elk especially."

Hitler threw down his brush. "Don't patronize me."

He looked over at the huge portrait of Frederick the Great hanging above the roaring fireplace. "Your wife came here in tears the other day. You seem to be prowling around the movie studio again, chasing starlets. I told you to stop that. She's a good party member."

Goebbels felt ice water pour down his back—the pang of terror palpable. Hitler, the prude, had indeed warned him. He thought he had covered his tracks nicely, but apparently not. "My Fuhrer, I'm done with that. I swear it. You know how women just seem to flock to me—against my will."

Hitler then wiped his hands and started to pace the room. "Have a seat, Herr Goebbels. I've discussed my plans with Reich Minister Goering. A massive art exhibition will soon come to Berlin."

Hitler paused, staring at the other paintings hanging on the towering walls, including the Cranach next to him. "Did you know, Herr Goebbels, you can detect madness in a person from the shape of their skull or the width of their nose?"

"Yes," answered Goebbels. "It's called 'phrenology.'"

Hitler returned to his easel, picking up his brush. "Bolsheviks," said the Fuhrer, "charlatans, pretenders—all this degenerate scum who call themselves 'Expressionists' or 'Modernists'—you can tell how mad they are by just looking at how close their eyes are together! Just by looking at the filth they paint!"

His patent leather shoes slapped the marble floor in an odd rhythm, as he marched away from his easel again, pacing the floor, his coarse voice shifting into an even more ominous growl. "Do you know what this scum really wants to do, Herr Minister?"

Blondie growled.

"No. What, my Fuhrer?"

"To spy on me; to degrade me. They want to see me copulate."

"I think that's obvious," agreed Goebbels, really pondering the unlikelihood of his strange boss achieving that particular biological function.

"I want to show you something, Herr Minister."

Goebbels panicked.

Show me something*! What on earth can* that *be?*

Chapter 18

Hitler strode to the closet next to the coat rack and removed a box. He carried it over to the desk. Goebbels looked on, wondering—with some misgivings—what could be in it. The minister hoped that it wouldn't be some weird sex object. Ever since the Fuhrer had become tight with one his secretaries, he had sometimes wandered into strange territory.

Hitler removed the lid on the box, extracting a small club and a spray can. He dumped the contents of the box onto his desk.

Goebbels nearly jumped out of his chair.

Large cockroaches scrambled over Hitler's desk as he picked up the can, and sprayed them. The few that had survived made a run for it. He smashed them with the club. A bead of sweat rolled down his forehead. He tossed down the cudgel and stared at his minister. "This is the key to saving civilization."

Goebbels scoured his mind to find a response to this surreal tangent. "You're much too quick and wise for me, my Fuhrer."

"Smash these degenerate artists like cockroaches! The turds they leave behind must be exposed to the German people—much as the exposure of an inoculation prevents disease!"

Goebbels sat frozen, eyeing the smashed insects. Hitler started pacing again as the minister regained his composure. He would try to get the Fuhrer back on track. He considered himself a practical man, not full of fanatical theories.

Women are emotional; real men, cold and logical.

To tell the truth, his boss sometimes showed an effeminate streak, and the minister felt that it was his duty to reel him in. "What a great notion, my Fuhrer, a *degenerate* art exhibition; ingenious! I assume this is *your* concept, not Reich Minister Goering's."

"Reich Minister Goering? No, no, did he say it was his idea?"

"Of course not. Not in so many words. As we all know, he likes to claim credit for things. But he's a grand, fat fellow anyway—" Goebbels loved to make the Fuhrer believe that others tried to steal his ideas, then take their part, to appear magnanimous.

Hitler resumed his painting with his small sable brush, placing his initials upon his finished piece. "Someday, this shall be priceless, like Da Vinci's *The Last Supper*. It'll be the centerpiece of our German Louvre."

He scowled at Goebbels. "It's my unshakable will that we also have an exhibition called 'The House of Aryan Art.' This one will open first, then they'll run simultaneously."

Hitler, as was his custom when in one of his bohemian moods, sat down sideways in a large leather chair, his feet dangling over the armrest. "All the great artists shall contribute to this national event. It'll glorify our heritage."

Goebbels resented that Goering, through intimidation, theft, and official confiscation, got all the good loot, and he little. Goebbels knew how to curry favor and satisfy his ambitions, and he also knew who might be able to help him control the art market— including both traditional and modernist pieces.

Most important, he realized how much Hitler loved Max Bauer's style—and the extent of the artist's ambition. Therefore, he sensed a great opportunity.

"My Fuhrer, I know just the genius to guide our efforts. The perfect curator and manager for our exhibits."

Hitler's eyes shone. "Who?"

"Max Bauer, the war hero."

"Yes, this man Bauer's a fine painter—another Cranach."

"I visited his gallery," said Goebbels. "Simple, Germanic and honest, imaginative and original—"

"Do you know that I saw Bauer during the war, Herr Minister?" Hitler ran his hand through his stringy, dark hair, which cascaded over his forehead. He kicked his feet. "We were in the gas ward together in Passau. We received the Iron Cross."

"I checked on him," said the minister. "He's broke."

"All the better," Hitler said. "Yes, Max Bauer's the one."

"In fact, I have a present for you," said Goebbels, "a landscape by Bauer. I'm presenting it to you soon."

Hitler clasped his hands with joy. "I can hardly wait, Herr Doctor, and for the exhibitions to open."

"And I will *produce* them," added Goebbels casually. Mentally, the little minister crossed his fingers at this self-serving, throwaway suggestion.

"Very well. We'll talk more of this later," said Hitler agreeably.

Joseph Goebbels, pleased at how he'd put one over on Herman Goering, smiled broadly. *Now, all I need is for Max Bauer to cooperate.*

He had little doubt that the ambitious artist would play ball.

Chapter 19

Frieda walked into the exam room and greeted Joel Roth, one of her oldest patients. She enjoyed this amiable businessman, who on occasion had brought her presents, including fine silk scarves from one of his department stores.

She noticed that the usually ebullient man seemed quieter than usual. She also noticed that he had a bruise on his forehead, but nothing serious enough to be of clinical concern.

Roth, gowned and perched upon the exam table, extended his right elbow and winced. "It still hurts. My hand's shrinking."

Frieda took his fist in her hands and spread out the fingers, examining the palm's medial surface, and the spaces between the knuckles on its dorsum. "I see atrophy of the short muscles of the hand, Herr Roth." She ran the pinwheel over the skin. "Feels sharp?"

"No, I can barely feel anything."

Frieda put the pinwheel back into her lab coat pocket and took a seat on the stool in front of him. "I told you to return in two weeks—not two months."

"What's wrong with the hand, doc?"

"The ulnar nerve's trapped. I may need to refer you to a surgeon."

Frieda saw that her patient looked more worried than she had expected. She rose from the stool and moved to her desk.

She charted as she spoke. "The surgery's simple, so don't worry. You can tell Sarah that once we release the pressure, the hand will be strong again."

"It's not that, Doctor Holtz. It's something else."

At the dour tone of his voice, she stopped her charting. "Well, what then?"

"I can't see you anymore. Neither can my wife."

Frieda put down her pen. "Why, for heaven's sake? Did I do something—"

"No, that's not it." Joel Roth looked down at the floor, letting out a deep breath. "The government says we can't use Gentile doctors."

"That's rubbish."

"They allowed me one more visit to close my account and get my records. I had to beg them for that."

"Those damn Nuremberg Laws!" Frieda said.

"Yes, that's it. At first, we just tried to ignore them. Now, they mean business, ever since the Berlin Olympics. No more putting on shows of tolerance for the foreign press. The other day, some Nazis roughed up our house and stole our art collection."

Frieda rose from her desk. She walked over to her patient, placing her hand gently upon his shoulder. "I'll still see you."

"*I* might risk it. But, your career's on the line—maybe more."

Suddenly, Frieda felt sick. She mulled over the horrors. One neighbor informing on another—a son informing on a father—the Gestapo coming in the night, then people disappearing without a trace, carted off to one of those horrible "detention camps."

"Just be glad you're not one of us," said Roth. "I never thought I'd say something like that."

"I understand, Herr Roth. I really do."

* * *

The clock in Frieda's office struck six as she sat at her desk, finishing her charting.

A knock sounded at the door; it cracked open, and the nurse's head popped though. "There's a call for you in the business office—it's on hold. Sounds important; the woman on the line's frantic."

Frieda jolted. "Who?"

"She wouldn't say; probably a patient, although it sounds long distance. There was a man in the background too; very upset."

Frieda nodded her head knowingly. "I'll be right there."

"By the way, Max is waiting for you at the cafe, next door." The nurse winked. "He's very good-looking, isn't he? Those bright blue eyes just kill me." The nurse disappeared.

Frieda shot up from her desk and then raced out of the room. She picked up the phone in the other office, closing the door behind her.

"What's the matter? Are you all right? *Austria*! I thought you were in Poland . . . " Her voice cracked. " . . . Why wouldn't they let you in? . . . Call me back as soon as you can. *Please,* be careful. Love you both."

She hung up. Frieda recalled the rumors that Hitler might invade Austria. She had never felt so desperate—or so angry. She walked out to get her coat, thinking also about poor Mr. Roth.

But the phone call was what really depressed her.

Her dear parents were now trapped in Austria.

Chapter 20

"Did you already order? Sorry I'm late, the model wouldn't stop fidgeting." Max took a seat at one of the Cafe Tambourine's small, colorful round tables, which resembled the musical instrument.

"You know, van Gogh met one of his lovers at a cafe decorated like this, all the rage in Paris at the time. Same name, too . . . "

Noticing that she ignored his small talk, he scooted his chair close to Frieda. Though the restaurant was dimly lit, he also noticed her puffy eyes and flushed cheeks.

"What's wrong?"

She looked absently into her empty plate.

Max took her hand. "What is it? Tell me."

The waitress stopped at their table.

"I'll have a pilsner," said Max.

"I'm not very hungry." Frieda pushed her plate away, and the waitress left.

Max sensed that she had received some bad news. Frieda, often taciturn and reserved, bottled her problems up inside.

"Something at work?" he asked.

She stared at him, the whites of her eyes pink from crying. "Yes, that's it."

"Tell me."

She hesitated, and then the words gushed out. "Herr Roth and his wife quit my practice. I'm forbidden to treat them."

Max saw her fingers shake as she fiddled with her spoon. "Forbidden? Why?"

"Why do you think?" she snapped back. "Sorry, Max." She looked around to see who was sitting around them. "They're not Aryan, but—*I* am."

"I thought that was it."

"Those bastards!"

Max had never heard Frieda cuss before. "Oh, *those* bastards," he said. He didn't know what else to say, except that she was right.

He also thought that the cafe wasn't the place to comment. You never knew who might be listening. He wondered whether there was more to her dejection than the news about Roth, as bad as that was. "What should we do?"

Frieda shook her head.

What *could* you do, Max wondered—grab a gun and start blasting? Blast whom, even if you wanted to? *Then* what? Night and Fog—or the chopping block, that's what.

Max felt useless. "Let's get out of here; go for a walk; check out the cinema."

As they walked down the street together, Max appreciated how the street lanterns reflected off the windows of the darkened stores that had already closed for the day. He headed for the Roxy Theater, located near Frieda's apartment, to see what was playing.

Lots of things have changed, ruminated Max, as he strolled with Frieda on his arm. He particularly resented the fact that since the takeover, films had changed—not for the better, either.

Famed director Fritz Lang had fled the country, and so had his beloved colleagues, Billy Wilder, the screenwriter and director, and Karl Freund, the cinematographer. Now, corny romantic comedies monopolized the playbills. Worse, hokey biopics about young Nazis or old German generals competed with them. Composer Kurt Weill and lyricist Bertolt Brecht had been driven out too.

Max and Frieda approached a large booth closing up for the night. A huge Nazi flag stood next to it on the sidewalk.

Young, brown-shirted SA recruits were packing up their papers and donation boxes. One strode up to a recruiting banner, resting in the middle of the sidewalk. Just at that moment, Frieda and Max had stopped to read its caption: "JOIN THE SA—DEFEND GERMANY."

The base of the sign rested next to Frieda's foot. With a shriek, she kicked the sign over, stomping on it. The Nazi charged her, knocking her to the pavement.

Max lunged at the trooper, kicking him in the knee and then punching his head. The trooper countered with a right cross to Max's nose, which he answered with a left hook to the temple. The blow sent the SA man reeling, crashing to the pavement.

Not having been in a fistfight since the war, Max was disgusted by the violence of it. Disengaging, he rushed over to Frieda and crouched beside her. She was still conscious but groggy, so he helped her to her feet and then looked her over carefully.

He saw that she wasn't bleeding, except for a small cut over her eyebrow. She appeared to have good eye contact and balance. Max noted that the scar on his left hand was bleeding slightly, his powerful left hook's impact having injured his palm.

He took her by the hand and led her quickly down the sidewalk. A whistle blew, and a black-coated SS man overtook them, halting their progress with his drawn revolver.

Max thought it best to take the offensive. "Why are you molesting us?"

"Destruction of property, assault—"

"He made a lewd comment to my fiancée here," Max insisted. He pointed over to the SA trooper he had just punched, the man slowly regaining his feet. "Don't make me discuss this with your superior—"

"And *who* would that be?" asked the SS officer.

The gun still pointed at him, Max slowly pulled out his wallet and handed the trooper the golden card. "That's who."

His eyes widened as big as saucers as he studied the card. "Herr *Goebbels?*" He put his revolver back in its holster. "How do you know the propaganda minister?"

"I'm—his artist," Max lied. He took out his business card and handed it to him as well.

The Nazi examined the card and then shrugged. "Well, no harm done. Let this be a warning to you." He stomped away.

Max wiped the trickle of blood from his nose, and whispered to Frieda, "That was close."

They continued down the street.

"I'd better look after that nose," said Frieda, looking at Max's wound. "How's the hand?"

"Fine."

Glad to see her alert and perky, he chimed in, "I'd better look after your eye. Come to think of it, *you'd* better look after your eye."

She pointed down the street. "My apartment's just ahead."

Chapter 21

"Just hold still," said Max as he applied the hydrogen peroxide to Frieda's cut. "I thought that *you* were going to do this."

"I can't stand blood."

"And you're a doctor?"

"I'm a neurologist, not a surgeon. It was bad enough cleaning yours."

Max continued to dab around her eye as she cringed slightly from the sting.

"—Nearly done." As he dabbed, his face moved progressively closer to hers. "Your eyes are the deepest shade of umber that I've ever seen."

"What the hell is that?"

"Get an art lesson—I have a few bookings left."

They sat on the white leather couch beside her coffee table. He placed the cotton swab on the table, next to the peroxide, wine bottles, and half-empty crystal goblets.

Max looked over to the phonograph next to the rosewood china cabinet. "Chopin?"

Frieda nodded, her eyes resting dreamily upon him, her legs curled up under her.

Max took a bottle of the white wine, and poured them another, noticing that she still wore the same cream-colored cotton dress that she had worn to work. He handed Frieda her glass, then took a long pull on his.

To his surprise, she quickly drained her glass too, holding it out for a refill. "Alcohol's not a very potent anesthetic," she said. "I need a lot."

Max glanced around the small but elegant apartment, as he filled both their glasses to the brim. It looked like a place where Frieda would live, he thought.

The plates on the meticulously polished, oak dining table, across from the living room, were spaced perfectly; the white leather easy chair and loveseat were arranged to obtain the best view possible from the third-story window and balcony, which overlooked the city. The kitchen—an alcove off the living room—although tiny, offered an immaculate cooking range and oven, below the white cabinets.

The crystal chandeliers cast soft light on the wooden floors, and the shaggy, expansive, butter-yellow rug sprawled in front of the fireplace. Fire logs crackled. He felt a warm buzz overtake him as his eyes continued to wander. The spotless white lab coat hung from the rack—the stethoscope bulging out of its pocket.

Max observed a painting hanging over the hearth—a portrait of an elderly, dark-haired man. "Your father?"

Frieda nodded.

Cautious, clinically clean, insightful—with a dash of passion and boldness, but no frilly excess—this was Frieda's home, all right. Rising from the couch, he padded over to the coat rack, and retrieved the stethoscope, putting it around his neck, and returning to his seat on the couch beside her.

"What kind of doctor are you?" she asked playfully

Max noted her slur from the wine before answering the question. "A lovesick one."

"Nice to meet you, Dr. Lovesick."

Frieda shook his hand, and then her grin faded. She removed her hand from his, shifting her weight on the couch, uncurling her legs, placing them gently on the coffee table. The firelight played with her honey-colored hair. After draining another glass of wine, she put down her glass, and unbuttoned the top of her dress.

"Well, you'd better *auscultate*." Her warm but impish smile ignited him.

"What does that word mean?"

"Listen to my heart, silly."

He placed the bell of the stethoscope on her skin, at the center of her chest, just above her bra. "I don't hear—"

"Try putting on the earpieces."

"Ah, yes, that would help—"

"What do you hear now?"

"Nothing."

"I know; I'm heartless," she said.

"Just what I want in a wife . . . " Max caught himself, but too late. He thought, *what the hell, why not joke my way into marriage? Besides, I do love her.*

She took the instrument off his neck and tossed it on the end of the couch. "So, I'm your fiancée, huh?"

Then the whole ugly event on the sidewalk that evening shot back into Max's head. Why had Frieda been so eager to challenge those hooligans?

"Something else bothered you today. Not just Herr Roth. I could tell."

"It's nothing, Max."

He took both her hands in his, looking into her eyes. "Whatever it is, I'm with you all the way."

Frieda kissed him softly. He put his arms around her, his lips moving over her smooth neck, then her chest, then back up to her lips, and then her eye.

"Ouch!"

"Damn! I forgot," Max said.

"I'll report you to the Medical Board."

She played with him, but he chose to be serious. "You know I love you Frieda, and I've loved you since the first time I saw you in your white coat and stuffy glasses, all serious and professional. I sensed the warmth underneath—and the offbeat humor. I saw the beauty outside and in."

Frieda stood up, pulling Max up with her. "That was quite a speech, Max."

He laughed. She did too.

She then led him past the china cabinet to the door of her bedroom, her manner now serious. "The truth is, Max, I love you too."

They disappeared through one of the two bedroom doors.

Chapter 22

Berlin, September 1937:

The trim young lady—a total stranger—boyish and radiant in her frilly blouse and dark slacks, studied Max's nude portrait. She touched the canvas, as if expecting the two figures in the painting to blush from a caressing hand. Her trim, strawberry-blonde hair lent her a sporty look; the vibrant complexion suggested abundant health.

"The nude is joyful," she said as she stepped back from the piece, "and sensuous. Not the old, dark woman though. She looks—disturbing."

Max noted that this well-tended visitor to his gallery, with the large, hazel eyes, had a tone of voice that changed with the capriciousness of mercury. She also smiled one second and then frowned the next, for no apparent cause. Despite this, she had a charming, vulnerable quality that drew him in.

"Are you alone in the gallery today, Fraulein?"

"I'm meeting a man. He suggested your gallery." She fidgeted with her hair. "A very important man—do you know Reich Minister Goering?"

"No," answered Max, choosing not to mention that he had once seen him at the train station.

Max looked up at the gaping windows in Slaughterhouse 1, noting that the light entered at an advantageous angle. It lit up the young bather in his painting. The fully clad matron, sitting on the boulder beside her—washcloth in hand—peered up at the girl, who bent over the water, pushing back her long, auburn hair.

To be sure, the maid's expression invited speculation, thought Max. As Max's eyes rolled over his provocative work, the phonograph played "Liebestod"— a lilting, haunting aria from Wagner's opera *Tristan und Isolde*.

"Here's Herr Goering now." She waved him over.

The rings adorning fat fingers, the plump body crammed into the expensive suit, and the round face—bloated and red as a child's balloon—all belonged to Herman Goering.

The Reich minister halted in front of the nude, beside Max and the young lady. "You there, Bauer, don't go selling her any of your bottom-drawer stuff," he bellowed. "We're here to purchase presents for the Fuhrer. You come highly recommended."

"Meet Reich Minister Herman Goering," she said to Max.

Goering held out his doughy hand. Max took it, feeling the sweaty, smooth skin—soft as a baby's. He bowed his head slightly. "I'm honored." Max wondered who had recommended him.

Goering looked around the studio, studying the few other patrons. He then ogled the nude painting. "I like it," he said as he drilled one bejeweled fist into the other. "The girl in the stream's magnificent."

Max, now getting a closer look at him than he did at the train station, noticed his carnivorous eyes, which bit like an arctic wolf, darting quickly from the painting to other pieces around the room, perhaps adding up the value of everything he could bargain or loot. His thin, blond eyebrows, perched below the brim of his stylish hat, with the rosy cheeks and delicate nose, seemed oddly girlish. Goering's polka dot bowtie and black fedora reminded Max of the fat gangster Al Capone. "Do you care to buy my painting, Herr Reich Minister?"

"How much?" Goering asked.

"I saw it first," said the fraulein, wagging her pretty finger at the Reich minister, her green-painted nails sparkling in the light.

"I'll give you the painting, Fraulein Braun, but allow me to do the buying," said Goering. "Men should handle these matters." He shook his head. "Forgive me, Herr Bauer, did Eva introduce herself to you? Eva Braun's one of the Fuhrer's social secretaries."

She glanced at Goering with a hint of apprehension. Somehow, Max felt that this woman had been shielding her identity from him, and the impetuous Goering had spilled the beans.

"Herr Goebbels has told me all about you, Herr Bauer," she said breezily. "I—"

"Goebbels doesn't know a damn thing about art," huffed the Reich minister. "I'm the one who has the biggest collection in the world—except for the Fuhrer, of course."

He slapped Max heartily on the shoulder. "Anyway, I'll pay you good, Bauer. I'll even invite you to shoot game at my estate—Carinhall. I hear you're quite a shot."

"Well, Reich Minister—"

"Reich meister of the hunt." Goering puffed out his chest. "Hundreds of my hunting laws are on the books in Prussia."

His eyes shifted to Eva Braun. "The Olympic authorities wanted Max to instruct our team in the marksman competition, but he turned them down. I want to see him kill a stag. "

"I don't hunt anymore, Herr Goering," Max demurred.

"Why not?"

"They can't shoot back."

Goering chuckled, his belly jiggling through his clothes. He looked around the gallery.

Max continued, "Well, the painting's yours, Herr Goering. It's seven hundred marks, but how about five hundred?"

"Wrap it up, I'll take it."

To Max, five hundred marks was all the money in the world. Perhaps he would have enough to marry Frieda. His gallery would survive, his reputation would grow, and his art would be famous. There'd be food on the table, but . . .

Eva Braun moved closer to Goering, slipping her arm though his, placing her hand on his formidable waist. She guided him closer to a landscape hanging on the wall, but her eyes were fixed on Max. "I feel so alive. I love the nude. You may paint me sometime, Herr Bauer."

Max thought it best to remain silent.

A tear rolled down her cheek. "I adore how the picture dominates me, yet allows me to enjoy my hidden thoughts. Even of . . ."

Max wondered whether the word she had stopped short of saying was "suicide." Something terribly wrong nibbled at this woman's self-esteem, he surmised. Perhaps an overbearing husband, or a controlling lover . . .

Eva's lip quivered. "Herr Goering, escort me home!"

"Of course, Fraulein Braun." He turned to Max. "Send the painting to my office."

Goering guided Eva out of the gallery, like a gentle father tending to a fussy child. Max could hear her sobbing from across the gallery. Max wondered how this strange woman could command such a fuss from this Nazi bigwig. He wasn't entirely overjoyed by his encounter with this offbeat duo.

But the money perked him up.

Chapter 23

"Gretel, I worry about Frieda. She's alone in Berlin. 'At least there's anonymity,' I say to myself, 'it's a big city.' I'm still worried."

"She'll be fine." Gretel grasped Albert's cold hand under the cover. "The hour's late. We need our sleep."

"She should've left Germany long ago. It's hard now, with no passport. The Nazis branded her as a 'subject'—not a citizen. I tried smuggling her out, but my contact vanished—"

"I know, I know. There now, please rest . . ."

Albert felt as though someone had been watching them the whole day. He cursed himself for allowing himself and his wife to travel in broad daylight.

First refused entry into Poland by hateful border guards, they had then sneaked on a train in East Prussia that spirited them south into Austria. Then they had slogged it out to Vienna—walking long distances—and using underground contacts that Albert had developed in Dresden.

"We'll pray for her," said Albert.

Mr. Steinberg lay there on the hard mattress with his wife beside him, both unable to sleep in the converted barn, which smelled of horse dung. Just outside of Vienna, this farm at least offered seclusion, thought Albert, without a neighbor's prying eyes to contend with.

Moreover, their daughter, living under a different last name since she had graduated from medical school, had set up a practice in faraway, crowded Berlin. Maybe things would turn out well, after all.

Albert looked around him. Moonlight, beaming through the tiny window, filled the hay-strewn loft. Every dark object reflected just enough light to project threatening apparitions, including imagined Gestapo truncheons.

"I hope a good country accepts us soon. Then we'll be safe," he whispered. "In the meantime, at least Austria's still free."

"Go to sleep." Gretel turned over in bed, her back to him, her fair hair flowing over the torn blanket. "Things are fine—for now anyway."

Albert closed his eyes and tried to doze off. But what was that sound just outside the door? *Oh, probably nothing,* he thought.

Then the door crashed in . . .

Four husky young men in dark suits grabbed Gretel and Albert, throwing them out of bed. All brandished guns.

"Get up, swine! Get your clothes on. One word and you're dead."

The men bound and gagged them, hustling the couple out of the dwelling, and into the trunks of two waiting cars.

"Did you contact our border people?" the Gestapo agent asked his colleague, slamming shut the cover on the trunk.

"Don't worry, we'll be back in Berlin in no time. Colonel Hock's waiting."

* * *

"Do you concede the match?" asked Siegfried Hock as he breathed heavily through his cage like helmet, the sweat dripping down his neck and under the white fencing outfit.

His fencing partner and adjutant—SS Sergeant Klaus Grog—middle-aged, heavyset, and panting heavily—bent over, resting his hands on his thighs. "I did a half hour ago, Herr General." He removed his helmet.

"You were one of the best fencers in the Fatherland, in your day."

"Not as good as you," Grog said. "You've improved."

General Hock opened the faceguard on his helmet, "I like the sound of that word: 'general.' Now, I can wear my ceremonial sword with my uniform," he said with pride. "Just like some of the field marshals."

"You deserve it, Herr General. The Fuhrer's pleased."

Hock looked around the spacious fencing room, the latest addition to the SS-Gestapo headquarters, located on Berlin's Prinz Albrecht Street. This central office and prison facility had been refurbished in 1933 using curious architecture. The edifice, with its mansard roof and long columns, looked like a hybrid between a haunted mansion and a mausoleum. Berliners—noted for their dark humor—joked that the design fit its grisly purpose.

Hock, glad that he had insisted on extensive sport facilities, implemented his credo that an SS man must be fit mentally *and* physically. After all, the moral fiber of the Third Reich depended upon it.

Headquarters had even been provided with its own garden-maze, like the old English estates. Publicly, this happy playground assisted the recruits during training; privately, it served a more ominous purpose for some of the higher-ranking officers.

"Our vacationers have arrived from Vienna. Let's meet them," Hock said, shoving his fencing sword in the rack and then removing his protective helmet.

Grog unzipped his charge's suit, then his own. He retrieved the general's black tunic and polished boots from the locker. Fetching the long mirror standing by the wall, he rolled it over to his superior. "Allow me, Herr General."

The adjutant assisted Hock as he dressed in his new uniform, including the wide, white belt and the coat with the silver buttons, adorned with the insignia of an SS general. He examined himself in the mirror, slicking back his hair.

"My cap, Klaus."

Grog placed the black SS cap, with the white "death's-head" ornament—skull and crossbones—on his head. "You look splendid, Herr General. I saved the best for last."

Grog presented the remaining item.

Hock's eyes flashed with joy as he saw the long, gleaming sword in its scabbard, with its silver waist-chain and buckle. "It's exquisite," he said as his minion applied the menacing weapon to his waist. Turning in front of the mirror to admire himself, his face glowed with self-satisfaction. It reminded him of the Germanic knights of medieval times, when Germany had fended off the Asiatic hordes.

He would be sure to wear his new uniform to the meetings at the splendid, triangular-shaped SS castle retreat—and cult site—near Wewelsburg, in Westphalia. It even had its own round table, just as in the legend of King Arthur.

He glanced over to Grog. "Aren't you forgetting something, sergeant?" Hock's cold, predatory eyes—with their buzzard like stare—burned through his lackey.

"I'm sorry, Herr General—yes, of course." He ran back to the locker, plucking out the white rose. He rushed back to the general, pinning the flower to the lapel.

"That's better," said the newly appointed SS Reich-Fuhrer of the Secret Security Service—the parent organization of the Gestapo—and second in command only to Herr Himmler. "Let's go; we'll see what the lads dragged in."

Hock looked forward to dealing with the partisan scum from Dresden.

Chapter 24

The SS rank and file called the dunking tank—tucked away in a huge dungeon, under the sports facility at Gestapo headquarters—"Big Gulp."

This stinking cesspool—with the bizarre hoist—had the distinction of being in its own class of depravity. It played on a prisoner's fear of drowning, not once, not quickly, but many times, over an extended period.

Albert Steinberg—his round, balding, battered head swollen and bruised—wearing nothing but a filthy burlap nightgown provided by the Gestapo, stood ten feet away from the filthy tank, next to three guards.

In strode General Hock, escorted by his adjutant, Grog, halting at the table, one hand resting on the handle of his sword. Taking a seat, Hock sniffed the air, narrowing his eyes in disgust, and then read the file in front of him.

It irritated him that no matter how hard the staff scrubbed with disinfectants, the residual stench of urine, vomit, and feces never entirely disappeared. The loss of many body fluids—not just blood—was an inherent byproduct of severe torture, and this violated the fastidious general's sense of cleanliness and order.

Hock didn't bother to look up at Steinberg when he spoke. "Who is your underground contact in Dresden? Where does he live?"

Albert said nothing, his head down, the only reaction to the question being his twitching eyelid, red and swollen.

"All right," said Hock with a smooth voice, "if you don't tell us, your dear wife *will*."

Albert glared at him.

"Yes, that's right," said Hock, "your sweet Gretel hasn't been touched yet. It's all up to you, Herr Steinberg."

"I don't know," said Albert in a fading, scratchy voice. "She knows nothing."

"You love your wife, don't you?"

Steinberg nodded.

"You know," said Hock nodding at Big Gulp, "murder's highly underrated."

The general rose, slowly approaching his prisoner, eyeing him carefully. "Your kind is the most dangerous. In marrying you, your wife soiled herself. She betrayed her people. I don't have much use for you, Herr Steinberg, or for your *frau*. Speak up!"

"I don't know! *She* doesn't know."

"She's a pig."

Steinberg spat at him, the bolus landing on Hock's shiny boot. Grog kicked the prisoner in the groin. Albert crashed to the floor.

Hock looked down at the wad of spit. Instead of anger, his wafer-thin lips parted in a cool smile. "Now, lick it up."

Steinberg didn't move.

"I *said*, lick it up—or I'll hang Gretel in front of your eyes— this very minute! I have the warrant here in my pocket."

As Steinberg crawled on the floor, doing what he was told, the general fingered the white rose on his lapel. "That's better. Get him up off the floor."

Grog did.

"Now get back in place!"

Grog pushed Steinberg back a few meters, removing his truncheon from his belt, keeping it ready.

Hock sat down and scanned the file. "This report says you have a daughter somewhere in Berlin. Apparently, she's a doctor of some sort. Tell us where she is. What name does she use?"

"She's in America—"

"You lie. Tell us. If you do, she lives. She dies if I have to find her myself."

"I don't know. My wife doesn't know!"

The general sprung from the table, drawing his sword, running his small, delicate hand lightly over its razor-sharp blade. He positioned himself directly in front of Albert. Placing the sword on the prisoner's shoulder, at the base of his neck, Hock then twisted his torso, cocking the sword, as if to initiate a beheading.

Steinberg closed his eyes, ready to die.

Hock swung the sword, stopping short of its target, but close enough for his victim to feel the cold steel. Steinberg screamed, then opened his eyes.

"Next time, it's all the way. Now tell!" Hock placed the sword back on the prisoner's shoulder.

Steinberg said nothing. The general cocked his sword. Still, he said nothing.

"Gretel hasn't been harmed. Not *yet*. I don't want to send her to a work camp. I'm sure you know what that is, don't you?"

"She doesn't know anything—let her go!"

"Very well," Hock said amicably, sliding his sword back into its scabbard. He nodded to a sentry. "The Big Gulp for Herr Steinberg."

The guards escorted Herr Steinberg to the tank, careful not to manhandle him too much, lest the pesky general severely reprimand them. They gently bound his ankles together, then his hands behind his back, and fitted the harness at the edge of the cesspool. They hung him upside down, over the stinking water, with the metal hoist, shaped like an upside-down J. Steinberg's head, swinging over the center of the pool, rested an inch above the surface.

"This is our procedure," explained Hock. "Your head will be lowered at one-inch increments—starting at the tip of your skull where it meets the waterline—every thirty seconds until fully submerged. After thirty seconds under water, you resurface for air. Each round, the period your head's totally submerged will be increased by thirty seconds—until you drown."

The general sat down, Grog standing behind him. "Begin!"

Herr Steinberg gurgled, choked, and thrashed for three rounds, never talking.

Presently, Hock looked at his watch. "I'm a busy man. He may not know anything."

Hock rose, snatching the file off the table, angrily stuffing it into his tunic pocket.

"Take him away. Let him rest and eat for a while. Prepare him for the hunt. Get the Rottweiler ready, too." The general strode out of the dungeon, with Grog close behind.

As Hock reached the exit, he pivoted, shouting at Albert: "Frau Steinberg will vacation at Sachsenhausen—at government expense. You have about one hour to tell everything—or you're *both* finished."

Chapter 25

When nighttime descended the hunt commenced. The exterior floodlights illuminated the sprawling, English-style maze-garden, its interior dark and forbidding. Like most of the German brass, Hock admired the British and their genteel customs. He had even hosted foxhunts.

The Rottweiler growled viciously, its teeth gleaming, the mouth frothy with drool, in anticipation of the kill. Hock stood ready, holding the leash firmly, as he prepared for the blood sport. He felt the smooth handle of his shiny new sword and then looked up at the ten-foot-high, ivy-covered walls of the maze.

The general petted his dog on the head as Grog stood next to him. About fifty meters away, Hock observed two SS guards holding Steinberg at gunpoint, at the other end of the maze—its bushy entrance brightly lit. The prisoner held a pistol. The general waved to the guards, and they pushed him through the entry.

Hock had set the rules.

Herr Steinberg knew that if he made it to the other end, he and his wife would be set free. If he died, she would "vacation" in the concentration camp. The general was unarmed except for his dog and his sword, but the prisoner was supplied with a loaded gun.

That seemed sporting to Hock, a critical requirement. The German knights had believed in fair play, and the general embraced some measure of chivalry as well. Besides, defeat wasn't an option.

Drawing his gleaming weapon from its scabbard, he ordered the guards to play music over the loudspeaker. He had chosen "O Star of Eve" from the Wagnerian opera *Tannhauser*.

The general took the leash from Grog, then led the dog into the entrance of his end of the maze. Entering, he could just see the ivy on the walls, and the path between them. In places here and there, enough light shone through to reveal more detailing, like a sharp corner, an alcove, a large stone on the ground—or the outline of a man's figure.

Hock let go of the leash, giving the beast its head. Having been trained to ferret out human prey over the past few years, the animal had become a highly valued hunting partner.

It ran ahead of him, the panting becoming less audible to Hock behind right angles within the deadly labyrinth. Despite intermittent snarling and growling, the dog had been trained *not* to attack if he found its prey, but only to point to it, by barking.

For the dog to do more wouldn't be sportsmanlike.

Hock heard a shot crack through the air, the bullet swishing through the wall of the maze, roughly fifteen meters away from him. He raised his sword, moving in the direction of the sound.

The sounds from the dog had disappeared entirely. Hock felt a wave of emotion come over him, fearing that his prized animal had been hurt. He couldn't stand the thought of a dog suffering. Rage then took over.

He raised his sword higher as he heard the faint ruffling of leaves nearby, not quite drowned by the inspirational music. As Hock turned the dark corner, he thought he heard heavy breathing. Not from the dog, but from the wheezing prisoner.

Then he could just make out a faint silhouette, slowly approaching him, the twigs snapping under Steinberg's feet. Hock froze, holding his breath. He cocked his sword overhead.

The snapping and ruffling sound came closer. Running out of breath, the general slowly exhaled. Another shot cracked in the air, missing him by inches. He could see a round object at eye level just in front of him, next to a right-angle turn in the ivy.

Hock lunged, swinging his sword with all his might.

In a split second, he heard a groan, a splat, and then a plop to the ground.

The general, with a sense of relief, had felt his sword slice through a soft target, with a bone core—like a baked ham. His hand felt wet. He reached into his pocket and retrieved his whistle, blowing it.

Suddenly, the interior lamps bathed the inside of the maze with blinding light. The general saw Steinberg's head lying on the leaves, not far from the rest of his body—and the pistol too.

Barely paying his dead opponent any heed, his attention focused upon a more important object lying at the end of the leafy corridor. Throwing down his bloody sword, he ran to his dog—kneeling down—sadly stroking its soft coat. It still breathed and moved slightly.

He screamed for the guards. "Get over here on the double! You can't let a creature suffer!"

Chapter 26

"Cooking's very much like painting." Max placed a few copper pans on the tile counter in Frieda's kitchen. "You start with quality ingredients." He removed the veal, onions, potatoes, milk, and butter from the icebox. "You construct your creation in your mind first. Then, with your tools."

"What if you burn it?" asked Frieda.

Max shrugged. "In the trash."

Chomping on a raw carrot, he removed the peanut oil and spices from the cupboard, placing them on the counter. He threw a large copper frying pan on the range and turned on the fire. "Put a dab here and a dab there of spice and herbs, setting the mood and flavor."

He sliced a carrot and popped a piece into Frieda's mouth. "Like yellow highlights in a landscape, you add a dash more spice, if necessary."

Max waved his hand over his painting overalls, the black one with the multi-colored stains, and deep pockets. "Last—" He plucked his suspender. "—you dress so you're comfortable."

Frieda folded her arms. Dressed in a loose, lemon yellow dress and brown slippers, she snatched a piece of cheese from the counter and nibbled on it. "I'm really not very hungry, Max. This cheese will do." Her flat expression alerted Max to her pensive mood.

She walked over to the easy chair in the adjoining living room and plopped down. "A bit tired, too."

While Max worked diligently on the meal, he chattered about the weather, football, his favorite foods, and the latest antics of his artist friends, careful not to talk about anything very important. He felt that Frieda had her hands full with her practice, and he wanted to distract her from it. She had also been very concerned about the Joel and Sarah Roth.

He poured two large glasses of Riesling, delivering Frieda's, and then resumed his chores in the kitchen.

"Mozart, anyone?" Max asked. He slipped the record on the phonograph. He left to use the bathroom and then returned to see that Frieda had finished her drink, but she didn't seem more animated.

Max breaded the veal and fried it in the sizzling butter and onions. "Tell me about your parents." He could see that he had hit a nerve.

"They're—fine."

"I know that's what's troubling you. You've held back," he said.

"They're in Austria now. Really, they're fine."

"Austria? I thought they were in Poland. Are they in trouble?"

Frieda paused, then continued in a flat voice. "Daddy's a little sick, that's all. Maybe the flu—Mama's tending to him."

Max didn't believe her. He strode into the living room with the china plates and silverware, to set the table. He wondered why she had lied.

"I tried to buy an Arnold Schoenberg record the other day, and the store said they didn't carry them anymore. No store does. They said it was too 'atonal'—whatever that means."

Frieda watched him cook. "It means, like some of your paintings."

Max brought the food to the table. "It's ready."

He took his seat. Frieda sat at the other end of the table, seemingly distracted. She studied the food but didn't take any. "You're quite the cook."

He helped himself to a dollop of mashed potatoes, veal, some peas, and red cabbage with a hint of bacon grease and vinegar. He pushed the serving vessels over to Frieda. "Eat."

She poked at her food, hardly taking any bites. "I hate cooking," she said absently.

Max steadily depleted his plate. "I know."

"All right then!" Frieda's voice exploded, her pent-up anxiety boiling over. "Daddy used to be active in the Social Democratic Party in Dresden, before Hitler came to power. Mama would help him. Now, his business suffers. The worry is affecting his health."

Max sensed that she still wasn't telling all. "Is there any way we can help?"

"That's sweet of you, Max."

"Is that all there is to it?"

Frieda dropped her fork. "Not entirely. I've been feeling unwell myself for the last week—morning sickness."

Max's eyes grabbed Frieda's. He felt a thrill consume him. "How long have you known?"

"A few days; it was confirmed by an obstetrician friend of mine."

He jumped up from the table. She stood to meet him, and then he hugged her. "No wonder you're not hungry. I feel like a fool. What will we name her?"

A tear rolled down her cheek. "How about *Max*ine?"

He smothered her with kisses, taking her hands, staring into her lovely brown eyes. "Please, *please* marry me, soon! Now! Right this second! Marry this worthless artist and bad cook. The offer comes with a certified guarantee."

"Let's hear it."

"I'll love you forever."

"Not the best time to start a family, is it, Max?"

Max felt her mind turning over, pawing through cobwebs. Frieda then studied his face. Her eyes shone, and she smiled. "Of course I'll marry you. Not this second, though, maybe a minute from now. I want a civil wedding, but in a big church, with a couple of good friends."

"I can't wait to tell Hans."

As Max's eyes welled up, he kissed Frieda's smooth hands, thankful to her for loving him. *My God—I'm a father!*

Despite his rapture, a lingering thought nagged him.

There's still a piece of the puzzle missing.

Chapter 27

SS Adjutant Grog placed the day's copy of the *Volkischer Beobachter* upon Siegfried Hock's fastidiously tidy desk. It rested next to the photograph of his pretty wife and four towheaded children—two girls and two boys—aged four to nine. Devoted to them, Hock spent every spare minute that he could in their presence, their welfare always his primary concern.

When recruiting SS men, he looked for this quality in his recruits. Only good family men need apply. Any man found cheating on his wife or consorting with "cheap" women was dealt with in the most severe manner—then expelled. An orderly life, with loyalty to one's wife and children, to one's country, to one's race, was prized above all else. After all, the SS motto boasted: "Loyalty Is My Honor."

The books lining the shelves of Hock's Spartan office sat in perfect rows between two golden bookends, shaped in swastikas. No dust or clutter marred the desk's pristine surface, all papers neatly stacked, the silver pens shining in their holders. Everything had to be in its place.

As Grog fussed about the office, attending to his sundry chores, Hock stood across the room by the window, playing his favorite piece on his violin: a solo portion of the Violin Concerto in D Major from Beethoven's *Fidelio*.

As the general played, he let his mind race, his memory expanding to fill its robust container. The melody, cool, precise, and yet sad in places, moistened his eyes and facilitated his ruminations.

Squinting through the bright afternoon light streaming in from the window, he admired the blooms on the white roses in the garden, which he had carefully cultivated. Hock, an amateur horticulturist with an expert's knowledge of genetics, enjoyed breeding roses with the purest, cool-white hue of any species of flower.

The perfect white rose symbolized his obsession and sacred duty: not to aesthetics, but rather to racial purity and mass genocide.

Having majored in biology and mathematics at Heidelberg University, he had quickly mastered eugenics—the study of human breeding—as well. Darwin's theory of evolution no longer held, he fretted, since human survival had become too easy, and breeding too indiscriminate.

"Survival of the fittest" had become largely irrelevant. This had led to a degenerate population pool and the dissolution of the genetic material where habitual criminals, gypsies, Jews, cretins, anarchists, and their ilk—essentially *madmen*—polluted the Nordic race, not only physically, but also *culturally*.

Indeed, the field of phrenology underscored this pollution. It had become en vogue in medicine and philosophy over the prior fifty years, and asserted that physical traits of some groups of humans could be correlated with adverse psychological characteristics. For instance, the shape of the head could predict criminality, insanity, or a low IQ.

Similarly, society's "ills," such as economic depression, inflation, prostitution, homosexuality and transvestitism—or any social "deviancy"—were the signs and symptoms generated by these madmen, these degenerates with the adverse physical traits.

Modernist art represented symbols of this degeneracy, and so did its offshoots, such as Impressionism, Cubism, Dadaism, and German Expressionism. Therefore, the general believed that these symbols must be ruthlessly eradicated.

That's where Bauer came in. He illustrated both good and bad traits. He represented a mystery.

Hock held on to a musical note, moving his fingers over the strings of his violin, his eyes closed, his body consumed with emotion from the music's sweet sentiment. He strode about the room in rhythm with the melody . . .

The holy—yet disagreeable—task of those saddled with the burden of eliminating human degeneracy and the problems caused by it was to liquidate large numbers of undesirables, since nature no longer did. World progress depended upon it. The Nazis were doing humankind a favor—the part of it that mattered, anyway.

The general wandered over to his desk, putting down the violin. He took a seat, straightening his black tunic and fingering the empty hole in the lapel. He opened the desk drawer and retrieved a fresh rose, carefully affixing the white flower.

He looked up at Grog, who pointed at the newspaper on his boss's desk.

"Second page," said Grog. "They found it. According to the Race and Research Department, that's the Steinberg daughter in the photo. She's a neurologist, living here in Berlin."

Hock picked up the paper. "I do believe you're right, Grog. Look who she's marrying. I wonder if Bauer knows he's marrying a kike—a half-kike, anyway. She had changed her name to 'Holtz' from 'Steinberg.'"

Hock threw down the paper, the headline of the column in large print: "ARTIST MAX BAUER AND PHYSICIAN FRIEDA HOLTZ TO EXCHANGE VOWS TODAY."

"It would be rude of us not to attend," said Hock.

* * *

"I do."

"I now pronounce you man and wife. You may kiss the bride."

Standing at the altar in front of the justice of the peace, Frieda and Max kissed each other in the old cathedral—the Kaiser Wilhelm *Gedächtniskirche*—just off the Kurfurstendamm. Max took the dignified official's hand, which had been offered in congratulations, then also shook hands with Hans Beckman—his best man—nattily attired, as usual.

Max led Frieda down the aisle toward the three-arched exit and the huge, wooden front door. He and Frieda had decided on a civil ceremony in this stone, multi-spired, mostly secular, Prussian landmark.

As the smiling couple strode arm in arm to the organ music of Felix Mendelssohn's "Wedding March"—still allowed despite the heritage of its composer—their faces glowed with joy.

The bride and groom waved at the handful of guests, including Lena and her grim-faced grandson, Paul—he attired in full Brown Shirt kit.

Victor, the railroad supervisor, and Frieda's nurse also lined the aisle. As Max scanned the interior of the historic structure with its vaulted ceilings and gorgeous stained-glass windows, he thought about Frieda's absent parents.

What happened to them? Why aren't they here?

Frieda and Max reached the blinding sunlight of the outdoors, descending the front steps of the cathedral that led to the parking lot and to the waiting Mercedes that Lena had hired. Max's gaze collided with the sight of black tunics and red armbands waiting for them below.

There stood General Hock, with his SS assistant. The general held up a piece of paper. "I see I'm too late, Herr Bauer." He handed it to Max. "You see the problem, I'm sure."

"Problem?" Frieda shrieked. "Who are you to come here and bother us?"

"I don't understand, Herr General." Max glanced down at the paper. He saw that it concerned the Nuremberg Laws of 1935. "What's this all this about?"

"Your wife has deceived you."

Max glanced at Frieda. He smiled at her reassuringly, then glared at Hock. "I don't need *you* to tell me about my wife, General."

"Apparently I do," he said as he snatched the paper back from Max. "You see, your wife's a Hebrew."

He nodded at Frieda, as if unmasking a mass murderer. "Or a half-breed, I should say. Her father—Albert Steinberg—is a full Jew. That means she's half—and consequently your marriage is technically unlawful."

Max looked at Frieda. She looked away.

"I know all about him," Max lied. He now knew what Frieda had been hiding.

"Her father was also a dangerous subversive—a member of the Dresden underground—"

"*Was!*" shouted Frieda. She lunged at Hock, Max restraining her just in time. "What do you mean, '*was*'? What's happened to him?"

Hock's eyes lit up with excitement. "Papa is dead."

Max took his wife's hand to comfort her.

Frieda, at first stunned, groped for words and then screamed, "My mother! Is she—"

"No," answered Hock.

"Where is she?" Max asked.

Hock ignored the question.

Max—instinctively—thought it best to get out of there quickly. "My wife's a neurologist. She's no subversive, Herr General. Unless you're charging both of us, we're leaving." Lingering would only ensure their arrest, he knew. Frieda and the baby would suffer the most.

Hock's eyes shifted, looking at the crowd that had formed around them. Hans, Lena, and Victor stood solemnly by, bearing witness, with scores of guests. Paul, not surprisingly, had disappeared.

"In two days, I start an important painting for Minister Goebbels—an official commission for the Fuhrer's new Reich Chancellery," Max said. It was a partial truth: The offer had been made, but he had yet to accept the job.

He observed Hock weighing his options, his eyes bubbling cauldrons of calculation and probabilities.

Then the general stood aside. "Take her and leave, Herr Bauer." His chilling eyes shifted to Frieda. "I'm sure we'll be meeting again, Frau Bauer."

They headed for the Mercedes.

"Oh, Bauer," added Hock.

Max turned.

"Remember, 'Until *death* do you part.'"

Chapter 28

Adolf Hitler, casually dressed in his rustic lederhosen, with edelweiss adorning his leather suspenders, stood by the huge picture window in his private study at the newly completed "Eagle's Nest." The new retreat, tucked deep into the Bavarian Alps, offered breathtaking views of the majestic Obersalzburg resort area.

Hitler's small pinewood desk, and thick, oaken bookshelves—crammed with cultist history books and offbeat philosophy tomes—stood in the corner of the cramped room. He toiled over an oil painting with a rare-for-him subject matter: human beings.

He loved to paint at that window and took up his brush almost every late afternoon, when visiting his southern redoubt. Through the glass, the hyper-vigilant Fuhrer noticed the winding footpath in the distance—at about five hundred meters away—partially obscured by the pines that dotted the area.

At least a dozen shades of green—with varying amounts of yellow and blue, depending upon the sunlight—offered a feast of color. The pure, clean countryside, not at all like the grime and squalor of degenerate city life, energized him. It rekindled his faith in the superiority of the German soul.

Biting on the fingernail of his left pinky, Adolf ogled another radiant oil painting—not his—but one already completed, resting upon an easel that stood next him.

The mere fact that he considered hanging it in his main reception area over the marble hearth spoke volumes about his high regard for it. Joseph and Magda Goebbels had gifted him the emotionally charged landscape, as well as the art-deco furniture that festooned the entire, castle like structure.

As Adolf enjoyed one of his favorite records, Wagner's "Das Rheingold Preamble" from *The Ring*, his milky blue eyes devoured the extraordinary piece by Max Bauer.

Bauer's pastoral scene symbolized the Fuhrer's motivation for dominating Germany and Europe. The burst of vibrant yellow played with the farmer's hut, providing a wholesome focal point and an implied promise of expanded *lebensraum*—more living space for Germany.

The bluish fields and purple valleys—although somewhat odd to the Fuhrer—nevertheless worked marvelously. The brush strokes, thick and zigzagging—like bolts of lightning—imbued the rich, impasto surface with a raw energy that he had seldom seen, let alone possessed as his very own.

Inwardly jealous of the artist's gifts, he nevertheless admired the Great War hero. *Creative expression on the canvas*, he thought, *is welcome, as long as it serves the nation's needs.* After all, he wasn't a blockhead. And this painting did just that.

Bauer's sixteen-by-twenty-inch masterpiece represented the natural world at its best. It had shunned—largely—the diabolical, un-German Expressionism that had infected Germany since the war, which he considered "madness." His heavy gaze, moist with feeling, shifted from the vibrant sun to the label on its frame: "*PEASANTS EARNING THEIR DAILY BREAD*, MAX BAUER, 1937."

I remember him, ruminated the Fuhrer, *from the gas ward. The chap across the aisle from me; he'd been gassed too.* A tall, blond, freckled fellow with a gentle, understanding expression, he had won the Iron Cross Second Class.

This is my man! The propaganda minister was right. He'll direct the art exhibitions.

The Fuhrer, on Goebbels's recommendation, had summonsed Max to the Eagle's Nest to bestow upon the struggling artist the chance of a lifetime. Naturally, as a painter, he had some quirks that needed mending. But the Fuhrer had resolved that he would be tolerant—to a point. With Minister Goebbels at his side, he would reorder the culture of the nation, thus bolstering its moral fiber. Art is as important to character, Adolf believed, as nutritious food is to a strong body.

Corrupt art, and you poison the character of the German nation. Art *is* politics.

Wasn't the alluring insignia—which he had personally designed for the party—proof of this? Had not Joseph Stalin, in Russia, accomplished the same thing for the Communists?

Of all the leaders throughout history, including Frederick the Great and Napoleon, he secretly admired Stalin the most; he suspected the Russian leader of being—like him—deep down, an artist. Unlike the sniveling English politicians, thought Hitler, Stalin had virtue. His masculine ruthlessness, his cunning, his uncanny intuition, and his manipulation of world opinion almost couldn't be matched. Almost, except for *him*, of course. Stalin had murdered millions of his own peasants—now there was a man to contend with!

At that moment, Eva Braun opened the door that led to the upstairs bedroom, striding into the study to join her consort. Completely naked, she performed a handstand, walking on her palms to the wall, against which she positioned her upside-down feet, performing vertical push-ups, just a few meters away from Hitler.

He glanced her way.

"Well, Fraulein Braun, I see you're in good spirits today."

Chapter 29

"Max is simply divine."

"Oh, so '*Max*,' is it?" quipped the grumpy Fuhrer.

Eva's sprightly voice echoed throughout the study. "The sunburst over the farm—*sumptuous*—isn't it?"

Hitler, not sure that he liked her without clothes so early in the evening, decided that this silly woman—so fond of using fancy words—deserved a one-syllable answer.

"*Ja*," he grumbled.

Eva pumped her push-ups. She spread her finely toned legs. "Now, don't pout."

"I'm not pouting!"

Hitler glared at her. "I told you not to walk too close to me around others, like at the reception yesterday."

"Oh, fiddlesticks—"

"People are talking," added the Fuhrer. "A great man can't be too careful with public displays of affection," he nagged.

"Yes, my Fuhrer—"

"Don't '*Fuhrer*' me! I remain single for German womanhood—their love is key to my power. I can't afford to make them jealous."

Shaking his head in exasperation, he changed the subject. "So, you like Herr Bauer's painting—this landscape here, do you?"

Eva walked on her hands to the middle of the room, springing off the rough, beige stone tile to land upright, squarely on her feet—in front of him—her smooth backside pleasingly visible as she performed her calisthenics.

"He's the best painter in Germany. Goebbels thinks so too," she said.

"Goebbels—sometimes his taste runs on the wild side."

"Nevertheless, Bauer's a genius," she insisted.

Her slim, boyish figure titillated him—more since she had changed her hairstyle to a short, clean, cadet like cut. Her lithe body and her clear, hazel eyes radiated youthful vitality and physical confidence.

She seemed to possess—he let himself admit—bits of masculinity that poked through her flighty temperament. He even suspected that her usual, dizzy-blonde persona might be just an act. He mistrusted clever women.

"Agreed," conceded the Fuhrer. "He's certainly a genius."

Hitler felt that Eva exhibited just enough girlishness—at almost twenty years his junior—to neutralize his fear of her boyish qualities. However, it was also this coquettishness that increasingly irritated him, rendering him—except on rare occasions—unable to discharge his manly duty.

"I'm painting, Fraulein. Why don't you go pester someone else?"

The Fuhrer then noticed Wagner's magnificent crescendo-decrescendo intrusion, straining to wave his hand to its haunting rhythm. Music had increasingly taken the place of sex—such as it was—as his physical release.

"Pity," Eva said. She bent forward in front of him, performing toe-touching exercises.

The Fuhrer had shifted his attention back to his easel, hardly noticing that she remained in the room. "What's a pity?"

"Bauer married a Jewess. General Hock told me."

He finished the touches on his portrait. The subject—a young mother holding her infant son—reminded him of Mary holding her baby, Jesus. His use of vibrant red on the mother's robe could be considered very bold, he thought. The painting reminded him of *his* mother.

"Fiddlesticks," said Eva. "He should marry whomever he wants."

Hitler picked up a filbert paintbrush, dipping it into a pile of vermillion paint. "Quit using that silly American word! I told you not to do that. Now here you go, saying it not once, but twice. Next thing you know, you'll be playing bongos."

"Don't be boorish, my *wolfschen.*"

"I told you not to call me that." Secretly, he loved that nickname—*little wolf.* "You'll obey me in all things."

He had mastered his mistress totally, suppressing any trace of rebellion, or so he had gathered. These childish outbursts represented pathetic gropes for freedom—foolish aspirations that he had always ruthlessly vanquished. Women craved domination, he believed firmly. He knew that she also craved punishment.

"I shall always obey you, my Fuhrer, to the end."

Eva's face flushed. She stopped exercising. She turned, facing her paramour with her head hung low. Her lovely lip curled down in contrition, completing an emotional right turn that never ceased to amuse him.

As always, she had capitulated. Hitler smiled. "Now, now, where's the happy little cadet . . . "

Eva wiped her moist eyes, then returned to her stretching exercises.

His gaze shifted from the easel to her body, running his eyes down her smooth, firm thighs and pelvis. She had just a bit of a tan line left from sunning herself nude on their private patio. Her broad, muscular shoulders, and narrow hips, charged him with excitement. To his surprise, he sensed a nascent tumescence.

Somewhat shockingly, she reminded him of an inductee during the war—a tall, lean boy with fair hair . . . Hitler then banished the disquieting thought.

"Maybe it's a good thing that Bauer has a Jewess," he continued. "There are only two possibilities, my child. One, he's of no use. Two, and more likely, he's a success with the exhibitions. It'll be easier to control him if we have something on him."

Eva Braun stopped her exercising, staring at him with sublime adoration. "You're very tolerant, my love."

That look of devotion—it's the same look! Why is this silly woman now reminding me of the woman in my painting—and my mother?

That emasculating notion shocked and perplexed the Fuhrer. He stared at his enigmatic mistress, paralyzed by the threat of fresh assaults on his fragile virility.

Adolf knew that Eva idolized him. He had figured that she was torn between domination and dependence, and he loved to drive a wedge between her dueling personalities, to capitalize on her weakness. Power, as always, is what mattered.

But, over the past few months, a new, troubling wrinkle had crept into this game—the sacred memory of *Frau* Hitler.

This must be some trick of Eva's. Maybe she wants to play that game again; I liked that, he admitted to himself. She must've known that the pain had titillated him.

He noticed a tear rolling down Fraulein Braun's cheek.

Oh no, fretted the Fuhrer, not another one of her mood swings.

"I've been bad. Punish me completely," she said in a barely audible, crumbling voice.

Hitler nodded absently as he painted. The truth was, he didn't like her talking about the spankings—their little secret—because that spoiled it. Weary of this drill, he would instead have her repeat the little routine that they had fallen back on several times before. *He* would be punished instead, just as when he was a child.

"Do you remember what you did last Christmas Eve?" asked the Fuhrer.

She slowly nodded, then smiled. "All right, if you insist, my Fuhrer."

"But not too hard," he firmly admonished. He studied the mother's expression on the painting, then glanced at her. "Like my mother used to do, Fraulein; you remember."

Her eyes sparkled. She strode over to his easel and jerked the brush out of his hand, then spanked his butt with one brisk swoop of her hand. "Like that?"

"Please don't!"

Grasping his belt, Eva jerked him across the room like an unruly dog on a leash. She led him to their private chambers upstairs, through the study's back door.

As per their usual playacting, the Fuhrer whined like a naughty schoolboy, walloped in the woodshed.

"After that, I've got a new game, *wolfschen*," she reassured him with gravel in her voice. "I stole some knickknacks from my doctor. You won't have to do a thing."

Chapter 30

Max sat in the back seat of the long, open Mercedes, the swastika pennant flapping on the black hood, as it whisked him up to Hitler's Eagle's Nest. The road, a winding and steep affair, unsettled him.

As the car sped up the mountain, he looked over the side, eyeing the infinite drop down to the valley floor. He had heard that at nearly a thousand meters long, this service road to Hitler's new retreat was meant to intimidate visitors, and it did. The car sped faster into a hairpin turn, tossing Max a few inches sideways on the passenger's seat.

The driver, a lean, dark-haired ruffian in uniform, glanced back at him, as if to see whether he was still there. Max then marveled at the resemblance between this middle-aged man behind the wheel and the Fuhrer himself.

The intense eyes, the shape of the head, the broad, fleshy nose, the unruly hair waxed to the side, and the toothbrush mustache—now a fad since Hitler had become famous—were all uncannily similar. Max surmised that the resemblance hadn't been chance alone, but perhaps a device to thwart assassination attempts using a decoy.

"How much longer, Herr—?" shouted Max.

"Bruno Meier, sir, the Fuhrer's chauffeur and valet. Not long at all."

Max recognized this terrain from his early teens, when—just before the war—his father had taken him to the mountains surrounding Berchtesgaden, to hunt stags.

He wondered why Adolf Hitler had invited him to his mountain retreat.

Max ruminated over the situation, possibly a dangerous one.

The honeymoon had been cancelled, and he moved into Frieda's apartment after the wedding. As her pregnancy progressed, he enjoyed doing extra chores around the apartment so that she could save her energy for the medical practice. After they'd received the harrowing news from Hock of her father's death, he had tried to console her and uncover the mystery surrounding Frieda's mother.

Then, the night before, two Gestapo agents had rousted them. They ordered Max to pack for a road trip, scheduled for the next morning.

Hitler had mandated his presence at his new retreat.

Max hoped the meeting was about his art, but there were other—troubling—reasons that were possible. Frieda being half-Jewish, could that be the problem? She had kept that secret from him for *his* safety, not just hers, knowing that it made no difference to him whatsoever. Perhaps this was about Herr Steinberg's underground activities or Max's friendship with Hans Beckman.

Maybe it's a trick.

Maybe Hitler won't even be at the destination. *Maybe I'm about to be murdered. Murdered? Why?* He didn't give a hoot about politics. *To them, I'm a blasted war hero. Goebbels even bought my painting!*

All these scenarios were unlikely, thought Max. This impromptu meeting with Hitler must be about his art, not a death warrant.

Presently, the car stopped and unloaded in front of a huge, arched metal door carved into a cliff. Over the entrance, the bronze initials "AH" welcomed them.

The driver pushed a button next to the door, and the metal panels separated, revealing a polished-brass, Venetian-mirrored elevator with a red leather bench.

Max examined himself in the mirror as Bruno whisked him up to the main floor, ascending the tall granite mountainside. Max's ordinary dark suit and tan fedora, another wedding present from Lena Krebs, seemed to him sufficiently respectful. By most accounts, however, Hitler enjoyed countless bohemian traits, including a fondness for casual, Bavarian getups. Max wondered whether he had even overdressed.

The elevator doors opened onto an octagonal, stonewalled reception room with a red marble hearth. Shocked, Max saw his recent landscape, *Peasants Earning Their Daily Bread,* perched over it.

Brass and ivory art deco furniture, with hunter green pads, offered a curious contrast to the drafty, stone—almost medieval—enclosure. Knights' armor, swords, battle-axes, and other weapons hung from the walls.

From this odd room, lined with small, square windows that overlooked the Alps, the driver spirited Max into an adjoining office-study, dominated by a large picture window. Two easels stood beside it. One displayed a painting of a mother and her infant child. The window overlooked a forest at about five hundred meters away, where a zigzagging, partially obscured path ran through it.

Next to the two easels stood none other than Adolf Hitler, his back turned to Max, hands folded behind him, peering out the window into the nearby foothills.

Chapter 31

Hitler cleared his throat. "It's been a long time, Herr Bauer."

Slowly turning around, the Fuhrer of Germany waved his driver away. As the door closed, Hitler carefully approached Max with a welcoming, outstretched hand.

"It has indeed, Herr Reich Chancellor."

Hatless, his dark hair greased to one side, dressed in a mustard-colored tunic with a Nazi armband, navy slacks, and patent leather shoes, the dictator appeared exactly as he had in the newsreels. His hand felt—somewhat surprisingly to Max—warm and smooth.

Max recognized little of the scruffy, raving soldier he had met in the gas ward of the army hospital nineteen years earlier, except for the strangely flickering luminosity of his blue eyes—and of course the toothbrush mustache.

Hitler placed his hand under Max's elbow, gently guiding him to his portrait by the window. "When I'm done with politics, I shall paint all day. As it is, I try to paint at my window here most late afternoons. The pre-dusk lighting is best, unless you're an early riser."

As he talked in an even, gentle, and scratchy voice, he clasped his hands behind his back, leaning towards Max in a gesture of sincere intimacy. Then Hitler placed his gentle hands upon Max's shoulders, peering into his eyes.

"I want you to feel at ease here, Herr Bauer. After all, war comrades need not put on airs. We both won the Iron Cross, after all."

Hitler moved close to his easel, waving at the canvas. "What do you think of it?" He wagged his finger at Max playfully. "Be honest."

Max, somewhat lost for words, hesitated. "Gracious, well, it has a certain—technical virtuosity . . . "

"*But*—" Hitler said. He nodded encouragingly. "Don't hold back, Herr Bauer."

"Well—"

"On the one hand, you don't want to insult me, and on the other you take me for a man who doesn't abide cheap flattery—which would make things even worse for you."

Max fired his critique. "Technical virtuosity's important, but your painting hasn't much feeling that goes beneath the surface of the canvas. That makes it flat."

Hitler frowned, then laughed.

For years, Max had heard all the vicious rumors about "The Carpet-Eater," and he had seen him long ago raving in the hospital, though he realized that war and injury could destabilize anyone. More recently, newsreels at the cinema presented him in a way that, to Max, depicted him as just another hell-raising politician, of which there had been many since the war—in many countries.

But in *person,* Max thought, this earnest man standing before him wasn't the homely neurotic who had been so pilloried in the press before the takeover. He possessed a strange energy and physical attractiveness that instilled confidence. So far, he didn't seem that bad . . .

"Herr Bauer. There are two possibilities. Either you're a great genius, or you're the greatest dauber of all time. Your landscape composition, hanging over my hearth, has not only accurate perspective, but also delicate balance. Most of all, it makes me proud to be a German!"

"You're too generous," said Max.

Hitler chuckled. "From one artist to another, you have the rare gift of artistic genius."

Hitler studied Max with appraising eyes, as if summing up his core being. "I see you're ambitious, Herr Bauer."

Max remained silent.

"You have a wife to consider, and a son coming too," added Hitler.

Max started slightly. *How did he know that? This man really checked up on me.*

"Yes, well, it may be a daughter . . . "

"One can only hope that it's a masculine child." Hitler slapped him on the back, not without some measure of charm. His restless eyes moved back to his painting, resting on the easel.

"You know, Herr Bauer, when I was a boy, I passed a pet store that had a nice little doggie in the window. We were too poor to buy it. Do you understand me?"

"Yes sir." It shocked Max to see Adolf Hitler's eyes well up.

"One day, the dog got out of his kennel and followed me all the way to school. It was very cold and icy that day." Choked with emotion, his host gritted his teeth and then continued. "Just as I was about to enter the schoolhouse, I heard him barking from the road. I could see his loyal little eyes shining."

Hitler moved his face close to the canvas, examining the mother in his painting. "A passing car hit the dog." His voice cracked. "The doggie died in my arms—his loyal eyes closing forever."

Max stared at Hitler, pitying the poor little dog; and his host also.

Hitler's extraordinary sincerity brought the maudlin story to life. Max had believed every word he said, without the urge to laugh, as he would have with Han Beckman telling it. It seemed impossible that this leader could be aware of—not to mention responsible for—the regime's excesses. Therefore, a few fanatics close to him must be responsible, he surmised.

"When I first saw your landscape, Herr Bauer, that was the first time I'd felt such emotion since that tragedy with the little dog."

Hitler slowly backed away from the painting. "You see—despite what you've heard, Herr Bauer—I'm a sensitive fellow."

He paced the room, his voice taking on a deeper tone. "I have a big job for you." Hitler chewed on his pinky nail. "In this job rests the fate of the Fatherland and of the great German folk."

Max, surprised at his own words, nevertheless blurted his response. "Yes, my Fuhrer."

"That word doesn't come easily to you, and I respect that honesty," said Hitler.

Hitler seemed to have the uncanny—and somewhat ominous—ability to read one's mind, Max thought. He wondered whether he dared to bring up the topic of Frieda's parents. But something told Max to wait. He needed to prove himself first, then broach the issue.

The Fuhrer of Germany, he realized with excitement, had something great in store for him, something that would empower his art and provide security for his family.

Chapter 32

Max had supper that night in the small commons, situated next to the Eagle Nest's well-stocked kitchen. He dined with a few visiting dignitaries from Hungary and a gaggle of Hitler's secretaries, including Eva Braun.

Hitler loved to surround himself with fawning females who could manage his limitless pile of details—which he abhorred. Ever paternalistic, he called them "my children." Eva, the life of the party, attired in her Bavarian dress and mountaineer hat—with a peacock feather stuck in its brim—shared ribald jokes with two pretty, thin, elegantly dressed English twins of noble descent.

According to the gossip around the table, Hitler and his entourage—including a couple of Nazi bigwigs such as Albert Speer and Rudolf Hess—had taken their meals in the main dining hall. The Hungarian princess sitting next to Max, adjusting her diamond tiara, informed him that the Fuhrer—a teetotaler and vegetarian—preferred that no meat be served at his table. Apparently, he couldn't stand the sight of animal carcasses.

Moreover, their renowned host was obsessed by movies, especially those featuring English colonial troops suppressing their brown-skinned subjects. After dinner, they were all—including Hitler—to relocate to a small theater for a feature film. An important announcement would follow. Max felt uncomfortable with the mad-tea-party atmosphere, so close to a focal point of such raw, immense power.

When they finished their food, a bell sounded from the kitchen, and a steward appeared. He picked a spoon up off the table and banged it against a glass. "The Fuhrer requests your presence in the cinema."

He led the guests through an arched door and up a short, dimly lit, spiral staircase built with thick stones, suggesting the entrance to a dungeon rather than a social venue. Max emerged in a pine-paneled theater, with seven rows arranged in a V. The seats faced a small stage with a large screen behind it. Diamond chandeliers softly lit the theater.

Max sat in the back of the room with the Hungarians, while the other rows—closer to the stage—filled with arriving guests. He noticed that the heavy adjutant, the man who had stood next to Hock at the steps of the wedding chapel, placed Eva Braun and her friends near him.

As Eva's lively eyes danced about the room, she noticed Max, waving to him. He wondered whether she was really just a clerical assistant, or rather something more intimate, perhaps even to Hitler. Max nodded to her coolly, refocusing his attention on the front of the theater.

The adjutant had made his way to the center of the stage, standing in front of the movie screen. "I'm Klaus Grog, adjutant to General Hock. Ladies and gentlemen, our Fuhrer." The guests shot to their feet, silent as a buried coffin.

Adolf Hitler, attired in the same outfit that he had worn that afternoon, slowly entered the room from the back. Unmindful of the guests, he sat alone in the short, front row, situated slightly below the raised stage. The guests retook their seats.

Max noticed a tall, angular man enter the room. Siegfried Hock cast Max a frosty glance. The general carefully selected a spot with no people around it, wiping off the seat with his handkerchief, before sitting down. Adjutant Grog left the stage, and took his place behind the general.

Max felt as though a dark cloud had moved over him. Maybe good news would chase it away. Presently, the lights dimmed, and the screen lit up. The piped-in music commenced.

Hitler jerked around in his chair, glaring at Grog. The SS adjutant, as if remembering something, bolted up the aisle toward the exit. The credits of the main feature flickered. Grog soon returned, handing a large box of popcorn to Hitler.

The movie was about to start—the one that had been touted by a dinner guest as one of Hitler's favorites.

To Max's amazement, the film *King Kong* filled the screen.

Chapter 33

Max had seen *King Kong* when it first came to Germany a few years before, one of the diminishing number of American pictures that hadn't been banned. He noticed that the enthralled Hitler didn't budge throughout the movie, except for moving his greasy fingers from the butter-stained box of popcorn to his overflowing mouth.

Max, revolted, could hear the crunching sound from his seat way in the back. His revered host appeared to be in a trance, totally mesmerized by the sheer magnetism of the giant ape, as it rampaged throughout downtown Manhattan.

When Hitler saw Kong scoop up the blonde actress—she wearing a skimpy, torn nightie—the Fuhrer's jaw dropped to his ankles. The ape peeled away pieces of the beautiful young heroine's clothes.

The Fuhrer angrily threw his popcorn down on the floor.

At the end of the film, Kong stood at the pinnacle of the skyscraper, swatting the attacking double-winged airplanes that buzzed around him. The girl—lying at his huge feet at the precipice of the Empire State Building—hung on for dear life. Mortally wounded by the attacking planes, the gigantic gorilla tumbled off the building, splattering on the street below.

Hitler shot up from his chair, his eyes glued to the screen. He waved his hand. The lights turned on, and the screen went blank. The Fuhrer looked shaken.

Turning toward the small audience, his grave expression highlighted his gruff, steady voice and intensely burning eyes. "Yes, the actor in the film is correct; *beauty* killed the beast, not the fighter planes."

"With us tonight," intoned Hitler, "is the wonderful young artist Max Bauer—whose work symbolizes the new spirit in our Fatherland—a new beauty. Stand up, Herr Bauer."

Max slowly got to his feet, not quite believing his ears. He nodded lamely to a few in the audience, not really knowing how to react to this praise, and then sat down.

Hitler clapped his hands. Attendants carried *Peasants Earning Their Daily Bread* onto the stage. He ascended the few steps to the center of the stage, eyeing the landscape.

"*This*, is beauty. The virtue of the simple folk toiling in the fields."

Max could see Hitler's face transform into a mask of escalating rage. "*Madmen* have stolen our beauty; charlatans pretending to be artists; Modernism, Dadaism, Cubism, all the crap of lunatics—degenerate scum! *Beasts!*"

Hitler's voice, like gravel mixed with tar, stuck firmly with its gritty, smothering, searing message. "The *beauty* of our new, nationalistic art destroys the beast!"

Hitler's mouth quivered. He pointed to Max's painting. "I hereby decree that the new House of Aryan Art shall soon open in Berlin. Max Bauer is appointed curator and one of the featured artists. He shall also host its opposite, The Degenerate Art Exhibition. This freak show will showcase the turds of the old German Expressionism. Minister Goebbels—now enjoying a short health leave—will serve as producer for these historic events. Congratulations, Herr Bauer!"

Hitler patted his hands together, and the whole theater exploded with applause.

Max sat stunned, his head spinning, as if caught up in a surreal dream. Who would have thought that *King Kong* would provide him with—through a bizarre metaphor—the opportunity of a lifetime?

Hitler then abruptly left the theater.

Instinctively, Max glanced over and caught the eye of General Siegfried Hock. Max thought that he detected a slight gleam of sadistic amusement, as a sated cat might display when toying with a mouse. Hitler's executioner nodded confidently at the personal challenge.

Max knew that he would embrace this generous—yet strange—commission, offered by the Fuhrer of Germany, and hope for the best.

Chapter 34

"I missed you," said Frieda.

"Did you find out anything more about your mother?" Max asked.

"Nothing. Did you?" she asked.

"No—not yet."

Max watched as Frieda removed her frilly dress, revealing her silk underwear, very white against her apricot skin. At nearly one month, her pregnancy didn't show.

He rested under the covers. It being Sunday morning, he had slept in, very tired from his trip. Glad to be back home, Max glanced around their apartment bedroom. The furniture, wallpaper, and linens—mostly in pecan and subdued, cream hues—suggested his wife's refinement.

As Frieda applied lotion to her body next to the lace-curtained window, Max enjoyed the sight of filtered sunlight bouncing off her silky skin, also illuminating the traces of gold in her thick hair.

"Tell me about down there," she said as she slipped under the covers next to him. "My imagination ran wild."

"It wouldn't equal the bizarre reality. Herr Hitler asked me—well, *informed* me that I would be curator of the new 'House of Aryan Art,' whatever the hell that is, and one other extravaganza."

Max studied his wife's reaction, hopeful that she would, at least, have an open mind. But Frieda sprang up from her pillow. "How could you work for that dreadful man? What about my parents?"

"We don't know what happened to them, exactly." Max turned toward her, propping another pillow under his head. "What's that got to do with my job?"

"Don't be stupid, Max!"

Her shrieking tone, new to Max, triggered a mixture of alarm and defensiveness. He could feel the tension building. "The money's fabulous, the exposure for my work incredible. This may mean friends in high places, too, something your mother could use right now. Most important—we have a child to think of."

"My point exactly! What kind of world do you want for our child? Do you know what Hitler's doing to innocent people? How about my father—how about *us*? How could you do this—especially with that *maniac*?"

Frieda jumped out of bed, throwing her clothes back on. "You should be fighting them, not joining them!"

"Stinking politics isn't my thing, Frieda. I hate it. I'm through fighting for anything! We'll find out where your mother is. Your dad—well—we'll try to get justice."

"Justice! Ha! Don't count on it . . . "

Max scrambled out of bed, snatching his robe off the bedpost. "We can work these high contacts to our favor, help other artists too. By modifying it, I can save German Expressionism from extinction—and my life's work."

"Is that so important?"

"To me it is."

"Why do they want *you*, Max?"

"Thanks a lot." Max threw a pillow at her. She ducked. He cooled down, and he could see—gratefully—that she had too.

"I don't know why they chose me," he said softly. "Some foolishness about 'blood and soil'—simple German peasants—sounds weird when I talk about it now. But there it is."

Max felt that somehow he had—inch by inch—been sucked into the whole mess and now had to make the best of it—cash in on what was good about it. Above all, he would see to it that they stayed alive.

He looked at Frieda, who seemed consumed by dread. "There's something else, isn't there, Frieda?"

Frieda sat back down on the bed. He sat down beside her. Her face red, her lower lip quivering, she buried her face in her hands, and sobbed. "Rumors, I guess," she managed to say.

"What rumors?"

"Ask Hans Beckman."

My God, thought Max. Hans—now there's a steadying influence. "Why Beckman?"

"He confirmed that my father's dead—executed—horribly by the Gestapo. My mother's—in *Sachsenhausen!*"

"That's the work camp, isn't it?"

"Yes. The *concentration* camp!"

Max scooped Frieda in his arms and hugged her. "If that's where she is, we'll get her out of there. We'll have to be careful, though. Hock is waiting for his chance to pounce. That bastard!"

Frieda kissed Max on the mouth. "I'm sorry, Max. I know it's hard. We have the baby, too. But I just have a bad feeling about all of this."

"I know. I'm beginning to have my doubts too. Let's just see how things go. I saw what happened at the Bauhaus, and I don't want us to end up hanging from a tree."

Chapter 35

Potsdam, September 1937:

The train stopped in Potsdam, a suburb of Berlin, noted as the true capital of Prussia and home to countless kings, including the Hohenzollerns. If only in spirit, it remained the nerve center of German militarism.

Max and Hans stepped down from their coach and made their way to the trolley. Glad to leave behind the smell of the train's coal dust, Max peered out the window of the trolley as he and Hans whizzed past the ancient, imposing structures of Potsdam. Loaded with mighty Gothic vaults and buttresses, Rococo swirls, and semicircular, Romanesque arches, their imposing style symbolized—to Max—the power and self-destructiveness of politics and war.

"I didn't think you'd come," said Hans, sitting beside Max, chomping his chewing gum.

"Someone at this meeting knows about Frieda's mother, right?" asked Max pointedly. "Please chew with your mouth closed."

Hans answered in an uncharacteristically low tone, furtively eyeing the other passengers. "That's what he told me." He spit his gum past Max's face, and out the window. "There. Happy?"

"Who is *he*?"

"Who?"

"The guy who told you."

"Professor Stallbun; he teaches sociology at Kaiser Wilhelm University in Berlin—he's originally from Dresden. Victor knows him too."

"Dresden, that fits—that's where Frieda's from. Will Victor be at the meeting?"

"No. This meeting's mostly a philosophy group, a high-toned gathering. They love to chat and toss rumors. Intellectuals, artists, professors, civil service hacks. I hear today there's a new member—some disgruntled general. Lena will be there too, you'll like that."

"Disgruntled about what?"

"The general? How should I know? Maybe he has hemorrhoids."

Max, not entirely pleased about attending this mysterious gathering—sarcastically known as the "Frau von Stoltz Tea Party"—gazed at the pointed spires of the Garrison Church, the burial site of Frederick the First, and the yellow, ornate Sanssouci Palace as a sort of consolation as the trolley rumbled past the historical landmarks.

Deposited on the cobblestone street a few hundred meters from their destination, Max felt, for late summer, a distinct nip in the morning air. Good thing he had dressed warmly in his ski jacket and thick woolen slacks. Hans, as usual, wore his dirty leather attire.

Arriving at Frau von Stoltz's mansion, a turreted, castle like structure sitting on a huge, wooded lot, Max figured that its aristocratic owner hailed from a very noble family. The frau opened the thick, oak door.

A tall, gaunt, unsmiling woman who wore her grey hair up in a bun, she glided along the vestibule's marble floor in a long, black muslin dress. Max observed that she wore no jewelry except for a large, wooden cross around her thin, heavily veined neck.

"The others are in the living room," she said in a rather nasal, patrician voice. "You're five and a half minutes late."

* * *

"The German Army must stand rock solid—uphold its most sacred traditions. I resigned—on principle—as chief of the general staff."

General Black looked self-satisfied in his dark suit and red tie, his roundish, gentle eyes—and refined features—resembling a minister more than a warrior. "The Nazis destroy our Christian foundation, our values. But we swore an oath of allegiance to Hitler, so what can one do?"

His soulful stare groped the eight other guests who sat around the huge, circular coffee table in the marble-pillared living room. Max observed the general fold his smooth hands on his lap, reclining comfortably in his chair, retreating into smug silence.

Max walked over to the refreshment table, ignoring the pile of scones and helping himself to one of the steaming mugs of English tea. The room, drafty, cold, and paneled with a greenish-grey plaster, complemented the dreary paintings—mostly dull battlefield affairs.

Mug of tea in hand, he took his seat next to a bald, quick-eyed man wearing a brown three-piece suit and a yellow bowtie. Count Siegfried von Spahn scooted his chair over to give Max more room.

"Business is good—very good, I might add," blurted von Spahn to his cohorts in his high-pitched, barking tones. "Large orders for tires flood our office—many of them from the armed forces." The jovial face betrayed a slight frown. "It's almost like Germany's at war."

"Quite right," said Frau von Stoltz pleasantly.

Max, glad to see Lena Krebs sitting in the group next to Hans, caught her eye, and winked. A tent like cover draped her huge figure. He wondered what her dimwitted National Socialist grandson would think of this august group of complainers, who seemed to enjoy their soul searching.

Lena bent forward in her chair, her intense stare drilling into the tire tycoon. "You know what *that* means, don't you? We *are* at war, mister! You're making that possible."

Von Spahn turned red, shifting his gaze from Lena to the hostess, as if appealing to a referee. Frau von Stoltz pursed her thin, wrinkled lips and quickly changed the subject. "Herr Inge, last meeting you recommended a book. Will you tell us more about that?"

Karl Inge—a high-ranking civil servant—sat directly opposite Max. "I read Nietzsche's *Notes From the Underground* again," said the diffident bureaucrat, "and it struck me that a man's free will and unpredictability make him uncontrollable . . . " He pulled a cigarette out of the pocket of his wrinkled suit, then waved it around unlit as he droned on. "The people will eventually reject the rigidity and oppression of Nazism."

"You took the words right out of my mouth," blurted Hans with his arms folded, his sarcastic tone raising eyebrows.

Max, who had been briefed by Hans regarding the other members of the group, felt a pang of boredom—but also apprehension. The loose talk in this group sounded treasonous, not philosophical or artistic, as Hans had claimed.

He recognized the mayor of Berlin, Helena Holbein, the only female mayor left in Germany since the takeover.

She whispered to the gentleman next to her, Professor Stallbun—the man who knew about Frau Steinberg, Max recalled. He figured he would catch Stallbun alone later and see what this elderly, sallow-skinned man had to say.

The good professor, a caricature of the prototypical German academic, wore his tweed coat with patches proudly, stroking his greyish beard and filling his pipe with tobacco. His tone smooth and precise, he addressed the others as though giving a lecture to his freshman class. "A pause in our meeting is long past due. Then we'll debate the pamphlets to be distributed at the university—so don't be late returning."

Max stood up and mingled, keeping his eye on the proud academic. Fighting the urge to get the hell out of there quickly, duty to Frieda's mother forced him to stay.

These people put their lives on the line for just empty talk.

He followed Stallbun out the French doors and into the courtyard. A path led them past one of the loveliest rose gardens Max had ever seen, a kaleidoscopic burst of color exploding from red, white, and yellow blooms.

"Excuse me, sir, I'm Max Bauer—Hans Beckman's friend. I understand you've got news about Gretel Steinberg. I'm married to Frieda, her daughter."

Stallbun eyed Max carefully, putting his lighter back in his coat pocket, as he puffed away on the sweet, aromatic blend in his pipe. "I'm afraid I've got bad news," he said, waving away the blue smoke.

Max looked around to make sure they were alone.

Stallbun shook his head. "Gretel is slaving away in a concentration camp."

The professor plucked a rose off one of the bushes, pulling off a petal, and throwing it to the breeze, watching it float to the ground. "Germany's beautiful, isn't it?" He ran his thumb over a thorn. "Sharp edges, though—"

"What else can you tell me?" asked Max.

"The mother cleans the latrines. She's also forced to work in the SS lab, located by the barracks. At least she's alive."

"I know that Gretel worked as a chemist," said Max.

Stallbun glanced around. He moved closer to Max, their eyes meeting. "We must protest. But I'm against violence of any kind. Killing's wrong. These men must stand trial . . ."

Max saw Hans walk into the courtyard. "Thank you, Herr Stallbun. I'll have to say goodbye."

"Will we see you again, young man?"

Max didn't answer, because he doubted it. He strode over to Hans. "You bastard! Why didn't you tell me? This is treason."

"You wanted to know more about Frau Steinberg, didn't you? What did you expect, a Boy Scout meeting?"

Max grabbed Hans by the elbow, yanking him along as he broke stride across the courtyard. They hurriedly exited the mansion. "The only thing they'll accomplish is to hang. A 'philosophy group' my ass!"

Hans protested, "Let's get off our butts and fight, Max."

"I'll tell you what we'll do. We'll work hard and mind our own damn business."

"Not me," said Hans as he halted on the sidewalk.

Max pivoted on him. "I've got a big job to do back in Berlin. I don't want to blow it. I also don't want to see your stiff body face down in some gutter!"

Chapter 36

The long-anticipated Great German Art Exhibition—also designated by Adolf Hitler as the House of Aryan Art—had finally opened after two years of frantic preparation.

Max had noticed the construction on this rectangular, multi-pillared, Neoclassical behemoth, shooting up along Ludwigstrasse. On this bright summer morning, he stood atop the long series of steps, ascending from the street to the structure's white portico entrance, festooned with hundreds of swastika banners.

Below Max, on the sidewalk, rested a marble podium where the Fuhrer—flanked by Goebbels, Hock, Goering, and a flock of SS guards—addressed his admirers over the microphone. The audience numbered about fifty thousand.

Dressed in his usual, mustard-colored tunic, Hitler shouted—in his coarse, scratchy tones—the purpose of the exhibit: "blood and soil" and how to protect it from the invading, subhuman hordes.

He screamed that "degenerate scum" who had infected national culture and spirit—especially art—would now suffer. This exhibition would serve as the antidote. Max viewed the festivities from the lofty porch, enjoying a well-earned respite.

Over the past few weeks, he had scoured every gallery, studio, museum, palace, and private home he could find, to extract from its owners the Nazi kitsch that filled the exhibition—along with pieces of some artistic achievement. Mostly representational paintings and sculptures, the exhibition offered few traces of Modernism. What Max couldn't bargain for, the SS Procurement Agency nabbed. Inwardly, he disapproved of these strong-arm tactics.

With hundreds of trumpets blaring, a huge parade that the newspapers called "2000 Years of German Culture" rolled past Hitler. Max observed long rows of floats, presenting golden statues from Nordic lore—from Wotan to Brunhilde.

Hundreds of German knights rode decorated steeds, the warriors brandishing silver swords, the shields emblazoned with golden swastikas. Then a float rolled by, carrying a huge bust of Adolf Hitler—the giant head alone standing over ten feet tall.

Fit young men, garbed in ancient Roman and Greek togas, held standards—with runic symbols and swastikas—as they marched past the throngs of cheering spectators. Hundreds of ballerinas performed in the street. Young children, dressed in German folk costumes, threw rose petals on the street behind them as they followed the parade route.

Then came the countless soldiers, costumed in sixteenth-century Prussian blue uniforms and powdered wigs, strutting with their swords drawn. Behind them trudged soldiers dressed in old Bavarian regimentals, carrying muskets.

The parade's finale featured implements of mass destruction. The latest tanks, artillery, and Luftwaffe planes rolled by, towed by huge army trucks. One motorized platform carried a prototype of the new "jet" fighter—the ME262—its futuristic form loudly applauded by the audience.

Countless modern troops marched by: some goose-stepping, black-coated SS regiments, others from all branches of the armed forces.

Max made his way into the exhibition through the huge double doors, weary from the festivities. Three of his pieces and one of Adolf Hitler's hung inside, as well as works from countless other artists vetted by the regime. These included such notables as Karl Truppe, Elk Eber, Wilhelm Hempfing, and Adolf Ziegler.

But truth be told, none of these art luminaries could hold a candle to Lena or Hans, he mulled, with some degree of agitation.

Chapter 37

Max and Frieda walked through the House of Aryan Art, the first time she had been on the premises. Not having been eager to see it, she consented—as a sop to Max's employers—to at least attend the grand opening—meeting him there in the late afternoon.

"This place is so vast, Max, like being inside an airplane hangar," Frieda said. "It's scary."

"It lacks any sense of proportion," he agreed. "The art pieces are buried in empty space."

They halted beside Max's masterpiece—*Peasants Earning Their Daily Bread.* Apparently, Hitler had donated it as the star attraction.

The event drew huge crowds. A throng of visitors had gathered around Max's oil painting, most appearing delighted, some even weeping at the overwhelming sentiment of the piece. Max beamed with pride, overwhelmed by the opportunity to share his talent with so many. Yet a pang of apprehension gnawed at him.

Hitler—flanked by Goebbels and Goering— approached him. The Fuhrer glanced at Frieda and abruptly changed course, probably to avoid meeting her, Max surmised. The proud dictator halted in front of Max's landscape, pointing at it with a satisfied smile. The spectators applauded. With his SS guards and photographers in tow, Hitler—with his cronies—quickly moved on to the other exhibits.

"Well, a snub's better than a beating," whispered Max to Frieda with a wry smile. "Did you see them avoid us? *Fine.* A fly on the wall's all I aspire to."

"Avoid *me,* you mean. Let's move on," said Frieda. "So far, your painting is the best thing about this mausoleum. How do I look in this tight dress—pregnant?"

Max scanned her trim figure, the sleek, black evening dress, pumps, and pearl necklace underscoring her sophisticated beauty. "Awful."

Glancing down the vast hall of exhibits, Max eyed the sculptures ahead.

Arno Breker—the brilliant sculptor—had scores of them within the gargantuan, white marble interior of the show, the polished floors reflecting the brightly lit, lofty, sienna-colored ceiling. As Max and Frieda moved along the row of nude statues, he observed the light reflecting from their supple, firm muscles.

Still and expressionless—except for a stern, high-cheekbone stare—the female figures, although of flawless proportion and shape, nevertheless seemed sterile.

"The Nordic ideal gone mad," Frieda commented.

"Well, it's strange all right, I can't deny that."

"Smut without any thrill," she added.

"Well put," said Max. "Just wait until you see what's coming up."

Aside from nudity, motherhood also dominated as a theme in the exhibition, mostly in oil paints. The mothers generally displayed babes sucking at their breast, or slung their arms around their handsome broods, or sat around a bedroom with their young daughters, brushing their long hair.

Moving along to the next space, Max and Frieda came upon another piece—this time a painting of a large hotel. The walls of the structure came together at a right angle, over a rectangular courtyard. The building's steep roof made of blue and orange brick, multiple chimneys and turrets, and arched entrance gave it a cool, Gothic look that suggested extreme loneliness.

Max thought it interesting. He read the label to Frieda. "ARTIST: ADOLF HITLER."

"I wouldn't want to rent a room in *that* place," said Frieda.

"Hitler submitted several paintings," explained Max in a very hushed voice. "Most of them awful. Surprisingly, this one's a little different."

"It looks desolate," said Frieda. "Mean and alone."

"It *feels* desolate, and that's not all bad."

Max loved it when Frieda disagreed with him, especially about art. That was one reason why he loved her so much. Art has no political requirement of its creator, he believed.

As it so happens, there weren't many famous artists that were both fascists and exceptional painters, he realized. But the fact that Hitler might have one or two decent paintings in his inventory wasn't impossible. In fact, the hotel piece would be passable in many second-rate art museums.

They came upon more oils from different artists, more landscapes featuring German families tilling the soil, German knights in shining armor, slaying infidels, syrupy "religious" pieces, and seemingly bored German families reclining about in their living rooms. Then there were more nudes.

The oil that drew the most crowds displayed a nocturne of Adolf Hitler, dressed in his lederhosen and knee socks. He stood alone in a dark forest, peering up into a wide beam of moonlight that terminated—from its bright, lunar origin—at his illuminated, solemn face. A halo effect enveloped his head, suggesting a Christ-like aura.

"Sheer egomania," said Frieda under her breath, her eyes darting around the room, making sure she wasn't overheard.

Max and Frieda, among the sea of bodies navigating the exhibition, threaded their way into the remaining part of the exhibition; this time they were confronted by an army of male sculptures. These immense pieces depicted martial themes.

Huge statues of nude, muscle-bound, sword-wielding warriors, with high cheekbones, chiseled noses, square jaws, and huge pecs, seduced the audience with rippling, outstretched arms. So, there it is, thought Max. Nudes and warriors, warriors and nudes, more nudes, mothers, more warriors, then nudes and mothers again. He laughed out loud.

"What's so funny?" asked Frieda.

"I have to know," said Max. "Why do war and pornography always complement each other—and then they blame motherhood?"

"You're really sick, Max, you know that?" She laughed too.

They both laughed again, long and hard. Good thing the place was crammed, thought Max, or some honcho might have noticed their irreverent merrymaking.

Frieda stared past Max. "Well, here's something that's not too funny. Don't look now, but our friend's right behind you, staring at us from the stairs across the room."

Max's smile faded.

"It's *him*, isn't it?" he asked.

"Yes."

"What does he want? *Me?*" asked Max.

Frieda shook her head, her eyes finding his. "*Us* . . . "

Max turned his head slightly, and through the heads and hats of the crowd between them, he gained a full view of the tall man across the room,

The eyes of General Siegfried Hock bore into him.

Max felt something he hadn't felt in nineteen years. His trigger finger had twitched.

Chapter 38

Berlin, October 1937:

"The Voss boy's ready to be examined."

"Thank you. Make sure he's disrobed to his shorts and then gowned. He has a concussion."

Frieda sat behind her desk, charting in the exam room, when her nurse brought in the next patient, young Wilhelm Voss, nine years old, with his taciturn mother. Dr Bauer asked him to sit on the exam table.

Frau Voss stood in the corner with her arms folded, looking down at the floor.

After studying his file, Frieda approached the child with a reassuring smile, placing her hand gently upon his shoulder. "I'll bet you're a fine ballplayer, Wilhelm."

The boy, tall, with a shock of red hair and freckles, beamed as he nodded. "I'm the top scorer."

Frieda sat down on her examination stool, looking up at her proud patient. "Your mom once told me that you won a trophy. That was a few years ago. You must be a big star by now."

The child blushed.

"She said you hit your head yesterday. Ran into another player. You were dizzy—is that so?"

As Frieda gathered more information for the medical history, she carefully peeled his gown down to waist level, examining him with her reflex hammer and pinwheel.

"Did you black out when you hit your head?"

"Yeah, I think so."

"How long?" Frieda ran the pinwheel over his arms and legs.

"A few seconds, I don't know. I don't remember."

"What were you doing just before your accident?"

"Don't remember."

Frieda wondered whether he suffered from post-concussive, retrograde amnesia. "Did you feel that?" She had run the pinwheel over both his palms.

"Yes."

"Both sides equally?"

"I think so."

"No double vision?"

The boy shook his head.

"How about headaches?"

"Yeah, I have those."

"Located here?" Frieda touched the side of his skull where he had been bruised.

"Yeah."

"Ever have them before the accident?"

Wilhelm shook his head. Frieda stood up and strode over to Mrs Voss.

The boy's mother, a large-boned, athletic-looking woman who wore no makeup, had a cutting voice. "Well, what's wrong? Sometimes he just stares into space."

"Frau Voss, did you see your son get injured?" Frieda crinkled her nose, whiffing the ammonia scent of horse dung on the woman's soiled, pleated dress.

The mother's eyes shifted continuously, avoiding eye contact with her. "I wasn't there."

For some reason, Frieda had never quite got on with Mrs Voss. She was on good terms with her husband, who, unfortunately, seldom accompanied his wife or son to the office. They had a small dairy farm just outside the city.

"Has your son had any nausea since the accident?"

"I don't know. Why do you ask so many silly questions?"

"I see. All right then."

Somewhat jolted by the mother's hostile response, she dropped her pinwheel. Frieda then noted something that she had not seen before. Frau Voss's necklace fell over her rumpled blouse. A swastika pendant hung from it.

When Frieda reached down to pick her instrument up off the floor, she heard the door squeak open. A pair of shiny black boots occupied her field of vision. As she straightened, her eyes climbed up the tall figure of the uniformed intruder—and stopped on the white rose.

Siegfried Hock, his silver sword accenting the jet-black uniform, stood squarely before her. Her mind raced back to her wedding day, when this terrifying man coldly informed her that her father was dead . . .

She rose to her feet as Hock stood silently, his arms folded, his gaze smothering her.

"Frau Voss," instructed Hock, "take your boy out of here."

"But—"

Hock tossed the mother a frosty smile. "You can't understand these things. Go, dear Frau." As the mother left the room with her son, he reassured her, "He'll be rebooked today, with another physician."

Frieda, feeling the blood rush to her face, tried to wet her dry mouth with her tongue, which was even drier. She put on a brave face.

"How dare you intrude here? What's this about? That boy's sick."

"Frau Bauer—"

"*Doctor* Bauer."

"Doctor *Holtz*—or I should say *Steinberg*."

Frieda felt ice-water flow down her neck.

"I remind you that the Nuremberg Laws of 1935 forbid non-German physicians to treat Germans, especially children."

"I *am* German."

"Let's not go there, Frau."

"I've treated that family since—"

"You don't qualify—"

"I graduated first in my medical class—"

"I know."

She froze. *This brute's been researching me.* The anger about her mother's incarceration in a concentration camp—not to mention her father's murder at the hands of the Gestapo—soon extinguished all caution.

"Is my mother well?"

Hock walked around the exam room, carefully noting its contents, including the medical instruments and the paintings on the walls. He turned on her. "You will discharge all patients for which the law applies."

"I want to see her."

"Look, Frau Doctor. Your husband's doing good work. Everyone says so—well, at least some, who are very important men. Let's be sensible."

Frieda noticed that Hock's eyes fixed upon one thing in particular, a celebrated Expressionist painting hanging on the wall titled *The Shout*. It featured the twisted, blue face of a woman standing in the middle of an empty street, covering her mouth.

The general frowned. "Ordinarily, I'd shut your office down permanently. But you'll only be fined. Your practice is closed for one month. I hope you appreciate that I handled this personally, instead of through normal channels."

"Please . . . " said Frieda, almost in a whisper.

She saw no reason to bring up her father. She wasn't sure that Hock knew what happened to him, anyway. Her beloved father was gone—now her mother must be saved.

Hock pointed to the painting. "By the way, did your husband paint that?"

"No. Please go."

"Get rid of it—today. I realize that your kind is fascinated by such filth." He donned his spotless white gloves. "I'll take my leave. Give my regards to Herr Bauer. Enjoyed our chat."

He moved to the door and opened it, then turned to spread his good cheer one more time. "Do you treat typhus, Doctor?"

"I haven't since medical school," Frieda answered, somewhat taken aback by the question. "I'm a neurologist."

"Too bad. Gretel's camp has an epidemic of it. One of her roommates weighs only fifty pounds." He smiled and closed the door behind him.

Frieda broke into tears.

Chapter 39

Berlin, October 1937:

The huge windows of Max's gallery—Slaughterhouse 1— trapped the soft, orange light of the setting sun, sprinkling the interior grey walls with a dappled, warm color.

Busy packing and sorting his inventory, he studied his new oil painting hanging from the ceiling. He wondered whether he dared transfer this piece to the House of Aryan Art and then ruled that out. The subject of the picture—a red horse gazing onto a Fauvist, purple meadow—might provoke disapproval by the regime or even get him canned from his job.

In fact, he had hesitated to hang it in his *own* gallery. It must have been Schoenberg's music—atonal and bold, playing in the background—that had given him the perverse courage to display it.

"I like the horse, you derelict," blurted Hans as he strode in from the other wing of the gallery. "He kind of looks like you Max, especially from the rear."

"Stuff it."

Max watched his friend hang his new painting, next to his own. Hans tied a knot to secure his work, and then jumped down from the chair. "Well?"

"It's one of your best," said Max. "You'd better not display it, though. They might arrest us."

"You've really lost your balls, Bauer."

Max studied his friend's new painting. Two green objects stood out on a red background. One, a skull, with weeds and worms growing out of its jawbones and eye-sockets; the other—lying next to it on the debris-cluttered battlefield—a German army helmet.

"On second thought, get that damn thing out of here, Hans."

"No."

"Now!" Max snapped. "If you don't take that down, *I* will. I'm expecting government couriers from the exhibition any time now. They're picking up a few of my pieces for . . ."

Max heard a crashing sound coming from the front door. Four SS men entered the room and strode up to the surprised artists. One of the soldiers, a hefty, balding man who wore the insignia of a sergeant, barked his identification. "Sergeant Klaus Grog, SS adjutant to General Hock." His bovine eyes fastened on Han's painting. "What's that up there?"

"A toaster," snapped Hans.

"Shut up, Hans." Max recognized Grog—General Hock's lackey. "What do you mean barging in here? Please leave."

"Stay out of this, Bauer. I'm collecting your paintings for the exhibition. Whatever else I choose to do is my call."

"The paintings are ready. I'll get them for you."

Max took Hans by the arm and led him away. As they passed in front of Grog, Hans abruptly halted, spitting on the floor, just missing the sergeant's boots.

"That's for you." Hans glared at the SS adjutant, his hands curling into fists. Max tried to jerk him away, but he resisted, stepping closer to the Nazi.

"Look here," explained Max softly to Grog, trying to defuse the situation. "I'm on commission from Minister Goebbels—"

"I know all about that." Grog pointed at Hans's picture. "Take that degrading shit down. I'm confiscating it."

As the troopers grabbed the painting from the hook, Hans lunged at them. Max tried to wedge himself between his friend and the guards, but one of the hulking figures pushed him back. The other two beat up Hans, then threw him to the ground like a rag doll, repeatedly kicking him in the ribs.

"Let them have the damn thing," shouted Max.

Hans slowly got up from the floor, his mouth bleeding, holding his side—his face grimacing in pain. As he stood there panting, wiping his mouth, one of the soldiers spirited his painting away. The other two lined up next to Grog, waiting for further orders.

"You pigs," said Hans, wiping the blood from his mouth.

"All right. I'll get my paintings for you," said Max to Grog. "Then go—"

Grog pointed at Beckman. "Arrest him."

Hans tried to make a dash for the door, but the two soldiers had him down on the floor again, beating on him. Max lunged at the soldiers, but Grog knocked him back with a powerful head-butt. Max crashed to the floor. He slowly raised himself, feeling dizzy.

"If you know what's good for you, stay out of this!" Grog screamed.

The troopers scooped up Hans—now unconscious—and carted him away.

The sergeant glanced at Max's painting. "That's yours, isn't it, Bauer?"

"Where are you taking him?"

"You know."

"Eight Prinz Albrecht Street?" asked Max.

Grog smiled and said nothing. He didn't have to: Max knew that the infamous Gestapo headquarters would soon host his friend.

Grog moved closer to Max's painting of the red horse. "Take that thing down."

Max wiped his mouth, noticing the blood on his hand. He felt weak in his knees. Grog had head-butted him hard.

"No."

"On second thought, give me that painting, or I'll arrest you too."

Max thought it unwise to battle them anymore. Retrieving Hans from the Gestapo took priority. He took the painting down from the hook. He was starting to put it in the trash, when Grog informed him, "I'll take that with me—for safekeeping."

Max reluctantly handed him the piece. "I'll get the other ones for the exhibition, Sergeant."

As he walked away to fetch the other paintings, he dreaded what lay before him. Extricating poor Hans from the Gestapo prison was what he had to do now, and it wasn't going to be fun.

Chapter 40

Hans Beckman dangled upside down over the acrid cesspool, his red curls disappearing under the grimy surface. His nostrils submerged, it would only be moments before his mouth would be too. As the hapless prisoner hung there—naked—with his ankles bound, and his hands shackled behind his back, he squirmed violently in an attempt to reposition his face out of the water.

Siegfried Hock sat at the table next to the tank, as Grog stood at his side. The general's new favorite Rottweiler—Luther—rested at his master's feet, slobbering, enjoying the juicy morsels of horsemeat that his master tossed down to him. After his other dog had died, he insisted upon pampering this one.

"Grog, this procedure's pointless. Beckman knows nothing, he's just an artist."

"He has information, Herr General." Grog nodded to the soldier manning the hoist, signaling another round of dunking. "He has subversive friends."

"Maybe, but Bauer's untouchable at this moment, unless we have something really big."

Hans thrashed in the putrid water.

Luther growled louder.

"That's all right, boy," said Hock as he leaned down to stroke his head. Hock nodded to the soldier manning the hoist. "Pull him up." Hans's head rose two feet above the water's surface.

"Now, Herr Beckman," said Hock in a loud but steady voice, "My sergeant here says you belong to a subversive organization. Your paintings prove that you're a degenerate, so what he says is possible. Tell me, who is your contact in the group?"

Hock carefully picked up Hans's skull-and-helmet painting off the table, as if shaking hands with a fingerless leper. "If you give me names, you'll be free to leave."

Hans coughed the water out of his trachea. "All right. Give me a minute," he said, still gagging and choking, sucking in fresh oxygen as fast as he could. "I'll tell you. My voice's weak," he grunted, almost in a whisper.

Luther showed his fangs and frothed at the mouth. "Now, Luther, behave. Go over to the prisoner, Grog. See what he has to say."

Grog moved close to Beckman, to hear the information. He grabbed the prisoner's hair to get his attention.

Hans cleared his throat. "Greta . . . "

"Greta *who*?" asked the sergeant in an excited tone.

There was a long pause from the prisoner, then: "—Greta Garbo."

Grog removed the service revolver from his belt, and whacked the side of the defiant artist's head with the butt of his gun. "Who's your contact?" demanded Grog.

Silence.

Grog whacked him again, blood streaming down the prisoner's head.

"Enough," pronounced Hock as he crumpled Hans's painting in his hands, tossing the wad on the filthy floor.

He patted his dog. "It's game time, isn't it, Luther?"

* * *

Dusk splashed the maze-garden with cadmium orange and Naples yellow hues, casting very long shadows that made its ten-foot walls appear even more forbidding. Near one entrance stood General Hock, holding Luther's leash with one hand and fondling the handle of his shiny sword with the other.

The formidable dog, resting on its haunches, licked his master's hand. Grog, standing at attention next to Luther, gazed at the maze's sharp-angled turns, listening to the faint noises coming from within the sinister labyrinth.

"That's Beckman, Herr General," said Grog.

"No, really? I thought it was the gardener." Hock, irritated that his music hadn't already been playing, glared at his adjutant. "Turn it on, Grog."

"Sir?"

"The music, what do you think I mean?"

Grog ran into a nearby guardhouse. Presently, the golden tones of "O Star of Eve" from the Wagnerian opera *Tannhauser* filled the air.

The lackey resumed his place next to the dog.

Hock looked over to the other entrance, with two SS guards standing next to it. They had just released Hans Beckman into the interior, armed with a pistol. The fastidious general removed his sword from its ceremonial scabbard, standing ready to initiate the hunt.

He ran his fingers lightly over the cold, steel edge of his weapon. "Maybe I should let Luther have him." He petted the dog. "What do you say, boy?"

The Rottweiler growled.

"No, I think I'll go it alone," decided Hock.

"But Herr General there's still some daylight—too dangerous."

Hock sheathed his sword. He removed his white gloves and put them in the pocket of his black tunic. He preferred the feel of the cold steel on his fingertips when he grasped the handle of the sword.

"It's sporting to give him a chance. This is getting too easy."

An SS guard rushed up to Hock. "Herr General, Max Bauer's causing a fracas in reception. He demands that the prisoner be released to his care. Himmler's called about it. Apparently, Goebbels called *him*—requesting Beckman's discharge on Bauer's responsibility."

Hock glared at the guard, biting his lip. He almost popped off with insults aimed at these meddling desk jockeys. *This damned art nonsense has gone too far*, he fumed. He had been afraid this would happen, hence his haste to execute the prisoner, and not just let him rot in prison.

All this handwringing for canvas and crusted pigments!

Nevertheless, he knew that Hitler took art very seriously and in fact painted daily. It would be stupid to go against this current. Besides, these flaky Expressionists were bound to screw up again, and he would be right there when they did. Impatience had never been one of his vices, and he wouldn't start now.

"Very well. Bring Bauer here. He can have this garbage. Fetch the prisoner."

Soon, Hock mulled, he would prove his worth to the Fuhrer. He'd be given his own ministry within the secret police. There would be no meddling into his new plan: disposing of tens of thousands, even *millions*, of degenerates—*efficiently*, as the Fuhrer had requested of him. The key would be the trains, the massive incinerators, and the "pesticide" gas, Zyclon B—for the shower stalls.

Then Max Bauer's tall, muscular frame strode athletically toward him, accompanied by the guard. Luther showed his sharp teeth.

"Take your friend home," blurted Hock as the artist halted before him.

The general hated to lose this round, but he knew that—one day—he'd get his chance to kill Max Bauer.

Chapter 41

"German men and women, peer into the face of death fearlessly, and in the end you'll have more respect for it. The era of intellectual filth is over. With these burnings, we consign to the flames the degenerate ideas that infected the German spirit. So, on this night you're doing well . . . "

Max and Frieda stood among the crowd in Berlin's Opernplatz square, with stunned silence. Their faces, and those of hundreds of others around them, glowed from the huge bonfire, only meters away.

From the huge pile of logs and burning books, the yellow and white flames shot up into the cold, autumn night. The conflagration appeared even more cataclysmic against the pitch-black sky. Max heard Goebbels's rich voice over the microphone, as the minister poked his finger in the air.

Crowds of college students—and Germans from all walks of life—threw thousands of volumes into the flames. Close enough to see the covers of the books, Max noted Ernest Hemingway's *A Farewell to Arms*, Sigmund Freud's *Civilization and its Discontents*, Erich Maria Remarque's *All Quiet on the Western Front*, Thomas Mann's *Magic Mountain*, and a biography of Albert Einstein.

To his disgust, he also observed the frenzied participants tossing in Dadaist and Cubist art.

"You see what this has come to," whispered Frieda. "Madness. *Bad* madness—*real* bad."

"Lunatics," said Max. He saw Goebbels leave the podium. A young Brown Shirt replaced him. As the recruit belted out the Nazi "Horst Wessel Song," the crowd joined in, the sea of twisted faces disseminating death like a mustard-gas attack.

"True believers. That's even scarier," said Frieda.

Max recognized that Frieda had, again, hit the nail right on its head. Her diagnostic skills for political infections were more acute than his. "Let's get out of here," he said.

As they started to leave, he noticed a young woman arguing with a Nazi trooper standing in the crowd. To his revulsion, Max recognized the young, husky fanatic.

The woman's flowing, brown hair, blazing eyes, and white blouse lit up in the intense glow of the fire. She screamed at the trooper—Paul Krebs—but Max couldn't make out her words over the noise. The hostile crowd glared at her.

The singing stopped. Paul slapped the woman hard. Max jerked forward to help her.

Frieda grabbed his hand. "Don't, Max. They'll tear you apart."

He stopped in his tracks, guilt from his hesitation overtaking him instantly.

Then the throng savagely turned against the hapless dissenter, backing Paul. They took turns punching and kicking her. Some laughed. They ripped off her clothes, and hoisted the young woman upon a smoking log, carrying her toward the fire as she screamed.

Max realized that—chillingly—they were going to burn her alive. Stripped down to her underwear and too weak to resist any longer, she accepted her fate, riding the log to the edge of the conflagration, to be thrown onto the inferno like a chunk of sirloin onto a spit.

Max bolted toward the impending atrocity, just as the Berlin civil police arrived. They halted the proceedings.

Max, making his way back to Frieda, noticed that the perpetrators hadn't been arrested. It appeared to him that Goebbels had called in the regular police to stop the killing, but not punish the criminals. *At least*, he rationalized, *he* did *stop it.*

"Let's get out of here," he said to Frieda. "I've seen enough."

Chapter 42

Potsdam, November 1937:

"Violence is wrong. The Nazis must stand trial and not be harmed. That's the right thing to do," Professor Stallbun instructed the assembled conspirators. "But they must be punished somehow."

Max, having taken up Hans's offer to revisit the Tea Party, made his way back to Potsdam, alone, to see what more its members had to offer. He had advised Hans to lay low until his encounter with Hock had blown over. Frieda, harassed at work and manhandled on the street; her parents destroyed; Hans, beaten up and tortured; incident after sordid incident on the street—all of this had convinced Max that perhaps this group deserved a fresh look.

He sat in the group around the table, studying the sallow face of the bearded, elderly man addressing them. Professor Stallbun continued talking in his civilized, educated manner.

"Yes, *trial*—for unconscionable crimes against humanity. *Humanity*, isn't that a beautiful word? What do you think, Frau von Stoltz?"

The gaunt hostess—dressed in black again—wrenched open her thin, wrinkled lips, as if invading an ancient crypt. "Why *yes*, Herr Professor, *humanity*. Ideas are more powerful than men—"

"Very pretty. But ideas don't kill people, their guns *do*," Lena Krebs testily interrupted. "What the hell are we *doing*? I'm sick of chitchat."

Frau von Stoltz—stiffening at the impropriety of Lena's tone—reminded Max of an owl, whose eyes popped open at the sound of an intruder. Her tired gaze searched those seated around her; the bony fingers fidgeting with the wooden cross dangling from her neck.

"I say it's time to splatter Hitler," Lena added.

Her remark stunned the others, except Max—and possibly one other.

Von Spahn, Inge, Holbein, and General Black had shown up again, but Max saw a face in the circle that he hadn't recognized from his prior visit. Yves, a dapper young dentist from Bern, Switzerland, who spoke fluent *Schweizerdeutsch* with a rich, melodious accent, had been introduced to him before the meeting started.

Yves displayed the intense, dark eyes, and fiery determination of a French revolutionary. Max couldn't put his finger on it, but something about this glib, young firebrand bothered him.

"Hitler's a pig!" insisted Yves, his grating tone reverberating throughout the group. His agile gaze hopped to Lena. "I have contacts in Switzerland that will supply guns. Money too. I can courier letters to important individuals, if you write to them for help."

Max sympathized with the young dentist's words to some extent. His attitude toward the government had begun to evolve. However, he had returned to the group primarily to question Professor Stallbun again, about Frieda's mother. He wondered whether passive resistance might help change the course of more moderate Nazis, Hitler included, steering them in a more responsible direction. Another war—the scourge of humankind—might even be avoided.

Nevertheless, still cautious, Max would choose his words carefully in front of the Tea Party. "*Passive* resistance—for Germany's sake—might be considered," said Max to the others. "Not attending rallies, speaking up for your neighbors, participating in activities to soften the harsh culture of Nazism, this will help guide the others—the moderates, maybe even Hitler—by *persuasion.*"

"Not all of us have the cozy relationships you seem to enjoy, Herr Bauer," said Yves. "I understand you're a big shot in that disgusting new art exhibition."

Max felt the blood rush to his head. His hands, resting on his armchairs, squeezed the polished wood almost hard enough to break it.

"Yes, I've been in the same room with Adolf Hitler," admitted Max, getting to the heart of the matter, "on more than one occasion, including a hospital room during the war." A few eyebrows rose. "He's coarse, I must admit. At times, he even seems brutal."

"You don't say," said Yves sarcastically. "You're very informative."

The group's members, their eyes shifting between the antagonists like the spectators in a Ping-Pong match, remained contentedly quiet. "In his speeches," continued Max, "Hitler says he wants peace. He loves art, too. Despite the contradictions in his personality, he might come around if persuaded to ignore the zealots that advise him."

"Well now, a *pacifist*. Coming from a war hero, who slaughtered hundreds, that's rich, I must say. We must *fight*—and now!" Yves looked around at the others, noting the lack of enthusiasm.

A few members voiced objections, but Max wasn't listening. He was too focused on the dandified dentist, the mouthy stranger garbed in his fine tailored suit and paisley bowtie. His slick, black hair and penciled, Clark Gable-like mustache looked too pretty for Max to stomach.

Max glared at the firebrand, feeling his cool slip away. "Armchair patriots and tea party heroes make my butt drag. We're about the same age," he said calmly to Yves, "but I'll bet you didn't even touch a rifle in the last war. People like you are always the most gung-ho to use violence—and to get *others* killed."

Yves smiled defiantly. "I'm Swiss—we were neutral."

"How convenient—"

"Now boys—" interrupted Frau von Stoltz. An agitated, but relieved, murmur emanated from the group. "Time for a break—and tea," said the civilized hostess.

* * *

Professor Stallbun sat on the stone bench in Frau von Stoltz's courtyard, sucking on his pipe. Max stood beside the bench, peering into the sea of vibrant roses, overflowing in the garden.

"We had to stop spreading the pamphlets at the university," said Stallbun. "The janitor turned in one of the student protesters—a nice, brave young girl."

"Will they release her?" Max asked.

"Who knows?"

"What about Frau Steinberg? Any news?"

"The camp is Sachsenhausen—the town just north of Berlin, next to the suburb of Oranienburg—is where they have her—"

"I know. How bad is it?"

"Bad, but she's well," said Stallbun, "as well as anyone can be in that hellhole. There was a typhus problem, but she never got infected."

"Frieda will be relieved to hear she's still alive," Max said.

The professor leaned forward, picking one of the white roses. "This camp has research facilities, and factories nearby too—which use the slave labor and nearby train terminal. Much of this information comes from Victor. Do you know him?"

Max didn't answer. He had never heard much about the camps. There had been rumors about detention facilities for political prisoners, but nothing one could put one's finger on. There also had been wild speculation about mass killings. However, most of those dissidents, some claimed, had been released.

Stallbun looked around furtively, noticing the tall, trim figure of the dentist slowly passing by them. The Swiss visitor nodded at the professor, while not acknowledging Max. He stopped to look at the roses.

"I prefer the red ones, personally," Max commented to Stallbun.

"I like the white better. I hate the thorns, though."

When Yves had seen enough of the flowers, he moved on. Max disliked the dentist but had no specific reason to hide his words from him—except prudence. Stallbun had had the good sense to play along.

"Frau Steinberg's not just a chemist—but a *research* chemist—once for I.D. Fobben," added Stallbun.

Max moved away from him a bit, avoiding the blue clouds of sickeningly sweet smoke wafting from the professor's pipe. "What's that got to do with anything, except maybe helping her to survive? "

"It may mean something else, also." Stallbun shifted his eyes and shook his head—hesitating. He stroked his beard nervously.

Max didn't like riddles. "Well, spit it out."

"Don't repeat this to *anyone*, except your wife, and then only if you must. Gretel Steinberg's working on a chemical called Zyclon B."

"So?"

Stallbun emptied his pipe. He looked at Max with a dour expression. "It's an industrial pesticide—used to exterminate *rodents.*"

Max didn't know what this man was driving at. His irritation showed in his voice. "I imagine a place like that has plenty of mosquitos and rats."

"It's a cyanide *gas.* It kills a lot more than rats."

"I've had my experience with poison gas, Herr Professor—in the war. I still don't follow you." Then, a notion shot into Max's head that horrified him, which he considered impossible.

"Yes, that's right," said the professor. "Maybe it's for something else."

Max then saw General Black and von Spahn approaching, engaged in lively discussion.

"That's von Spahn coming," said the professor in a hushed tone. "I don't trust him. Good day, Herr Bauer."

Stallbun cut off their conversation and walked away.

Max wondered whether the professor had a good reason not to trust von Spahn.

These days, can you trust anyone?

Chapter 43

Berlin, December 1937:

Nazi cuckoo-land had done it again, Max thought. *This must be a dream.*

As he stood in the huge, dark room, in his respectable business suit, waiting for his meeting with Dr. Goebbels, he looked up at the immense, circular stage, with a girl twirling upon it.

To Max's surprise, the piped-in music blared to an anarchic, primitive beat. The girl—tall, blonde, with toned, oiled muscles, and poured into a diaphanous, one-piece bathing suit—spun around the stage, her tap-dancing in perfect rhythm, as the bottom-lit stage accentuated the lithe outline of her sensuous body.

On the chest of the skimpy bathing suit, a black swastika with a white, circular background, sparkled in glitter paint. Before Max knew it, he had been whisked away by an attendant into another huge, dark soundstage, this time in the presence of his host.

"What do you notice about the actresses in this scene?" asked Goebbels, sitting on a director's stool next to a movie camera. "I'll give you a hint. It's all about contrast."

Max, standing beside the propaganda minister, groped his mind for the right answer. He knew that Goebbels liked testing him.

"I need you to help me with something else, Herr Bauer."

Max's eyes fixed upon the actors on the set. "I'm surprised that you're directing a Sherlock Holmes movie," said Max, preferring to be as tangential as the minister.

"Holmes? Why not," retorted Goebbels, dressed in a white suit with a cranberry-colored tie. He shifted his fawnlike eyes between the two women on the set. One of them—the younger and shapelier, noted Max—took a bath as she bantered with her homely maid. "The first Sherlock Holmes film wasn't filmed in England. It was made right here in Berlin," he added testily.

Goebbels had invited Max to the UFA studio, Berlin's most famous, to join him on the set of its latest movie: *The Man, Who Sherlock Holmes Was*. Although Max didn't like the minister, the fact that he had intervened to save Hans Beckman's life couldn't be disputed. Therefore, Max hadn't refused his summons to meet at the studio, rather than the art exhibition.

Max unbuttoned the top button of his starched shirt, the key lights in the studio unbearably hot. His eyes darted around. The only signs of other workers were the tips of their lighted cigarettes, glowing from the rafters and ladders that surrounded them.

Having imposed dead silence on the set, Goebbels nevertheless felt free to banter as he wished. "As I said, I need you, Herr Bauer."

"Do you mean some detail with the Aryan Art Exhibition?"

"Not exactly."

The bathing actress stood up from the bath, her wet body covered in suds. "Get back in and do it again!" shouted Goebbels. "Only less suds! Herr Bauer, the Fuhrer's pleased with the exposition. The reviews are wonderful."

"Well then—"

"Have you noticed the contrast I was talking about?" asked Goebbels.

It shot into Max's head, as he observed the dowdy minion drying off the young girl: the stark difference in beauty between the two women. "Loveliness beside homeliness."

"Yes, that's it, Herr Bauer. The star in this movie—although attractive—isn't what I call beautiful. She's a—friend—so I made her a star. To make her appear beautiful, I casted her maid as ugly as I could."

Max found the concept twisted and brutal. "Yes, Minister, I see."

"Cut!" shouted Goebbels to the crew. "Lights, fifteen-minute break!"

His liquid eyes poured into Max's. "You're smart, Bauer, and you'll do yourself a favor by listening carefully."

The rafters became noisy again, the overhead lights brighter. The minister, barely five feet tall, jumped down from the stool and scribbled production notes in his ledger.

"The House of Aryan Art is the antidote to cultural disease. Displaying degenerate garbage to our people in an exposition—simultaneously—makes the inoculation more potent."

"I see," said Max, holding his nose mentally. "Herr Minister, I'm flattered, but I have my hands full already—"

"Allow me to persuade you, Herr Bauer." Goebbels waved off an attractive, dark-haired woman who had stopped to ask him a question.

Max knew the name of the woman, a renowned female director who had recently made a hit film about the Olympics of 1936. As an amateur movie and photography buff, he recalled her cinematic innovations. Her reputed, chummy associations with top Nazis had soiled her reputation among many artists.

"I'm offering you, Max," continued the minister, "the job as curator of our new exhibition. It's called 'Degenerate Art.' It'll open in two weeks. The Fuhrer's very excited about it."

"Minister—"

"You can expect more pay with the position."

Max realized that he had better be careful, since Goebbels always expected to get his way. To disappoint him could prove lethal.

Moreover, he wanted to broach the subject of Frieda's mother. The only other person he could approach was Hitler himself, which seemed much more difficult a proposition. On the other hand, the additional curatorship would inevitably put him at loggerheads with many of his Modernist colleagues, and the very idea of censoring—let alone banning—any kind of art horrified him.

"Herr Goebbels, I'm sure you could make a much better choice—"

"There'll be massive publicity in movies, newspapers, magazines, and radio," countered Goebbels. "Soon, I bet they'll even have the new sensation—called 'television'—covering it, just as they did during the Berlin Olympics."

"What about my other duties—"

"You'll combine the two positions. The public will love it. One ticket buys admission into both."

Goebbels's restless eyes shot about the studio. "As national curator, you'll receive an exclusive on all art placed in state buildings and monuments. Naturally, I'll be in charge of acquisitions. From that, you'll choose the pieces. Anything else, Herr Bauer?"

"I need to ask my wife. She's three months pregnant—"

"I understand," said the minister with a twinkle in his eye. "Mark this, your *personal* problems will be overlooked. We in the regime generally take care of our own. But some aren't so sympathetic. Take General Hock, for example."

Their eyes met like a locomotives colliding at full speed. The threatening subtext screeched at Max. He chose not to bring up Gretel Steinberg, the timing now being wrong. He'd get this damned exhibition going first.

"I volunteer, Herr Minister: The Degenerate Art Exhibition it is."

"Good, I thought so," said Goebbels as he glared at the crew. "All right, back to work!"

Chapter 44

Sachsenhausen concentration camp, December 1937:

Siegfried Hock stood stiffly, looking down on the human filth assembled before him, in the "progressive" concentration camp that truly reflected his "values"—and, he would ensure, those of the SS. As he stood with Adjutant Grog and his Rottweiler, Luther, on a small hill in front of his office and staff quarters, his cool stare blew over the hundreds of emaciated prisoners assembled before him.

The general, more chilling to them than the nippy, late-fall air, delivered his usual before-breakfast speech. On its huge, triangular lot, Sachsenhausen contained a dozen barracks and scores of roads—both inside and outside of its towering, barbed-wire walls. A schoolhouse, factories, laboratories, a railroad station, and a German Nationalist Congregation chapel also dotted the snowy grounds. Hock took pride in another of his construction marvels: the "white cottage," situated next to the guard tower.

This massive, brick cube—its interior lined with steel and exhaust vents—served as the clandestine prototype of a massive, new "hygiene" facility, where prisoners would receive their "delousing" showers. Among the emaciated and head-shaven wards, all clad in identical burlap, black-and-white striped uniforms, the general appreciated the one significant, colorful difference in their attire.

This ornament had been designed not so much as to recognize specific groups, but rather to rob the inmates of any trace of individuality. Triangular pieces of cloth, each of a different color, were sewn onto the chests of the prisoners' "uniforms," according to a perverse hierarchy.

At the top, criminals, such as rapists, murderers, and habitual thieves, wore white triangles. Communists wore red ones; homosexuals, pink; Jehovah's Witnesses, Freemasons, and the occasional Jesuit priest, purple; and at the lowest rung, Gypsies and Jews displayed yellow triangles.

During the earlier stages of the camp's existence, fatal beatings of prisoners had been haphazard and "wild"—more or less according to the whims of the SS guards. Executions were performed in a trench, usually by mass shootings. Hock had put an end to most of these sloppy, chaotic acts of violence.

Slaves from the camp toiled in nearby brickworks, to implement Adolf Hitler's grandiose scheme to rebuild Berlin, with most inmates starving to death—or succumbing to disease—within three months of arriving. Hock had been horrified by this inefficiency, especially involving *skilled* labor.

As he stood in front of the starving humanity, the general searched out the tall, fair woman in the first row of white triangles: Gretel Steinberg. Her skill with chemical compounds would be immensely valuable to the SS laboratory and key to his success with the "final solution." Moreover, he knew that if a war came, as had been assured by his contacts in the Wehrmacht's general staff, then the population of undesirables at Sachsenhausen—and other camps modeled after it—would increase a hundredfold.

He therefore had his work cut out for him.

As the general addressed the assembled prisoners, Luther, apparently agitated by his master's loud pronouncements, showed his teeth. The dog's additional stress worried Hock, but he continued anyway.

"Due to overcrowding, public health is of utmost importance. Therefore, many of you will undergo additional sanitary procedures, such as delousing, disinfection, and vigorous cleansing, in the showers that have been generously provided."

The general interrupted his speech to make sure that Grog fed Luther his treat. He then resumed his discourse, scanning the filthy prisoners, many of them eyeing the dog's snack with envy. "Some of you are educated scum. Ask yourselves, if we intended to kill you, would we go to all this expense?"

Hock loved that one. It had always worked.

At that moment, one of the pink triangles, standing in the front row of his group, dropped to the ground in front of the SS guards, unconscious. Jerking the leash out of Grog's hand, Luther charged him. Savagely attacking the sick inmate, the Rottweiler chewed viciously on his leg, shredding his bloody trousers.

"Luther!" screamed Hock. He glared at his adjutant. "Fetch him!"

Grog dashed over to the dog, pulling him off of the victim. He inspected the lifeless body, lying on the ground.

"It's dead, Herr General."

A murmur rose among the groups of prisoners. "Silence, you filth!" commanded Grog. He strode back to his general, standing at attention. "What should—"

"Drag him away, you fool!" screamed the general. He dropped his voice so that only Grog could hear. "Keep an eye on prisoner Gretel Steinberg. She's in the white triangle group—in the front row. Make sure she gets her proper rations."

Grog executed his orders to his subordinates and then returned to his boss's side, as the general resumed his address.

"Resist these sanitary procedures, and you'll be shot. Your relatives will complete your sentences in your stead. Most that know me well say that I'm a civilized fellow. I'll leave you with this last piece of advice. The same that's posted over the entry gate to the camp: 'Work makes one free.'"

Out of the corner of his eye, Hock noticed the camp physician for the white triangles—SS Captain Elsa Mensch—fussing over the dead prisoner, again being a damnable nuisance. Her dowdy figure and porcine face—with a nose that resembled a snout—housed weepy eyes, with two yellow dashes painted above them, simulating eyebrows.

Unfortunately, fretted Hock, this meddling, churchgoing spinster—related to Heinrich Himmler by marriage—was about to waddle her way over to pester him again.

And she did. "General, I protest. This prisoner died of starvation," she said softly in her syrupy, emotional voice. "This is not only unsanitary, but *inhumane*. Why treat any creature this way?"

The SS insignia on her bright-pink tunic—a makeshift uniform for female physicians assigned to the camps—sickened the general, especially with the ridiculous Christmas ornament of a smiling reindeer affixed to it. This homicidal, paranoid Bible-thumper, with her thickly painted, neon-red lipstick and greasy hair, fancied herself a compassionate soul.

What a joke. Hock knew this lowbred harridan's true nature—her sadism was too much even for him, turning his stomach. "I'll keep that in mind, Captain Mensch. Make sure your prisoner— Gretel Steinberg—has everything she needs in the lab."

The doctor waddled back to the dead inmate.

"Yellow triangles, you stay put," shouted the general. "The humans are dismissed."

The SS guards dispersed the other groups of prisoners, herding them to their workstations. An army truck drove up and parked, with two soldiers quickly raising the cover on the back, emptying the vehicle of its contents.

Other soldiers unloaded fire logs and petrol, building a pyre in the middle of the assembly area. Hock delighted at the mountain of horse dung lying there on the ground, next to the truck, masquerading as art.

All over Germany, his troops had raided private homes and galleries, and many museums, collecting subversive paintings and sculptures. Now, some of the scum that perpetrated this fraud against the nation would toil to burn it. *The humiliation is complete*, mused Hock.

"Torch it!" he snapped.

The overwhelming majority of the sixteen thousand Modernist and Expressionist pieces that had been slated for the new Degenerate Art Exhibition were now confiscated, and the exhibition was now complete. *After that horror show has ended*, the general ruminated, *most of its rubbish will be burned also, except for a few paintings to be auctioned abroad for hard currency—to fund the humming munitions factories.*

Hock, after enjoying the fiery spectacle for some minutes, bent down, taking his handkerchief out of his pocket, and wiped the prisoner's blood from his dog's mouth. Grog assisted his general, wiping the dirt and bloodstains from Luther's fur.

Hock turned on his minion viciously. "How dare you let him loose. Do you realize what you've done?"

"My general—"

Hock's voice cut savagely. "You've exposed him to tainted blood. God only knows what diseases it carries."

Chapter 45

"Do you know what the Nazis scribbled on the wall above my painting? And in *brown* finger-paint—like shit on an outhouse," asked Emil Nordling in a crumbling, desperate voice, having cornered Max on the opening day of the Degenerate Art Exhibition.

Max broke the haggard artist's grip on his collar, gently removing the wrinkled, shaking hand. "Easy, Emil," he said. Max looked around at the other visitors in the crowded, dark, and narrow gallery, converted from a defunct sewage-treatment plant. "Keep your voice down."

"I'm a marked man," said Emil.

Max glanced up at the graffiti next to Emil's painting, hanging on the chipped, pockmarked wall: "INSOLENT MOCKERY OF THE DIVINE."

Nordling's mildly surrealistic masterpiece, *The Christ*, dangled there, like most of the other art that had been displayed— unframed, crooked, dimly lit, and illuminated by a bare light bulb, hanging from a wire, as if it were the star attraction in a horror show. This crucifixion scene, constructed in bold, Fauvist, complementary colors, had been the iconic symbol of German Expressionism's modern Christian art.

Nordling had expected his pieces to hang in every church in Germany. Instead, the exact opposite had happened. He had been banned by the new regime.

"Emil, I had nothing to do with this. Go talk to Goebbels," said Max. He pointed up at the huge sign—painted in slanting, crooked, black letters—hanging near the entrance to the cramped gallery: "DEGENERATE ART EXHIBITION."

"This exhibition bookends the House of Aryan Art," Max explained. "It's meant to show the public that if you don't want that kitsch, you'll get this," added Max as he pointed to Emil's painting. "I'm sorry you got in the middle."

"Goebbels won't talk to me! No one will. Modernist, traditionalist, it doesn't matter. I'm a leper. You're in the middle too, Max."

Max shrugged, but Nordling had a point. He found it hard to sympathize with the aging painter, since his predicament had been largely his own fault. Nordling—an early party member—had been the darling of the Nazi elite, until one day Hitler happened to see *The Christ* hanging in a Nazi art museum.

Reputedly, it plunged the Fuhrer into a rage; he had ordered his minions to confiscate it—and all of the artist's other work. Since then, an outcast, Nordling had been shunned by one and all, unable to make a living. A renegade in one's own flock is treated harshly indeed.

This new show included 650 paintings, sculptures, and prints by 112 artists— primarily German—and Hitler showcased them like a bearded lady in a circus. That very morning, Max recalled, the Fuhrer had opened this grotesque gallery with an inflammatory speech, to an amused throng of attendees.

"Chatterboxes, dilettantes, and art swindlers," he harangued, "are now exposed to the public, to be compared to our majestic House of Aryan Art."

This meant that the works of such luminaries as George Grosz, Paul Klee, Ernst Ludwig Kirchner, and others—and notable foreigners such as Pablo Picasso—would now be exposed to the light of day, like so many cockroaches.

"Just remember, Max, I won't be alone," said Emil ominously.

Max watched Emil—who had made a valid point—as he limped away, a broken man. He climbed the narrow, zigzagging staircase to the exit. Max saw him duck his head, so he wouldn't hit it against another haphazardly mounted work—a huge, wooden sculpture of an Expressionist Jesus.

Alone, Max strolled the drafty, dingy rooms of the exhibition. Layers of paintings rested on the filthy walls beside more derogatory slogans. He observed patrons grinning as they read them:

"AN INSULT TO GERMAN WOMANHOOD . . . "

"TOO EXPENSIVE AT ANY PRICE . . . "

And the one Max found the most insulting . . .

"MADNESS BECOMES METHOD . . . "

However, some patrons looked on in shocked silence. Frieda had refused to attend. Not surprised, Max greeted the news with relief. He didn't want her to be a part of all this.

His eyes shifted to the two new guests far across the room. A short, dark man stood next to a tall, blond one. The tall man carried a rolled-up canvas under his arm. He left the room, disappearing into the gallery's interior.

Max realized that General Siegfried Hock and Joseph Goebbels had just arrived at the funhouse.

* * *

"Goebbels had to go to an interview. I brought some tape, Herr Bauer. Will you help me mount this refuse on the wall?"

Hock, attired in a dark, pinstriped business suit with his shiny, patent leather shoes, unrolled his sixteen-by-twenty-inch painting, placing it against the wall situated next to the public latrine. Beside it rested the once venerated *Familienbild: Family*, by Johannes Molzahn.

"My addition to the exhibition will interest you." As the now agreeable Hock continued, tearing strips of tape from the roll he had fished out of his pocket, Max held the diagonal corners of the canvas against the wall. "I stole it from the mansion of a rich department store owner," the general said slyly.

The shocked, red-spiral eyes, buried in a greenish complexion, hit Max like a sledgehammer. His Modernist portrait of Herr Roth hung chillingly in front of his very eyes, the perfect evidence—and place—to plunge him and his family into danger.

"I might point this one out to the Fuhrer as a particularly egregious example of Bolshevik madness." Hock stood back from the picture. "We couldn't get the name of who painted it out of the original owner. But the initials 'MB' are etched there on the bottom right. Do you have any idea who that might be, Herr Bauer?"

Hock's buzzard eyes froze Max. He noted—at close range—their homicidal glint.

Max squared his shoulders in front of him. "Indeed I do. It's mine. The man in the portrait is Joel Roth, a friend of mine. What happened to him?"

"Is that so? I'm shocked, Herr Bauer. Though you seem to be drawn to that kind."

"He's a good man."

"He *was* a good man."

The impact of that evil statement exploded in Max's head.

Hock smiled. "Come now, Herr Bauer. Is this any way for the Fuhrer's artist to comport himself?"

Max opted to defuse this cat-and-mouse game by taking a chance. "The muse of the painter is unpredictable, General, but in the end, he's as good as his best work. And Goebbels covets that work. So does the Fuhrer—who is also an artist. Artists understand each other, do *you* understand me?"

Max had hoped that his masterpiece landscape would serve as his trump card.

Hock paused, seemingly considering his options. Max could feel the spiked wheels of his mind turning, the general hopefully deciding that he probably didn't have enough goods on the Fuhrer's protégé—and fellow artist—to destroy him. Not *yet*, anyway.

Hock reached up to Max's painting and ripped it down. He handed it to Max. "My compliments, Herr Bauer."

The general straightened his black tie. "Give my regards to your lovely wife. By the way, I may have another painting—a red horse. It has similar initials. I'd hate for that to get into the wrong hands."

Max watched the general as he strode away. Having just dodged one bullet, he took the general's not-so-veiled threat seriously.

Chapter 46

Berlin, January 1938:

"Doctor Lindorf, who's the next patient?" asked Dr. Frieda Bauer, as she unfastened the top button of her long, white lab coat, uncomfortable in the chronically overheated neurological ward of the hospital.

"Eric Sneiderman, Frau Professor," answered the young woman with the short, white coat, traditionally worn by the medical interns. The training physician nervously fumbled through her chart, standing among the small group of pupils, of which Frieda served as the attending physician.

They had been moving from room to room—doing rounds—halting at the doors of specific patients along the dim corridor, its grey linoleum reeking of ammonia and bleach.

"All right, Lindorf, you present this patient to me. Then we'll go inside and examine him," said Frieda.

The intern gulped, looking around desperately at the others, seemingly unprepared. "Ah, a thirty-three-year-old male; bricklayer; fell off a scaffold; cervical injury—"

"What level?" snapped Frieda, known not to be a pushover with the trainees.

"The—sixth cervical, I think, Frau Doctor."

"How do you know?"

"The X-rays, for one. Also, he can move his thumb and index finger somewhat, but not his pinky or middle fingers so much. He has some feeling in his shoulders, but not below."

"All right," said Dr. Bauer agreeably, "what else?"

The intern turned pink and silent, obviously drawing a blank.

Frieda got her off the hook. "What about his vitals?"

"Oh, his stables are vital," chattered the young woman, instantly realizing her gaffe. Her face turned pinker.

The students burst out laughing, howling with delight, their nervous exhaustion relieved by their colleague's blooper.

"I guess if he has *horses*, they are," Frieda threw in with a smile. The laughter increased, and she continued, "OK, shut up all of you. Soon, it'll be *your* turn instead of hers."

She gently put her arm around the young woman and guided her, with the others, through the door, into the patient's room. "Good job presenting the patient, Lindorf," said Frieda, "now let's get on to the exam."

* * *

"Yes, Doctor, that's fine," whispered the paralyzed man, stripped down to his waist, as he lay supine in his hospital bed.

Frieda looked around at her students. "Notice that the ribcage doesn't expand as he inhales. The intercostal muscles are paralyzed, but the diaphragm is spared, so quiet respiration is preserved at this cervical level of injury—"

As she heard the curtains tear back, Frieda spun around.

There stood SS Adjutant Grog with his Gestapo guards. He forcefully pushed a few students aside, grabbing Frieda by the arm and dragging her outside the room. The stunned students were frozen in fear. In the hallway, two of the SS guards slammed her against the wall, her head smashing against the hard tiles.

Dizzy, Frieda maintained her footing, her field of vision filled with Grog's savage, piggish face. "No Jewess doctor is allowed to treat Aryans—no matter the age or gender. Do you understand? That's now the law—inside or outside a hospital!"

Despite the pain and terror, Frieda found the words. "I have staff privileges—"

Grog slapped her face. "Shut up."

Frieda noticed that two of the young guards averted their eyes, probably in shame. The bigger of the two had even jerked forward slightly, seemingly attempting to come to her defense, but froze—resuming his rigid stance. Another guard, however, sneered.

She felt the warm blood trickle from her lip. "This patient needs me!"

A small crowd of concerned nurses and doctors had now formed around the grotesque spectacle. Grog glared at them. "Get out of here! Back to work, or you'll be arrested."

They slowly dispersed.

Grog then composed himself. "General Hock wouldn't approve of my—*enthusiasm.* But he's not here. Do we understand each other, Frau?"

Frieda nodded.

He patted her softly on her cheek. "Good girl. Now, close your office for good. No more big money. Then go home and make some sausage for your husband. Women and doctoring don't mix— even with *your* kind."

Chapter 47

Max looked out the frosty window of his studio, savoring the sunset—what little of it he could see between the lofty buildings, their steep-angled roofs covered with fresh snow. He loved to paint landscapes that depicted a late afternoon or early evening sun. Backlighting, the juxtaposition of warm hues with cool ones, contrast, and shadowing—all were at their best at dusk, even better than at sunrise.

He studied the people on the street—small stick figures blowing white puffs into the frigid winter air. From a distant perspective, people were easy to reproduce on canvas, and lent richness to scenes. If only they were so easy to deal with in real life, he mused.

It struck him how many of the pedestrians down there on the sidewalk had uniforms on and how the majority of the vehicles were military transport. There had been talk about Germany swallowing up Austria and rumors that Italy might go to war to protect her.

Max ambled back over to his easel, putting the finishing touches on his portrait of Adolf Hitler. He fished his favorite number-eight filbert brush and his silver palette knife out of his overalls pocket. He held the knife up to the light, enjoying its finely honed sparkling patina and its sharp edge. He mused that, like many tools, it could be used for both good or evil—ugly or beautiful—purposes.

He plopped down on the stool beside his easel. Next to his eleven-by-fourteen-inch stretched-linen canvas rested a photograph of Hitler, dressed in his mustard-colored uniform, with his arm out in a Nazi salute. This served as his model.

Hitler's countenance in Max's painting—meant to be generously flattering— reflected gentle understanding and sensitivity. His luminous blue eyes oozed empathy. Although the piece definitely couldn't be called Modernist, it did have certain, subtle qualities of tone and hue that hinted at Impressionist—and even Expressionist—emotion. Max hadn't been directly commissioned for this piece, nor had Goebbels or another of Hitler's paladins requested it. At first, he had marked it for the Aryan Exhibition.

In a bold move, Max had decided that his painting would be a special gift, from him to Hitler—*personally*—in order to lobby for the New German Expressionism—*his* kind. It embraced tolerance for a broader, less representational expression. It also embraced Modernist elements, minus the overtly subversive, political undertones that had so angered the establishment.

Goebbels might be of help too, and prime to pump for information, he hoped.

Max felt confident. After all, the Fuhrer had heaped praise on him for his great job on both exhibitions, which already had received over three million guests. Moreover, Max realized, he might also be able to intercede on behalf of Hans Beckman, who—due to his clash with Siegfried Hock—remained in mortal danger.

Of course, there was Gretel Steinberg to think of . . .

Max turned around when he heard someone enter the studio. He saw Frieda approaching him, her white lab coat splattered with traces of blood, her lip swollen.

He threw down his brush and rushed over to her, taking her in his arms.

"Who did this?"

She pushed him away and rested on a stool, unbuttoning her coat.

"I was mugged . . . " Her eyes welled up with tears. "On— the way home."

Max took a seat next to her, his voice calm. "Why is your purse still slung over your shoulder? Why wasn't it stolen?"

She shook her head.

"It was Hock, wasn't it?"

She averted her eyes.

"I thought so," said Max. "Are you all right?"

"Nothing serious," she responded.

Max jumped up from his chair, and rushed over to the cabinet. He reached deep into the back of it, and pulled out his Walther PPK .25-caliber pistol—his old army firearm. This was the first time he had handled it in years.

He stuffed it in his pocket and headed for the door.

Frieda chased him down before he reached it, grabbing him by the arm. "No! It was his adjutant—Grog—*not* Hock. You're not going down to Prinz Albrecht Street! You'll never return, Max—the Gestapo will kill you!"

"We'll see about that—" Max tried to break away, but he couldn't escape Frieda's strong grip. "Let me go."

Frieda tried to push him away from the door, but he pushed her aside instead.

She slapped him, getting his attention.

Stunned, he then calmed down, realizing she was right.

"It's partly my fault. I can't treat Gentiles—*any* Gentiles—*anywhere*. Since I'm half Gentile—I can't treat Jews, either." She lowered her head. "I lost my hospital privileges. They closed my practice. I tried to fight it, and he . . ."

He kissed her on the cheek. "All right . . . "

Max put the gun back in the cabinet, then took her gently by the hand. "Let's talk about this."

Frieda had been through a horrific ordeal—and he didn't want to upset her any more. He led her over to the center of the studio, and they both took a seat on the sofa.

As usual, she seemed to read his mind. "It's not your fault, Max, it's theirs." She patted him on his shoulder, then smiled. "I'd better tend to this lip."

He knew whom she meant. Yet he had gotten the two of them mixed up in all this business with the Nazis, and now he had a tiger by the tail.

Max stood up, protectively escorting her to the bathroom across the studio, placing her before the sink. He opened the medicine cabinet. "Not much, but there's some bandage strips and hydrogen peroxide. Cotton balls too."

"I'll manage," said Frieda as she treated her cut. "We seem to be old hands at this."

"How's the baby?"

"Fine—no problems."

"Thank God for that, at least." At four months pregnant, she hardly showed it.

He handed her the implements as she dressed her wound. "I wonder if Hitler knows about this attack by Grog," he said.

"Why not?" She dabbed her cut with cotton.

"I don't know. I want to see Hitler. I've got something for him."

She finished up on the lip, placing a small strip near the corner of her mouth. "I hope it's a bomb."

"It's a masterpiece and very flattering," said Max. He had to protect the other things in his life that mattered far more than his art: Frieda and the baby.

He showed her the portrait of Hitler. She studied it carefully and then walked over to the window, peering out at the traffic lights below.

"What's going to happen to us, Max?"

"I don't know."

Chapter 48

Sachsenhausen concentration camp, March 1938:

The white triangle on Gretel Steinberg's lab coat meant that her treatment in the concentration camp had been relatively mild, despite the standard starvation rations: five hundred calories of watery bean soup per day, one hundred calories of rock-hard "bread" made from sawdust, and sweepings from the SS kitchen. Six hundred of her "roommates" shared only one hundred bunks, in their unheated barracks, each bed five feet long and three feet wide, with no covers and no linens—just wooden planks.

The overflow of humanity fought for places to sleep on the filthy, sawdust-covered floor. With no running water, and an uncovered six-foot hole dug into the ground serving as a toilet, the stench and flies—with only two windows the dimension of breadboxes—had nearly driven Gretel mad. Despite all this, the violent separation from her dear husband was what had shattered her world. She knew that those monsters had murdered him. Moreover, Frieda's welfare tore at her.

Is my daughter safe? Has the Gestapo discovered her identity? Is she even still alive?

These torments almost completely sapped Gretel's will to live. Hock's stooges had already interrogated her as to Albert's underground contacts, which she had known nothing about. Albert had never shared this information—to protect her.

At first, she had also been questioned about Frieda and offered them nothing. Then, somewhat distressingly, they stopped asking about her. *Why?* She figured that either they already knew what they wanted to know, or, God forbid, her daughter was dead.

Gretel knew that the job in the lab offered her a measure of protection—but for how long? In this lavish "research" facility—located next to both the commodious SS barracks and the chapel within the campgrounds—she had been provided extras, such as a hot shower, a daily sweet roll, fresh water, and a clean, disinfected uniform that she wore under her white lab coat.

Guilt gnawed at her. She fretted over the other inmates, especially the yellow triangles. On occasion, she had been able to exchange a few words with them. They informed her about *their* conditions, which were much worse—unthinkable, let alone unspeakable.

How could Germany produce a beast like Hitler?

Gretel sat on her stool over one of three white marble counters that held beakers, jet flames, Bunsen burners, glass tubing, several small ovens with windows, and shelves of multicolored chemical reagents—all under vacuum hoods. The scent of bleach and other chemicals still bit into the temperature-controlled air.

Gretel wondered what kind of research would warrant such an expensive workroom and in the midst of such squalor. Then, in strutted SS Lieutenant Gerhardt Schroeder and Lab Director Bruno Roost, both men also wearing long white lab coats, and both middle-aged and of medium height. They sported short-cropped brown hair and thick eyeglasses.

Except for the pronounced scar lining the lab director's cheek, thought Gretel, they seemed as interchangeable as newborn twins. They headed over her way and, as usual, stopping first to admire the large glass bottle sitting on the middle counter. It held three predatory snakes, usually devouring each other. Gretel supposed that this gruesome spectacle reinforced the two men's twisted brand of Darwinism.

She rose. The two officers halted in front of her. As usual, the SS lieutenant said nothing. Director Roost picked up the pointer from the chalkboard hanging on the wall, and loudly tapped on the chemical symbols scribbled in chalk, as if jabbing one of his wards.

"Frau Professor Steinberg, the chemical compound we now possess needs stabilization at these ligands. When the metal canisters are opened and exposed, gas is released. The cyanide then filters down to the target organisms. Cell respiration consequently ceases. Understood?"

Gretel nodded, studying the schematic diagrams. "I think so. You want the compound to be safer for the staff, to diffuse rapidly, and not to activate until exposed to a destabilizing source."

"Yes, that's it." The animated director pointed at the last set of figures on the chalkboard. "In a mammal weighing sixty-eight kilograms, death occurs within two minutes of inhaling seventy milligrams of hydrogen cyanide gas."

Gretel said nothing. She wondered what mammals this man had in mind. Few of those in Germany had the mass of sixty-eight kilos—except humans, of course.

Then, one horrific thought shot into her head, which she instantly devalued, due to its wild, unbelievable nature.

Still, in the back of her mind, the notion lingered . . .

Out of the corner of her eye, Gretel saw the pink mass of SS Captain Elsa Mensch, waddling over to join them, her round, moist eyes undulating over her like a slippery eel. Her meaty hand grasped a box of chocolates.

Gretel noted the pink wooden truncheon that she carried, tucked under the white belt of her SS uniform. A swastika pendant hung from the SS captain's chest.

Mensch halted in front of Gretel, ignoring the men. "I require that you to join me for chapel." She raised the box of candy. "For the children—they're waiting outside." She spread her lips in a twisted smile, showing her crooked, lipstick-smeared teeth. "The service starts soon. We must hurry," she added with a flattened affect.

Elsa put her arm gently through Gretel's, warmly guiding her out the door.

Gretel had the urge to remove her arm, but something warned her not to. When they got past the front door, she noticed a group of small children standing in the street, listless, emaciated, and some nearly bald from protein deficiencies. Bruises and sores covered their little faces. Their small, filthy uniforms displayed yellow triangles. Many of the swarthy youngsters were barely able to stand, let alone walk.

"Gypsies," said Elsa, as she jabbed her finger in the air, as if pointing out penguins in a zoo. "They'll enjoy the pretty chapel."

She removed a hair comb from her tunic pocket. "This is for *you*."

Gretel took it, not knowing what to do.

"Wear it."

"Yes, Madame." She stuck it in her matted hair.

"*Captain*," corrected Elsa firmly.

"Yes, *Captain.*"

Elsa ripped open the box of chocolates, presenting it to one of the living skeletons, "Be careful," she warmed the little boy, "don't eat it too fast. You might make yourself sick."

Gretel studied the chapel as they all approached it together on foot, next to a huge, white-bricked, cubic structure called "the cottage." The chapel, a small, beige, wooden building, with a sunny porch and a stained-glass window, had a silver cross on top of its steeple, topped by a golden swastika.

Gretel recognized the emblem of the German Nationalist Congregation. Having imprisoned and tortured thousands of dissenting Catholics and Protestants, the regime had formulated this more "reliable" Christian denomination, to massage the sensibilities of the more pious adherents to Nazism.

Whatever might happen, Greta knew that she had no choice but to go along. She hoped that she still had Frieda to live for—and perhaps, some day too, liberation.

Chapter 49

"'Render to Caesar the things that are Caesar's, and to God the things that are God's.'"

The pastor of the German National Congregation smiled broadly at his flock, about thirty parishioners, sitting in ten rows of wooden benches, in front of the nondescript pulpit.

The acronym "GNC" in gold letters rested upon the plain, cream-colored wall, beside a Nazi flag. Pagan and runic symbols hung there too. The clergyman delivering the sermon wore a plain, dark business suit, with an Iron Cross commendation pinned to his chest.

"In closing," continued the pastor, "remember, as you go about your duties, our work is to end humankind's futile striving, and recognize that only certain people have been anointed to emerge as pre-eminent—and to inherit the earth. Attaining this divine goal humanely, and efficiently, is our burden . . . "

Gretel felt—sitting in the front pew—Elsa's greasy stare, as the Nazi matron turned her head toward her, her small, pink SS cap tilted ridiculously on her head. She sat in the same row as Gretel, but on the other side of the children, who had been placed between them.

Captain Mensch reached out to the youngsters happily, handing them pieces of candy. Lethargic from disease and chronic malnutrition, they either devoured the candies or, being too weak, ignored them.

Elsa then stuffed one in her mouth, chewing on it loudly, her red lips agape enough for Gretel to watch the gooey, sweet substance churning. This reminded Gretel of one of those orange fish, with the big, sucking mouths, she used to see in fountains—before this horror. Nauseated, she observed Mensch closing her eyes, then mumbling under her breath as she put her hand over her heart, lost in some twisted Nazi prayer.

"Therefore go about your work joyfully. Praise be!" the pastor concluded as he held his palms up, one hand of which, noticed Gretel, missed three fingers.

Elsa stood, helping the children up, gently ushering them and Gretel to the aisle and out the door. She took Gretel's arm as they strolled, with the children straggling a few paces behind them, just like a big, extended family. Outside, when they reached the edge of the gravel road lining the front of the chapel, Gretel saw an army staff car waiting. Two huge trucks were parked behind it.

Roost, the lab director, got out of the staff car to greet them, as did armed SS guards from the trucks—including two soldiers with police dogs. Elsa distanced herself from Gretel at the sight of the men, removing the pink truncheon from her belt.

She pointed the club at the staff car. "We'll go in that."

The captain addressed Director Roost. "Put the children in the trucks."

She distributed more candy to the children, and then patted some of them on the head, explaining, in a maternal tone that seemed alien to her, "You're going on a fun ride. You'll be cleansed—no more bugs and lice. Won't that be nice?"

Gretel stood there frozen and silent, with the Gypsy children. Her anxiety mounted.

Why all the soldiers?

Elsa turned on her, the piggish eyes flickering with uncustomary excitement, her usually flat voice infused with energy. "This field trip is mostly for your instruction, Frau Steinberg. You might want to take notes."

* * *

The staff car stopped beside a long, deep ditch next to a deserted dirt road, a few kilometers outside of the camp's entrance. Gretel, the lab director, Elsa, and the SS recruit who drove them there all disembarked, the army trucks having parked close behind.

The midday sun beat down. Gretel heard the sickening sound of the children wailing from within the trucks. The SS troops, having gotten out of their trucks, bantered—petting the guard dogs and laughing—as if attending a Sunday picnic. Gretel, standing in the other group, noted the deadly machine guns that the soldiers held ready.

One man in plain clothes—apparently a mechanic—fitted flexible, metal tubing from the trucks' exhaust pipes to an opening in the side of the trucks. The cargo areas were entirely enclosed, with no vents.

"Did you know, Gretel, that I'm a trained nurse?" asked Mensch. "I enjoy helping sick people."

The SS captain had never addressed her by her first name before. "Yes, I'm aware of that, Captain."

"Outside the walls, you may address me as 'Elsa.'" She smiled at Gretel and then looked over toward the trucks. "I'll get them out of there. We'll strip them too. I'll take their pulses, respiratory rates, and blood pressures, and you'll record them," she ordered. "Do you understand?"

"Yes."

"After we're done, you'll examine the interiors of the trucks. Please note the design and position of the intake channels. It'll help you design the interior of the white cottage. Now, get to work."

Everything from that point on—to Gretel—assumed the slow-motion blurriness of a surreal and wicked dream. Her remaining sanity told her that such things weren't possible, but her senses violently disputed that . . .

She couldn't allow herself to understand that she had been forced to be a part of it—and to some extent, the cause of it. Motion followed motion—fact followed fact—the consequences cascading, that's how she remembered it later.

As they worked, Elsa Mensch ordered that music—Brahms's "Lullaby"—be played on a bizarre phonograph system, with loudspeakers on top of the trucks. It helped to "calm" the anxiety of the children as they exited the rear of the trucks, explained the Nazi matron. Elsa helped them remove all their clothing.

Gretel scribbled the blood pressures and other vitals into a notebook as the SS captain obtained the data; all the while, the youngsters who still had the energy cried out, their whimpers mixing with the savage growl of the police dogs and the sweet tones of the music.

"Start the trucks," shouted Elsa to the drivers. "Full throttle!"

The children had been assembled in two lines. "Now, children, it's time to be disinfected. File back into the trucks and wait."

Elsa screamed at them when they hesitated, ordering them to accompany the guards over the gangways that led from the muddy ground to the interior of the trucks and through a small metal door. When candy didn't work anymore, the children—who realized, instinctively, that hygiene had nothing to do with their situation—needed persuading with vicious dogs and rifle butts.

The last victims were dragged or carried by the troopers, and then tossed into the trucks' interior, like sacks of potatoes. The heavy doors were then slammed shut and bolted.

The huge engines of the trucks shifted into overdrive, roaring and humming, but they weren't loud enough to drown out the screams of the youngsters inside. Gretel floated over the whole thing like a ghost, remembering later that the victims had stopped screaming only after twenty minutes.

After the doors were thrown open, Gretel—at gunpoint when she couldn't be coaxed—climbed into the interior of the trucks, scribbling in her notebook just what she saw. Nauseating images pummeled her consciousness.

The carbon monoxide-gassed children—their small, naked bodies bluish and bleeding from fresh wounds—had formed a pyramid, the apex ending at a few tiny cracks in the truck's ceiling. Traces of air had penetrated the tops of the trucks at those points. Gretel realized that the stronger children had fought their way to the top of the pile, to seize a few more seconds of life.

An SS solider—pistol in hand—dispatched one child that somehow how remained alive. Other soldiers unloaded the bodies and threw them into the ditch. They then buried them with lime. Some still twitched. Gretel realized that they were being buried alive.

"What did you think?" Elsa asked Gretel in an upbeat tone. "It's a shame," she continued, as she shook her head, her greasy hair shifting under her pink hat. "But someone has to do it."

Gretel, devoid of words, just shrugged.

"The gas needs to filter down better," Elsa said. "That's where you come in." She placed her hand upon Gretel's shoulder, patting it gently. "The Zyclon B will be different, more efficient. See how important your work is?"

Gretel couldn't find thoughts, let alone the words, to respond.

My God, is this the purpose of my work in the lab?

"Don't worry. It's always like this at first," Elsa reassured her in a nurturing voice. She stroked Gretel's hair. "You can cry on my shoulder, if you like. I'll have the strength for both of us."

Chapter 50

Max had become bored with the endless grandiosity and pomp of the Nazi Neoclassical architecture, with its sterile, symmetrical shapes, tall columns, and the low-pitched, triangular pediments, all suggesting Old Prussia or a Roman conquest. The building that housed Joseph Goebbels's Reich Ministry of Public Enlightenment and Propaganda offered no exception.

A massive, rectangular structure—situated in the 18th-century Ordenspalais, across from Hitler's Reich Chancellery—it contained offices that controlled all aspects of German cultural and intellectual life. Max sat waiting for the minister in his palatial suite, eyeing the millions of marks' worth of oil-nudes adorning its walls.

The interior of his office enchanted Max even less than the building's exterior. Decorated in an ornate, frilly, Rococo style, it suggested a horrifying mixture of a French nobleman's tasteless chateau and a cheap Parisian cathouse.

Max sat in front of the huge desk, his painting resting beside him on the thick, ivory carpet. He had planned to personally present Hitler with his new portrait. He then substituted a more realistic approach: Herr Goebbels would present it for him. The main reason, however, for Max visiting the minister that day was to take up with him the delicate topic of Gretel Steinberg. If he got nowhere, then he'd try the Fuhrer directly.

So there he waited, dressed in his best suit, checking out the gaudy ministry, until his eyes skidded upon his inspired painting—*The Smiling Pig*—which hung in a gold frame, next to the black velvet curtains.

The giant bronze door to the office opened, and the diminutive figure breezed in. Goebbels headed directly to his desk, oblivious to his visitor. His limp seemed more pronounced than Max had remembered it.

Taking a seat in his red leather chair, he silently fumbled through his mail and movie magazines, lost in thought. His brown, fawnlike eyes shifted to the appointment book sitting on his desk.

After a few minutes, Max forced a cough.

"*Yes*, Herr Bauer." Goebbels still hadn't looked at him, his eyes glued to his papers instead. "What can I do for you?"

Max picked up his painting and unwrapped it. "This is for the Fuhrer. I was hoping you'd deliver it to him for me." He placed it on the desk.

Glancing at it, Goebbels slowly reached in front of him, lifting it to his appraising eyes, studying it carefully. Slowly, his large, liquid stare spilled over to Max.

"Well," said Max, "do you think he'll like it?"

"Do you realize what you have here, Herr Bauer?"

"Well, no, sir." Max braced for the worst.

The minister cleared his throat, his rich, deep voice solemn: "*Mona Lisa!*"

Max tried to hide his sense of relief.

"This painting of yours invokes the Old Masters—and its modest size gives it even more power—like a stick of dynamite. The image of the Fuhrer will live forever, through you, Max Bauer. You were highly recommended by me, so I'm not surprised at all. The Fuhrer will thank me! I'll be honored to present this to him."

Goebbels rubbed his hands, placing, with great care, Max's painting back upon his desk.

"Minister, there's an issue that's very dear to me. It involves a personal, family matter of grave—"

"Do you mean your wife?" Goebbels spit out without missing a beat, as if expecting the topic all along.

Max continued, "Not exactly. I'd like to discuss her later. My mother-in-law is a Gentile, who had been married to a full Jew—"

"I know all about Frau Gretel Steinberg," snapped the minister. "General Hock briefed me. I also know about what happened to Frieda."

"We don't know where Gretel is," Max lied. "If she's detained, I'd like to get her out."

Goebbels leaned back in his chair, wedging his fingers together, cracking his knuckles. "She's in a work camp—in good health. We hear she gets along with her superior very well. They seem to have bonded."

Max could hardly wait to give his wife the good news. "Minister, do you think—"

Again, the quick-witted Goebbels rejoined with happy news. "I'll have a word with Herr Hock. We go back a long way. When Frau Steinberg's done with her assignment, we'll see what we can do to get her sentence commuted. I'm pretty sure the Fuhrer will agree to it."

Max could scarcely believe his good fortune. Perhaps he had been vindicated in his willingness to play ball with the Nazi brass. Perhaps his style of the new German Expressionism would have a chance.

Maybe Hitler and Goebbels aren't maniacs after all.

Chapter 51

"Gretel, this is the most important area in the white cottage." SS Captain Elsa Mensch shoved her pudgy finger into the air, pointing at three small holes in the white-tiled, ten-foot ceiling. "That's where the disinfectant's introduced into the chamber."

Gretel saw that the spacious, cubic structure, with shower spigots lining the concrete walls, had no windows.

"The chamber?" asked Gretel.

Despite the murder of the Gypsy children, despite the lab discussions, despite Elsa's hints connecting Zyclon B to mass murder, she still clung to faint hope that hygiene lay at the core of her technical responsibilities, not executions.

"I mean the shower room," clarified Elsa.

Gretel studied the strange shower facility, also noting that there were no toilets or sinks. Wide-bore, high-pressure hoses rested in coils on the galvanized-steel floor, which had numerous heavy-duty drains. The "dressing room"—partially visible from the showering area—had no chairs or benches.

"Those vents house the canisters for Zyclon B, don't they?" asked Gretel.

Elsa nodded. "Make sure the metal canisters fit the channels and that it's air-tight for the prussic acid," said the finicky captain.

"Where do the prisoners disrobe?"

"The inmates strip in the shower room, where their valuables are collected," explained Elsa.

"What do you do with them?"

Elsa pulled the pink truncheon from her belt and hit it against the wall. "Don't ask so many questions!"

The captain's reaction confirmed Gretel's suspicions. She knew full well why the incinerator bordered the cottage, with—what looked like to her—an adjoining door, which stood about ten meters away. Its function had become very clear.

To Gretel, the floor just fell through her consciousness. The situation wasn't only pathological and criminal beyond all imaginings, but absurd. Both of them knew that this facility had nothing to do with lice. Surely, Gretel figured—especially after the Gypsy atrocity—Mensch must know that *she* knew the real purpose of the showers.

Why this ridiculous dance with the truth?

Somehow, danger no longer mattered. Gretel's outrage exploded. "The reason for the incinerators is to dispose of the corpses—not the clothing!"

Captain Mensch's face flushed, as if her snout had finally been pushed into the dirt. At first, she ignored the insolent remark.

Then she seemed to change her mind. "Yes, of course, to burn the gassed corpses, of course," she uttered matter-of-factly. "I told you this operation's efficient."

Gretel stood there, in frozen silence.

Mensch pointed to a valve. "The gas vaporizes here and goes through there—at room temperature. Shortly, we expect the capacity to be in the hundreds of thousands—all of them liquidated." Elsa's expression shifted to the blankness of boredom, the topic no longer interesting her. "By the way, the chapel bake sale's tomorrow. We need strudel. You may use the SS kitchen."

"But the gas—"

"It's imperative that the gas be quick and volatile enough to spread quickly," badgered Elsa, "without escaping from the chamber. That's it, understand?"

"Yes—I understand."

"Are you OK with strudel or not? I want a firm answer."

"Fine."

"I've saved some real butter for you, none of this ersatz crap."

"Real butter," responded Gretel absently, feeling as if trapped in a nightmare.

Elsa's stupid little SS cap and the smeared lipstick nauseated her. And something even more sickening . . .

I'm an accomplice to this sadistic fiend's massive crime.

Gretel held her abdomen as she bent over, turning her head. The vomitus exploded out of her mouth. She wiped her lips with her sleeve when she was done. Mensch, stunned, put her arm on Gretel's shoulder, which the prisoner pushed away.

Rage consumed Gretel, uncontrollable and fierce. "This is mass murder!" she screamed at the captain. "You're a monster!"

"Who do you mean?" asked Elsa, stunned by Gretel's tone.

"The Jews, the Gypsies! The thousands—*millions*—of human beings you intend to murder!" shouted Gretel. "Frau Captain, this is a sin against God!"

Elsa shook with rage as she digested the gravity of Gretel's outburst, her mouth quivering. "God? *God*! This is God's *plan*, you fool. Don't you know anything?"

Gretel looked on with horror as the SS matron's piggish eyes—usually indolent—flashed savagely. Her thick tongue curled up in her gaping mouth, wedged between the yellow, red-stained teeth, as if she were in the grips of a seizure. Like a pot boiling over, Elsa's murderous energy had found its release.

She clutched her pink truncheon and beat wildly upon Gretel's head, swinging the weapon in powerful, wide arcs. Gretel reeled, her battered face absorbing more blows, until she hit the floor. As she lay helpless and unconscious, Elsa kicked Gretel in the head.

The livid SS captain then composed herself, catching her breath. She glared at the body on the ground. "No bake sale for *you*."

* * *

Adjutant Klaus Grog escorted Max and Frieda as they strode along the narrow gravel road. It wound under the huge sign at the main gate of Sachsenhausen, which greeted prisoners with the ominous words, "WORK MAKES ONE FREE."

They had come that cold, early spring morning to extract Frieda's mother from the squalor of the concentration camp, a trip that had been facilitated by Goebbels. The Fuhrer had loved Max's portrait of him, and the minister had been eager to reward the artist.

Frieda, now almost six months pregnant, wore a heavy, woolen overcoat that barely fit her expanded girth; Max, his old ski outfit, with the heavy jersey. Most of the sparse snow had melted. Nippy morning frosts, with unseasonably warm afternoons, had taken hold.

The massive stench of rotting bodies and refuse—even more repulsive when mixed with the swarms of flies—hit the couple like a sledgehammer. Max grasped Frieda's hand as they made their way into the camp's grim interior, both eyeing the stark rows of barracks, the guard tower, and the tall, barbed-wire fences. Frieda—carrying parcels of food in her large purse—quickened her steps in anticipation of the reunion with her mother, rapidly approaching her barracks.

Grog led them into the dim interior of the structure, carefully stepping along the creaking baseboards, between the endless rows of empty, filthy bunk beds. As he trudged along, the corpulent adjutant nearly fell through a rotten board. He grimaced as he sniffed the foul air. When the trio rounded a tight corner, Frieda screamed, spinning around to grab Max, burying her head in his shoulder.

Grog walked up to the figure dangling from the ceiling, next to Gretel's bunk.

Frieda had realized that her mother, her pretty face blue and cyanotic—her tongue purple and protruding—had hung herself, using strips of cloth cut from her uniform. When Grog cut her down with his knife, her lifeless body thudded to the ground

"She did that *herself*," Grog commented acidly. He tucked the knife under his belt with a cruel smile. "She'd been depressed for a while, not eating a thing. I wanted this to be a surprise."

With Frieda in his arms, Max glared at the sergeant, his fists ready, but held back.

Frieda slowly turned toward the harrowing sight of her mother's rumpled body, sprawled upon the sawdust floor, with crimson rope burns around her slender neck. She bent down, reaching out to stroke her hair.

At that moment, Frieda vowed to herself that she would live to see Hitler—and all his evil—destroyed.

Max guided her gently away from the body. "I'm sorry—too late."

Frieda embraced him, sobbing.

Grog, looking at his watch, announced, "I need breakfast. We can burn her in the incinerator, or you can carry her home in a gunnysack. Which one do you want?"

Frieda lunged at him, ready to claw his eyes out. Grog quickly stepped aside, and Frieda, missing him, lost her balance and fell forward, tumbling down onto the crossbeam of a bunk bed. She smashed her abdomen against a metal joist. Max had rushed toward her, trying to break her fall, but it all happened too fast.

Frieda's pelvis was seized with pain that had, at the same time, both a cramping and ripping quality. As Max crouched over her, helping her up off the floor, she felt warm blood ooze from her vagina. The pain grew blinding in intensity, and she also felt violent contractions.

In the terror of the moment, she realized that she was about to miscarry. She knew that even if they could get her to a fully equipped and staffed emergency room within the next thirty minutes—an impossible task—the fetus's chances of survival approached zero.

She also knew that *she* might not survive, either.

The likelihood of her child's death made her scream with anguish. Max took her in his arms. His love would keep her alive, she reassured herself.

Chapter 52

"We know that's your painting, Frau Krebs."

Siegfried Hock sat at the table facing the Big Gulp, with Luther the Rottweiler and Adjutant Grog at his side. He waved at the painting on the easel standing next to him. "You worked on it recently, in Max Bauer's studio. It's a Spanish town—the one bombed by our allies."

Lena Krebs, hoisted upside down and wearing only a burlap sack, dangled over the cesspool, her mouth just three inches above the surface. Having just been arrested for painting one of her anti-war oils, she was being "vacationed" by the Gestapo. Her increased size made the torture look even more grisly.

Pablo Picasso had already painted a more modernist version of the Guernica outrage, the grim landscape receiving international praise. Hitler, who had secretly ordered the bombing, had been livid with rage. Therefore, Hock swore that he would root out any other subversive renditions surfacing within the German art community. One of his many informants had implicated Lena.

"We know that you're attending a subversive group, Krebs. We're on to your questionable associations. For instance, the Communist painter Hans Beckman."

Grog interrupted. "We've got her grandson—"

"Shut up," snapped Hock. He continued, "My adjutant, and my dog, are too impulsive." The general looked Grog's way. "Aren't you?"

"Yes sir." Grog nervously fed Luther a morsel from the table.

"I was addressing Luther," snapped the general. The dog barked at the sound of his name.

"I want the names of the others in the group," Hock demanded. "Then you'll tell me about their crimes."

Lena said nothing.

"All right then. This is a lawfully assembled tribunal. Grog, dispose of this trash."

The adjutant took the painting from the easel and then dumped it in the middle of the cesspool. Grog then resumed his place beside the dog.

"That's where this dreck belongs. You'll go to the bottom too," Hock said softly to his prisoner. He stood up from the table. "Now talk!"

Lena remained silent.

"What about Max Bauer? Is he involved in a plot to attack the government?"

Lena finally responded. "I'd rather have my painting at the bottom of a filthy sewer, than in a Reich gallery."

"Brave words, Frau Krebs." The general glanced over at the guard near the pool's edge, next to the hoist. "Submerge her entirely. Three minutes."

"Three, Herr General?"

"Three."

Downward went Lena's body, the waterline passing over her bottom lip, down to her thick neck.

At first motionless, Lena then thrashed. Presently, a mass of bubbles came to the surface. Then they disappeared altogether, and the prisoner's body dangled motionless.

Hock looked at his watch. "Ninety seconds. I thought she'd do better than that. Take her up."

Her head cleared the water's surface.

"Cut her down!" ordered Grog.

"No matter," Hock continued, "we have other informers. At least she won't be painting anymore. Bring in the young SA recruit."

Grog left the room and escorted in a large, uniformed young man into the dungeon to stand before the general.

Hock nodded toward the wet corpse lying motionless on the ground. "You may dispose of her as you please," he said to the young recruit. "Your dutiful service is noted."

The visitor saluted. "If you please, sir, I don't want the body. She's a traitor."

"She'll get the incinerator, then."

Paul Krebs glanced at his grandmother. "I tried to talk sense into her, Herr General, but she was just too stubborn."

"No, not *stubborn*," said Hock wistfully with the utmost respect, "something *you* wouldn't understand. More than any man I've ever met, she was *brave*. At the end, she became a true German again. "

Chapter 53

Vienna, Austria, March 1938:

Vienna's Heldenplatz—or Heroes' Square—served as home to the beautiful Hofburg Palace, with the huge statue of Archduke Charles nearby, mounted on his steed. Also, the resplendent city hall, with its towering Neo-Gothic spires, charmed Austrians and foreigners alike.

The Neoclassical Vienna Art Museum stood next to those landmarks, securing its world-renowned art treasures. It consisted of famous statues, tapestries, and oil paintings—including Modernist and Expressionist masterpieces—as well as traditional German fare and favorites from the Old Masters.

Beside the geometric, modern-looking Stock Exchange—across the street from the museum—the *gemutlich* Glockenspiel beckoned. This ancient clock and tower, with its dancing, lederhosen-clad dolls that popped out of the little doors at the clock's apex, had entertained passers-by on the street below, every day since 1870—at precisely noontime.

The rustic figures twirled to the tune of "The Blue Danube." Tourists loved to climb the tower's narrow staircase to see the dolls up close, while enjoying the magnificent view of Vienna from one hundred feet high.

The view from the Vienna Art Museum wasn't bad either, where Max had been assigned to inventory art, and Reich Marshal Goering served as his supervisor. On this bright, spring day, Max enjoyed the wonderful, second-story panorama of Hero's Square, through the museum's huge picture window.

"Be careful, Bauer, the Fuhrer's watching you," warned Herman Goering as he evaluated—with a contingent of SS guards—the hundreds of art pieces he had assembled in the museum.

"On the one hand," the Reich minister added with his customary bonhomie, "you're Hitler's man; he worships you." Goering fingered the huge sapphires and diamonds wedged within his heavy, golden rings. "On the other hand, you're *trouble*. There's your wife for one thing, and her damn family for another, and rumored associations with questionable individuals. A few of your paintings have raised eyebrows—you may be sure of it."

This was the first time, Max realized, that such a high-ranking Nazi had reproached him and warned him of Hitler's wrath. He had been depressed enough by his visit to the concentration camp. This admonition from Goering didn't help matters.

Having closed the museum to the public for "inventory," Goering sat at a huge oaken table, with paintings and tapestries spread upon it, where he affixed colored labels. He threw the discarded pieces into a massive pile on the marble floor.

Another pile, more candidates for the Degenerate Art Exhibition back in Berlin, filled a giant trash bin. The Reich minister ordered his flunkies about, moving paintings between piles, throwing away rejects, and bringing in fresh pieces from the lower floor.

"I can assure you, Herr Goering, that these concerns are overblown," Max said. "As for the Fuhrer, he complimented my work."

Those words came bitterly to Max, and he inwardly felt sick at spewing them—especially considering the recent death of Gretel, and the loss of the baby. Now, there was Frieda's safety to consider . . .

"That may very well be true," the Reich minister responded.

As Goering continued, Max ruminated over his situation.

He and Frieda had agreed that the regime had grown warlike and oppressive. The rumors about a possible invasion of Austria— and Italy's counter-threat—had persisted. Then, there were the deaths of their loved ones . . .

The death of Lena Krebs, under mysterious circumstances, so very recent, haunted Max. Frieda favored direct action. *He* had urged caution and compliance. Now, he had his serious doubts about that course . . .

"I've noticed a lot of soldiers marching today, Herr Reich Minister, is something afoot?"

"You'll see," Goering said as he marked a painting with red chalk. "Today is a very special day. Why else do you think I'm here? I'm grabbing, while the grabbing's good."

Max stood across from the Reich minister, beside the tall, ivory pillars that straddled the entrance to the museum's cafe, picking through hundreds of candidates for the House of Aryan Art. He marveled at Goering's attire, this time his strange uniform a hybrid between a postmaster and an eighteenth-century grenadier. Max could smell his overpowering, fruity perfume from across the spacious room.

"I love art, Bauer," said Goering dreamily. "It allows me to connect with my sensitive side."

"What I don't understand, Herr Goering, is how the curator here is going to allow us to borrow all this art and ship it off to Germany."

"That Communist bastard, you just let me deal with him." Goering glanced at his diamond-studded watch. "It won't be long now."

"I'll inform Herr Goebbels about the loan of these art pieces," said Max. "He'll want a list as soon as—"

"Keep your mouth shut, Bauer. Goebbels can go to hell. You'll help me choose the most valuable pieces. They'll be auctioned off in Switzerland. Most of this crap will go to the fire."

"You'll destroy them?"

"Of course."

"When will the Expressionist pieces be incinerated?"

"Not long, maybe about eleven months," Goering said, "when that Degenerate Exhibition winds down. Then they'll be crammed in boxcars in Berlin bound for Sachsenhausen."

Goering sprung up from his chair, waddling over to where Max stood, inspecting his inventory. "Keep your hands off it. Do you understand me, Bauer? No tricks. If you cross me, believe me, I'll know how to handle you—"

Before Max could reply, he saw a tall, dark figure rapidly approaching from the stairwell.

"Herr Goering!" shouted the intruder.

Max saw the curator of the Vienna Art Museum march into the room, halting in front of the Reich minister. "Explain yourself! My assistant informs me that you're stealing our art—hauling it to Berlin," said the dapper young Austrian with the walrus mustache.

The SS guards moved toward the intruder, but Goering put his hand up. His cobalt-blue eyes bulged with rage. "You scoundrel, you! *Me,* explain myself to *you?* This art belongs to the German Reich. Right at this moment, that's yours truly!"

The curator stood his ground, firmly replying, "This is *Austria,* sir, and *I* run this state museum. Unless you can show me otherwise, you'll have to leave immediately—*without* the art."

Goering drew his pistol and fired it into the curator's temple, the brains splattering over the oil paintings lying on the floor, the curator's limp body crashing to the floor.

"There, I showed you," said Goering, holstering his gun. "Communist bastard!" He glared at the guards. "Don't just stand there you dolts, take care of this!"

The guards dashed to the body.

Goering screamed, "Not *him,* you imbeciles—the paintings! Some have blood on them. Clean them off—carefully!" He straightened the blue cross hanging around his neck—Germany's highest military decoration—the Blue Max. "Handle them gently!"

At that moment, a loud blast cut through the air, shattering the picture window overlooking the square. Max heard many more blasts, his ears smarting from the deafening noise. The popping of gunfire reverberated.

Goering glanced at his watch, then slapped Max on the back. "It's starting!"

"What's starting?" Max asked.

"The *Anschluss,* you fool!"

He waddled to the broken window, with Max not far behind him. "See there, Bauer? It's begun. Hitler's invaded Austria. Now, it's part of the Reich!"

Max, looking out the widow, saw tanks crawling up the street toward the museum. An unruly mob filled the boulevards.

So, the rumors had been true. Germany was smashing Austria.

Chapter 54

Goering and his SS detachment had skipped out with the truckloads of stolen art, leaving Max to sort the paintings and attend to the bloody corpse. The mob outside the window had grown louder, chanting, "We want our Fuhrer," repeatedly, for nearly an hour. As Max cleaned the blood off the white marble floors, he heard Adolf Hitler's shrill voice over the microphone outside, addressing the throng—about a hundred thousand strong—in the square.

"I have come home . . . "

Max caught bits and pieces of the dictator's speech as he rummaged through the reject pile that Goering had left behind. One painting particularly saddened him, staring him in the face—one of Lena's anti-war pieces.

"Your cultural pollution is over . . . "

Hitler's noises, glorying military aggression—in the Fuhrer's own words—enraged him.

"Austria is now part of Germany—the criminals, Communists, and profiteers can now be dealt with . . . "

Lena's painting—that he had just found—had plunged Max into a depression, her disappearance tormenting him. He knew that Hans Beckman had vowed to kill her Nazi grandson, Paul, whom he suspected of being an informer. Max understood Hans's rage, his own feelings also morphing into violent impulses of retribution.

Somehow, the wholesale slaughter of the Great War seemed less nauseating to Max than before. Hitler's sickening words ceased.

Max then heard screams coming from the window. He dashed over, hanging his head out, the view of the square now a hellish nightmare. Hitler and his entourage were nowhere to be seen. But . . .

Hundreds of brown-shirted Nazi youth jeered, as men and women—along with their children—were forced, on their hands and knees, to clean the sidewalks with toothbrushes. From the obscene signs and banners held by the troopers, Max realized that these poor victims were mostly Jews.

One young man burst through the crowd of onlookers, to help a woman who lay on the sidewalk, motionless, her toothbrush still clutched in her hand. Three SS men beat the Good Samaritan with their clubs. They dragged the woman away, like a bag of trash.

As the public address system blasted Wagner's "Ride of the Valkyries," Max observed, across the street, a wild horde of revelers, fiercely pounding on the doors of the Stock Exchange. The rioters shouted: "Jews out!"

They bashed in the door. The swarm rushed in. Presently, they carried out, on their shoulders, dozens of trapped victims—most dressed in dark suits—fighting and squirming, attempting to free themselves from the grip of the mad crowd.

These hapless stockbrokers, transported by the mob to the nearby Glockenspiel, were carried up to the top of the tower. It being noon, the dancing dolls had just come out, twirling and dancing to the charming music, blaring from the old clock.

Max looked on with horror as the terrified hostages were systematically thrown though the little doors, bouncing off the ledge that held the twirling dolls. They tumbled to their deaths from one hundred feet, splattering on the pavement, as cheers from the spectators rang out.

A garbage truck then pulled up, dropping its ramp. The SS guards clubbed Communist hostages that had been taken in the nearby park—some holding red banners—forcing them into the back of the truck. The vehicle sped off.

Max left the window, running into a deserted room facing the interior courtyard, the absolute quiet greeting him like an old, warm friend. The art hanging on the wall soothed him.

It reminded him of his escape in the trenches—with his sketches.

But maybe he no longer wanted to escape . . .

Chapter 55

Potsdam, July 1938:

Max sat in the drafty living room of the von Stoltz mansion, listening to—with the other conspirators—the soft, careful words of the refined hostess, whose syllables floated past her lips like tiny, evaporating bubbles. "Well, General Black, I'm not so sure your news isn't most distressing. Perhaps you would explain to us your concerns."

Max glanced at the others, their chairs again formed in a circle around the huge table, nicely sipping on tea and eating little cakes. According to the gossip that had already circulated, von Spahn—the industrialist—had been murdered by the Gestapo. Lena, of course, was also missing—probably murdered by Hock. Hans Beckman, too hot to handle due to his blatantly subversive art—not to mention his arrest and torture at the hands of the SS months before—had sat out this visit to Potsdam.

Yves, the dapper young dentist with the quick, dark eyes, and bellicose words, sat opposite Max, next to the ebullient and bejeweled mayor of Berlin, Helena Holbein. She had dressed as if attending a high-society soiree.

Professor Stallbun, the philosophical civil servant Karl Inge, and the intellectual General Black, none of them exactly firebrands, completed the circle.

The general's sensitive, round eyes—widened with purpose—his smooth hands placing his teacup on the table, offered sobering words. "My friend in the army's general staff informs me that Czechoslovakia's next, now that Austria's gone."

His meaningful stare rolled over his confidants. "The British are alarmed. An English contact assures me that when Hitler attacks the Czechs, France and Britain will fight. Then Stalin will join them, and eventually America too. It means the utter destruction of Germany."

"When might this attack happen?" asked Mayor Holbein.

"Anytime."

"That's it," said Yves as he slapped his thigh, "we kill the bastard. What about you, Herr Bauer?"

Max detested this Swiss dandy. "What about me?"

"Don't you think it's time to put down your paintbrush and pick up your gun—?"

"Now Yves, don't put him on the spot," said Karl Inge. "I've read in the classics that—"

"Oh shut up about that," interjected the usually sedate Stallbun, to Max's surprise. "This isn't a book club—"

"Why don't we kidnap him instead, and hold him for trial?" added Mayor Holbein, pushing back the long curls falling over her forehead. "Who's in favor of that?" She lamely raised her well-manicured hand, seemingly disappointed that no one else did.

"The trial's a good idea," said Stallbun, "but where would we hide Adolf Hitler—even if we nabbed him?"

"I want to hear what Max has to say," said Yves, his stare full of mischief. "Well, Max—are you ready to *do* *s*omething?" He grabbed a piece of cake off the table.

Max's eyes flashed at his adversary. He suspected that the dentist wanted to goad him into action, but why? *Maybe he wants to incriminate me?* He recalled from the last meeting that Yves had offered to courier letters between the Swiss underground and the group's members. *He seeks evidence in writing,* Max thought. *Maybe he's spying for the Gestapo.*

Max stood up. "I'm going to the W.C. Too much tea." He defiantly stared down the dentist as he left.

After relieving himself, he made his way out to the rose garden. Max stood before the lovely, multicolored flowers. *Why are flowers so perfect and people such shits?*

Eventually, the professor joined him.

"I don't like him either," said Stallbun, without preamble. "I must tell you, my friend. I feel guilty about von Spahn. I suspected him of duplicity. Now he's dead, at the hands of the SS. I don't know what to do, Max. We must *try* something, don't you think—to rescue the Fatherland from this maniac?"

Max's eyes met the professor's. He thought he saw pain in them.

"What does Victor think about apprehending Hitler?" asked the thoughtful academic.

"Victor?" asked Max, confused by this non sequitur.

"The railroad man," added Stallbun—"the friend of Hans Beckman's—"

"I have no idea," answered Max.

"We need action. Let's do *something*," Stallbun insisted.

Max mulled the problem over. "No. I'm not interested," he lied. "In fact, I'm quitting the group."

Max had truly intended to quit.

He knew that these people were all talk, even the old professor. Moreover, they were sure to get caught. But he wasn't—at this juncture—sure that no *action* should be taken—even decisive, violent measures to stop Hitler.

But Max resolved that if he ever did assault the regime, it would be massive—and it would be *alone*. "Goodbye, Professor," he said.

Max left, fuming. His urge to give the offensive Swiss dentist a proper goodbye had been resisted, with considerable difficulty.

Chapter 56

Berlin, August 1938:

Paul Krebs, now an SS adjutant to one of Himmler's top generals, had been well rewarded for his spying activities, not only on his grandmother, Lena Krebs, but also on other Expressionists and Modernist dissenters, many of whom were also pacifists, Communists, homosexuals, and Social Democrats—Nazi targets for liquidation. Through his grandmother, he had rubbed elbows with many and knew their names.

His informant activity had accounted for numerous arrests, and he had been rewarded. One perk that Paul had grown to relish—and had been provided by Himmler's SS—was codenamed "*Lebensborn*," a furtive organization that promoted increased birth rates for racially desirable couples, in or out of wedlock.

Hock, a prudish sort who disapproved of extramarital affairs, hadn't provided Paul with this particular bonus, but Himmler—the general's boss—had.

In Berlin, famous mansions lined a street occupied by old, Social Democrat luminaries, and rich industrialists—some Jews. By 1938, there were no more Jews living on that street.

Their dwellings had been refitted as high-class apartments, most of which housed young women—from any Germanic country—who possessed traits consistent with the program's breeding requirements. Authorized SS recruits, such as Paul Krebs, had free access to them.

The state paid for maternity care, babysitting, obstetric and gynecological care, and even abortions, when the authorities feared the babies to be "substandard" in any way. Prudishness, bothersome Christian values, or "frigidity," were dealt with harshly, and the girls who gave birth to the most desirable children were duly rewarded, with expensive gifts and vacations.

Paul liked to visit one mansion in particular, which had double rooms. He had persuaded the occupants—a tall blonde girl from Holland and an athletic young redhead from Silesia—to service him simultaneously. One evening, with the art deco lamps turned low, three glasses and empty bottles of champagne sat on the silver coffee table, as the phonograph played a banned American jazz record.

"Do it faster," screamed Paul, as he lay supine on the bed, flopping like a hooked mackerel on a sailboat deck. The redhead crawled off of him after he had finished. She turned toward her friend. "Well, how were we?"

"I was bored," said the blonde.

"I'm too tired," Paul chortled. "I need more champagne. I'm thirsty—it's too hot in here—open a window."

He sat up, trying to get to his feet, but wobbled, falling back down on the bed. "Well, go get my drink!" he screamed at the girls.

After opening the window, letting in the cooler, but still muggy, night air, the girls sauntered into the kitchen to fetch more hooch.

* * *

"The swine's in there, on the bed. He's out of it," whispered the redhead to the young man, who had just popped out of the kitchen closet.

He dipped into the pocket of his black leather pants and then counted out the bills, handing them to the blonde roommate. "There," he said, "get yourselves to the train station right away—you'll reach the border within a few hours."

They hugged him, his unruly, red hair falling over his forehead. "You'd better get going," said Hans Beckman.

He pulled out his switchblade, flicking it open.

The steel gleamed in the kitchen light. As he walked over to the door that led into the bedroom, he barely heard the girls leave through the back door. Cracking the door open, Hans saw his target lying on the bed, seemingly unconscious.

The artist's Persian slippers didn't squeak a bit as he slowly approached Paul, readying his weapon. Hans took the extra pillow, resting at the foot of the bed, and positioned it over Paul's face.

He thrust the blade deep into the base of Paul's throat, jamming it through the cricoid cartilage and the bone behind it, severing the cervical spinal cord.

Paul went flaccid immediately. Hans withdrew the blade a bit, and then jammed it upward, toward the jaw, for good measure—severing all the soft tissue he could.

Paul gasped, gargling blood, and choked; and then he died.

Hans wiped the blood off on Paul's chest. As he walked to the door and out into the hall, he calmly put the knife back in his pocket, then descended the dark stairwell. It was very late. He was too tired to notice the movement in the shadows, three doors down.

A man was watching him go down the stairs.

Chapter 57

Berlin, September 1938:

"I shall smash Czechoslovakia—erase it from the face of the earth! Even the British won't be able to swallow my Godesberg Memorandum!"

The Fuhrer pounded the map on Joseph Goebbels's desk, as his savage blue eyes shot between the propaganda minister and General Hock, both frozen to their chairs.

"It's my unshakable will that the Czechs be destroyed!"

Both men nodded vigorously.

"This will not be a nice war like the last one," promised the Fuhrer. "It'll be fought with immeasurable harshness."

Hock glanced at Goebbels beside him and, seeing that the propaganda minister had remained silent, spoke. "I suppose, my Fuhrer, that the French and the Russians will let Britain fight alone."

Hitler screamed, "The French can't even fuck their own women, they're so sissified! The Russians don't even know how to use toilets! I don't give a fig what they do."

Goebbels knew that the Fuhrer was playacting. As usual, he'd lather up for a few hours, then find a way to get what he wanted by bluffing—and not armed conflict.

Or maybe this time he's serious?

The propaganda minister couldn't tell. He'd spoken to Goering and the generals, and they had strong misgivings about taking on the Allies so soon.

Goebbels worried that the British would win and then take away all of their nice homes, and possessions—not to mention their girlfriends. *And we'll be left to hang for war crimes! I'll work on the Fuhrer later,* he decided. *I'll let him cool off.*

Adolf Hitler's gaze shifted to the vast assortment of expensive oil paintings hanging from the ornate, frilly walls in the propaganda minister's office. It halted on one piece that caused him to bite his lip. Its showy gold frame, next to the picture window, with the black velvet curtains, only served to heighten its offensiveness.

"What's that?" asked Hitler.

Goebbels saw him glancing up at Max Bauer's painting of the smiling pig. A bolt of fear surged through him. *My God! How could I be so careless as to let the Fuhrer see that damned thing?*

"What's *what*, my Fuhrer?"

"That degenerate pornography!" He pointed directly at the smiling, yellow pig in the purple straw, with the green sky over the barn.

Goebbels, who had been pointing out his latest art acquisitions to all the top Nazis, hadn't had one complaint—not even from Himmler. Now, he faced *this*. "Oh, that—" he said nonchalantly.

"How dare you!" continued Hitler. "You're the guardian of our culture, Herr Goebbels, and you hang this shit on your wall?"

Hitler strode over to the painting and ripped it down, studying the piece closely in his hands. "The artist initialed it 'MB' in the corner here." He walked over to his seated minions, jabbing his finger at the initials. "Who's that? You can tell from his brushstrokes that he's a homosexual."

Another shock wave reverberated through the propaganda minister. Of course, the Fuhrer knew the answer to his own question—*and he's trying to catch me in a fib.* Before he could decide on the best answer, Goebbels—to his horror—heard the truth come from Hock's lips. "The 'MB' stands for Max Bauer, my Fuhrer."

"Yes, of course," retorted Hitler, "Bauer? *He* painted this? It's not possible."

Goebbels rose from his chair.

"My Fuhrer. I'm sorry. I hadn't realized that my curator put it there."

It didn't surprise Goebbels that Hock would spill the beans about *The Smiling Pig*, given his dislike of the gifted artist. "It isn't Bauer's usual style, as you know," Goebbels added. "I only had time to glance at it in the pile—"

"Shut up!" Hitler threw the piece on Goebbels's desk, breaking a vase. "I order you, Herr Minister, to assemble in this office one hundred Reich farmers—immediately! Ask *them* if that looks like a pig! A pig doesn't smile! What's this world coming to?"

"I understand, my Fuhrer, I apologize for this outrageous oversight."

The blaze in Hitler's eyes had worn off a bit, and he sat down in the easy chair that Goebbels had bought for him to use during his visits.

"Has he painted any others like this one?" Hitler asked, seemingly hoping for a negative answer.

"No," said Goebbels quickly, "not to my knowledge."

"Yes, he has," interjected Hock as his tall, lean body rose from his chair. "Here, my Fuhrer, please review this."

The general pulled out a piece of folded canvas from his black tunic, then strode over to Hitler's chair, unfolding it and placing it in the Fuhrer's outstretched hand. "This garbage was taken from Bauer's studio."

Goebbels rolled his eyes. His mouth turned to cotton. He recalled that Hock had wanted to show him something before they had met with Hitler that morning, but he hadn't had time. *It must've been about this damned painting that he just handed to the Fuhrer!*

"The painting's named *Red Horse, Purple Meadow*, my Fuhrer."

Hitler studied it for a moment and then turned white. His eyes flamethrowers, he boiled with rage as he could hardly spit out his venom. "My God! Madmen! Degenerates; Can't I trust anyone? Yes, this turd also has the 'MB' initials."

Hitler popped up from his chair, screaming at Goebbels at the top of his lungs. "I want all this shit rooted out; every last charlatan who calls himself an artist and paints this trash is to be arrested!"

"Yes, my Fuhrer," said Goebbels.

"This horse contemplates the view of the meadow," said Hitler in a shocked whisper, as if he had just seen a ghost. "Is the horse a tourist?"

There was no answer.

"I repeat, is he a *tourist*?"

Hock snapped to attention. "Yes, a tourist," he agreed. "My Fuhrer, I've just received a report that Bauer visits a subversive group."

Hitler started to shake. His coloring went from red to purple. "Get Bauer! Bring him here!"

"My Fuhrer, please, let's get more facts first," suggested Goebbels in a reasonable voice. Goebbels wasn't surprised when Hitler, his moods given to roller coaster changes, calmed down, taking a seat again on his padded chair.

The Fuhrer's voice softened. "I had my heart set on Bauer painting my great legacy to the German folk: a huge portrait of *me*. He's the only one to do it! Now, the people will be cheated."

The Fuhrer hung his head, closing his eyes, massaging them with one finger. "What exactly did he do in this subversive group, General?"

Goebbels had only a split-second to decide to either defend his protégé or condemn him. *Let's see what the facts show*, thought the minister. *After all, I recommended Bauer. He worked under* me. *The Fuhrer really idolizes him.*

To throw him under the bus right then might backfire. The minister also had realized that when it came to artists he loved, the Fuhrer often favored leniency. Hock probably knew this too, he figured. *Therefore, he'll be careful about what he says, and not make wild charges.*

"Well," answered Hock, groping for words. "He really—"

"Herr Hock," interrupted Goebbels, "how many times did Bauer attend this group?"

Hock hesitated. He looked over at Hitler, who now glared at him. "Well, only a few times. Our informant also says that he quit."

"I see," said Goebbels in a lawyerly fashion. "Did he propose any violent action against the regime?"

Goebbels could see the general's eyes shifting, seemingly working to make up his mind about how aggressive to be. The fact was, Hitler's expression now looked hopeful, not accusatory, and the powerful SS general would be foolish to oppose the Fuhrer's inclination.

"No, he didn't. He suggested the opposite."

Out of the corner of his eye, Goebbels noticed Hitler's faint smile. The minister knew that Hock had been out to get Bauer, but this mud just wasn't bad enough to stick, and the general knew it.

"I'll bet he didn't even know what this social meeting was about when he started going there," assured the propaganda minister.

"Yes, Herr Goebbels might be on to something," said Hitler blandly, obviously getting bored by the topic.

"My Fuhrer," said Goebbels gravely, "Bauer's been naughty and needs to be punished." He glanced over at Hock's neutral expression. "I think we can rehab him. You and I are progressives, my Fuhrer, and your artistic prowess adds to your brilliance. As always, your wisdom will guide me."

Hitler rose from his chair. "I must go attend to more important matters. Herr Bauer is no longer national curator—that includes the Degenerate *and* Aryan Art Exhibitions. You, Goebbels, will see to it that he paints no more subversive trash; he's on probation, until I release him."

Hitler's gaze landed on Hock. "Bauer's gallery and studio are to be closed until further notice. He can paint at home if he likes. If he missteps again, it's the end for him."

Hitler marched out of the room.

Goebbels looked over at Hock. "Good try." He wiped his forehead with his handkerchief.

Hock shook his head. "Congratulations. Bauer's a lucky bastard."

Chapter 58

Berlin, October 1938:

"There will be a big shipment of looted art in March—maybe six months away. The boxcars will hold the whole legacy of the German Expressionist movement. This includes most of the Degenerate Art Exhibit," said Max as he watched Victor sitting across the desk, in his station office, rolling a cigarette with his thick fingers. "If we don't save it, the Nazis will burn it."

"So what?" said Victor.

The railroad foreman brushed off his dirty, navy blue uniform, looking out the third-story window onto the smoky tangle of glistening train tracks, threading through the glass-domed station. Hans Beckman, wearing his greasy, black leather overalls, sat next to Max, both facing their co-conspirator.

"So what?" repeated Hans incredulously. "Victor, the paintings—"

"Screw the damned paintings." Victor turned his head from the window to Max. "Divert the train to save this garbage?"

"*That's* what Hitler calls it," said Max.

Victor paused.

"Now there's a *great* reason to save it," said Hans.

Victor and Max laughed. A pregnant silence followed, the kind, thought Max, when friends pondered a profound truth.

Hans, his strong voice—as usual—louder than necessary, added, "There's a stowaway in the boxcar, too."

Max nodded. "A Jewish woman named Sarah Roth. She escaped before she could be carted off to a concentration camp. Her husband disappeared months ago."

Victor blew a large ring of smoke at Hans, then flicked the ashes on the floor.

He stood up, and walked over to the window to close it, then retook his seat behind the desk. "Max, most of this art was stolen by Goering, right?"

"Yes, and Goebbels. There were others, too."

"The woman, yes. But do we really want to risk our lives for paintings?" Victor asked.

Max glanced at Hans, who shrugged.

Max thought for a moment. Not sure he could explain, he'd try. "You're right. Paintings aren't worth it—to me, or to you, or maybe not even to Hans, sitting here." Max gestured to his friend, who had pulled out his switchblade, carefully peeling an apple that had been sitting on Victor's desk.

"But to millions of others—in future generations—yes, it's worth it," Max continued. "Even only if it's a small percentage of those generations—it's worth it to *them*. This art is the soul of Germany—the one that counts. If creative expression dies, we all die . . ."

Max stood up and walked over to the window, looking down on the travelers crowding the gangplanks. "It's what kept me going in the trenches. It'll help me to do what I may have to do."

Max then turned from the window, to face the other men. "I didn't mention the best reason."

"And what's that?" asked Victor.

"I included a few of my paintings to sell. I'll get rich. After that big speech, I deserve it."

Victor smiled. The big foreman pushed back his small cap. "All right. Where will the train be heading?"

"Sachsenhausen—one of General Hock's babies," answered Max.

"That bastard!" spat Victor.

Max sat down. "Goering has a shipment of art—priceless pieces—that will be bound for an auction in Zurich, about the same time."

"Yes, he's had many before," offered Victor. "The next one's maybe sometime in early spring."

"Right, well, you switch the bill of lading between the Sachsenhausen and Zurich freights," Max continued, his eyes fastened on Victor, "since they're about the same time, maybe delay one train a little somehow, if you have to. Your Swiss contacts in the underground can stop the one carrying our stuff, after it crosses the border—before Zurich—and empty the boxcars. They can stash it someplace safe."

"What about the SS guards on the train?" Hans asked.

"Last shipment there were only two," answered Victor. "We can handle that. This plan might work. I'd love to screw that swine Hock. Goering, too. I wish I could see the look on the general's face when he finds out."

Victor looked at Max. "How's my friend Professor Stallbun doing?"

"All right."

"A good man."

"Be on the lookout for another guy," said Max. "His name is Yves, and he's supposed to be a dentist from Switzerland. He says he has contacts in the underground. There's something about him that's not right."

"Never heard of him," said Victor. "That's odd, too, because usually I get wind of everyone involved."

"By the way, I may have another stowaway for you," Max said in a throwaway style. The two men, by their knowing expressions, seemed to have been expecting this news, thought Max. "With this train diversion, the Gestapo will probably suspect me. Frieda needs to get out of the country. It should've been done long ago. Her train better leave first."

Max stood up to shake hands with Victor. "Hans, let's let your boss get back to work."

Hans sliced the last bite off the apple, and then threw the core in the garbage can. He fingered the blade. "I volunteer for the two SS guards."

"It's a deal," said Victor.

Chapter 59

The Slaughterhouse 1 gallery had been a great success. Since Max had become national curator, sales soared, adding nicely to his salary. The exposure for his art had been broader and more powerful than he had dared to dream, with his notoriety climbing to dizzying heights.

Frieda had used the great inflow of money to help run charity clinics, somewhat softening the impact of her lost medical practice and the tragic loss of the baby—not to mention her father and mother. Hans Beckman had continued to paint, but only innocent, landscape watercolors—at least temporarily. He called them his "little paintings."

Max—knowing all about the murder of Paul Krebs—felt that Hans was a marked man. Having recovered from his torture, Hans had worked more hours at the train station, helping Victor disrupt Nazi shipments. Placing a small coin in the oil line of a locomotive, altering the train's destination by misfiling its papers, and tampering with the track's switching stations had all proven to be effective.

Then, the big roust came. The SS closed Max's gallery and studio, and his job as national curator was suspended. Many of his paintings were confiscated. Goebbels had not returned his phone calls. He and Frieda had feared for their lives. Max continued, however, to paint in their apartment.

The weeks passed, but no midnight visit from the Gestapo had materialized. In due course, Max found out that Hitler had seen one of his more Modernist-leaning paintings and had gone berserk, ordering the punitive measures. The story of Emil Nordling had played all over again—it seemed. The old man had warned him . . .

Consequently, that cold morning, he packed up—with Hans—the remaining items left in his shuttered gallery, before locking it up—probably for good.

They sat around the table in the lobby, upon which two bottles of expensive brandy rested, beside Max's folded newspaper. Struggling to believe that his best friend had only turned twenty-three, Max filled two glasses, raising his for a birthday toast.

"Here's to Paul Krebs," Hans said. "He can say 'Heil Hitler' to St. Peter."

Hans laughed. Max, however, didn't appreciate the young Communist's loose words. "Shut up, Hans—at least not so loud."

"The place's empty."

"How do you know?"

Hans shrugged, draining another glass of brandy. He picked up the newspaper, unfolding it, throwing it down in front of Max. "Look," he said with a slur, "this is really why I came over here."

Max studied the bold headline on the first page: "WAR OVER CZECHOSLOVAKIA LOOMS!"

"This time, Germany will be destroyed," said Hans. "I told you we should kill Hitler—"

"That talk will get *us* killed. I'll die for action, not hot air," snapped Max. "But I'm starting to think—"

Three shots rang out as the door to the lobby crashed open.

SS troopers flooded the gallery, kicking over furniture and smashing—with their rifle butts—the few paintings that had been left. SS Adjutant Grog followed on their heels, accompanied by more Gestapo toughs.

They strode up to the surprised artists who had jumped up from their chairs, observing the destruction with stunned silence.

Grog's eyes met Max's. "We're not here for *you*, Herr Bauer." He pointed at Hans. "Arrest Beckman."

The soldiers lunged at Hans, who attempted to make a run for it. They chased him down, knocking him to the floor. The rest descended upon the hapless young artist, kicking him as he lay on the ground.

When Max made a move to help his friend, Grog grabbed him, shoving a pistol into his temple. "If you resist, Herr Bauer, you die, and so does *she*."

Max froze, consumed with both rage and sorrow, looking on helplessly as the soldiers dragged Hans away. Grog tossed a triumphant smirk over his shoulder as he followed his underlings out, leaving Max alone with his morbid thoughts. This time, Max knew, Hans wouldn't leave the prison alive, no matter what he did or to whom he talked. Anyway, his influence had evaporated.

The price of being at loggerheads with the regime bit hard. The murder of Paul, Max concluded, had its name written all over this raid by the Gestapo. Now, Hans would pay the ultimate price. He may even talk, but Max doubted it.

With the soldiers gone, and his best friend with them, Max sat and poured himself a large brandy, draining the glass. He stared into the blank wall.

He felt like murdering someone.

Chapter 60

"Your painting of the smiling pig is degenerate horse dung. I was shocked. You're on notice, Herr Bauer—another infraction like that, and I can't guarantee your safety, or your wife's." Goebbels sat behind his huge mahogany desk, lighting a cigarette.

Sitting across the desk, Max fought back his anger.

"This seditious group of old frumps that you visited—are you done with that?"

Max, not really surprised that the minister had been fully informed about his activities, shrugged. "I quit it months ago."

"Yes, and you were innocent of any wrongdoing. That bunch is all talk anyway," continued Goebbels, "so I won't bother to question you further. Your grungy friend Hans Beckman suckered you into the whole mess."

"No he didn't," Max shot back, unable to mask his testiness when hearing his friend's name.

Goebbels ignored the remark. Max had suspected that there was an informant within the group. He thought about the Swiss dentist. *No wonder Goebbels knows so much.*

Max asked cautiously, "Can you tell me what's happened to Hans?"

Goebbels forcefully snuffed out his cigarette, saying nothing. Max felt that it served as a symbol for his friend's fate.

"Just consider yourself lucky, Herr Bauer. You must redeem yourself in the eyes of the Fuhrer. Then your welfare will be assured."

"Redeem myself *how*?" responded Max.

"You're not to repeat any of what I have to tell you," warned the minister. "Your life depends on it."

Goebbels, wearing one of his outrageously expensive three-piece suits, stood up, then strutted about the office with his hands clasped behind his back, shooting his eyes between Max and his new Nazi kitsch cluttering the walls—undoubtedly meant to mollify Hitler.

"I understand, Herr Minister."

"If the Fuhrer's happy, I'm happy," explained Goebbels. "Paintings, music, and victory are the only things that makes him happy. I can supply him with the paintings, therefore I must obtain the best ones possible," said Goebbels in a soft, almost fatherly voice. "At this moment—he covets *yours* more than any other. That makes you useful to me. As your star rises, so does mine."

It crushed Max that he couldn't apply any remaining influence with Goebbels to help poor Hans—too late for that, he knew. Moreover, he would risk his life—and, more importantly, Frieda's—if he tried.

"The Fuhrer's rebuilding Berlin," explained Goebbels. "Not too long from now, there'll be a new 'Fuhrer Pyramid' in the middle of Berlin—three times the size of the original pyramids in Egypt. A gigantic oil portrait of the Fuhrer will hang in that monument—in its top floor. Guess who the artist will be?"

Max couldn't believe the megalomania of such an enterprise. "Why me?"

"He's obsessed by your talent, that's why. But to get back in the Fuhrer's good graces, Herr Bauer, you'll do a lot more than paint that portrait. From now on, you'll only paint art that is consistent with National Socialist principles. The only way to rehabilitate you is to follow my plan."

"Plan?"

"You'll paint a full portrait of Hitler's mother—which *I* shall present to him. That's critical. I have one of her old photographs, for you to use as your model. He worships her memory."

"Is that all, Herr Minister?"

"Not entirely. You'll be invited to paint the Fuhrer's full portrait—as a preliminary to the one in the pyramid. The one you painted of him before was magnificent, but he wants a closer perspective, this time. Also, he requires a portrait of his close friend—who also idolizes you."

"Who?" Max asked.

"Never mind, Herr Bauer, the name isn't important. But your painting must please her." Goebbels looked uncomfortable. "If the Fuhrer likes it, you'll paint *his* portrait for sure, soon after hers."

So, Adolf Hitler must have a girlfriend, Max surmised. Then he remembered the pretty and vivacious—and unstable—Eva Braun. "I'll do my best, Herr Minister."

Max realized that if he botched this, he and Frieda could very well end up not only destitute and harassed by the Gestapo, but also in a concentration camp. His ability to divert the train laden with art—and with it Frieda's means of escaping Germany—might go up in smoke, as well.

Goebbels sat down again, locking his eyes onto Max's. "You better be at the top of your game, that's all."

As he sat there, Max's rage welled up inside him. Hans Beckman's face surfaced within his consciousness. He threw caution to the wind, taking a chance. "About Hans Beckman—"

"You'd better keep your mouth shut about that." Goebbels lit another cigarette. "You and your lovely wife might join him. Besides, Herr Beckman is attended to, as we speak."

Chapter 61

Hock drew his sword from its scabbard. The sun had set, and the garden-maze behind Gestapo headquarters looked especially forbidding, just the way he liked it for his blood sport.

"Turn on the music, Grog. Give me Luther first."

Luther, seated on his haunches beside his master, growled viciously, sensing his dinnertime. The adjutant gave his boss the leash, then scurried away.

Hock, having saved a few tidbits from the dinner table, fed them to his hungry dog, whetting the beast's appetite for the chore at hand. "O Star of Eve," the general's old standby, again filled the air.

His sword and dog ready, he approached the entrance to the maze, the other entrance having been traversed by the prisoner just minutes before. This time around, noted Hock, the prey had a knife at his disposal, not a pistol. Apparently, the detainee liked using knives, so now he could use it again. That scum didn't deserve a more sportsmanlike end, anyway.

Grog returned, catching up to the general before he disappeared into the labyrinth. "Watch out for this one, Herr General. Beckman's a wily bastard."

Hock bent down to pet Luther. "Want to soften him up, boy?" Luther, a special breed of Rottweiler, who stood nearly as tall as a pony, fought his leash, snarling and snorting for action. "I'll let Luther say 'hello' first, eh Grog?"

"A fine idea, Herr General."

Hock took off the leash. Luther dashed into the maze, sniffing out the trapped prisoner. Screams and growls competed with the din of Wagner's masterpiece.

"Sounds like he found something savory," chortled Hock. "I'll give the dog a minute, then finish this artist off myself."

Hock listened to the fascinating sounds of death, mixing with the celestial music. The breaking of twigs, the ruffle of dry leaves, Luther's grunting, growling, and panting, the cries from the victim, all signified to him the essence of life: fighting to the death—the stronger foe prevailing.

Beckman represented the worst form of vermin—a traitor to his own kind, ruminated Hock. He had handled the torture admirably, though. The scum had given up nothing during the most horrendous torture, including any information about Max Bauer. Despite this bravery, Hock would give no quarter.

Then, except for the music, the maze fell silent.

"Luther! Come on, boy! Come back!" shouted Hock.

He heard the dog panting again—the heavy paws rushing, traversing the maze, to return to his master. Luther finally appeared at the entrance. The general, at first surprised, shook his head with pride.

The beast moved slowly over to Hock, seating himself beside the general, his coat bloodied from a small knife wound to his massive leg. The general shoved his sword back into its scabbard. He glanced toward the maze, the ivied labyrinth still silent except for Wagner's music.

"Fetch the vet, Grog. Luther has a cut." He petted the huge head.

Grog's eyes widened when he saw what Luther had brought back.

"Drop it, boy. That's it. Leave it alone," murmured the general softly. "That was quite a tote, wasn't it, boy?"

On the ground lay Hans Beckman's leg, chewed off at the hip, strips of bloody burlap clinging to the torn flesh.

"He's still in there," said Grog, "—probably bled to death by now."

"I *said*," snapped Hock, "get the *vet*! Then drag the body out of there. I don't want flies."

Chapter 62

Berlin, November 1938:

"Hans Beckman's dead, murdered by the Gestapo."

Although no surprise, Professor Stallbun's confirmation plunged Max into despair—then a slow, seething rage. As the plodding academic sat on the couch in the apartment living room, his precise, careful words swept over Max, like a cold breaker at a Baltic beach resort.

Sitting opposite his guest on the easy chair, Max's violent hatred—no longer merely loathing—erupted. "Hock tortured him to death?"

"Who else?" Stallbun stared at Max, nodding. "A contact within the Gestapo said that Herr Beckman suffered—sadistic torture—then dismemberment."

The shattering news made Max's insides burn. "Hans told me, but I wouldn't listen."

"I'm sorry to tell you this, Max."

"I don't know what to say," Max continued. "He was a better man than all of us put together. He was right all along."

Mentally, he had already said his goodbyes to his friend, the emotional energy already invested. Powerful memories, however, remained, which fueled his fury. Max noticed Stallbun's hands trembling.

"What are we going to do, Max?"

"*Do?*"

"We must fight!" said the professor.

"Fight. How?"

Stallbun took his pipe out of his coat pocket. "You're a war hero, for Christ's sake; you ought to know."

"You sound like the Swiss dentist." Max realized that channeling his violent impulses into action couldn't involve an old windbag like Stallbun.

The professor's smooth hands fiddled with the unlit pipe sitting in his lap. "I think the Gestapo's on my tail. I know I've been followed."

"When?"

"Every day," said Stallbun. He sucked nervously on his pipe. "Now! In fact, I'd better go soon. I may have been followed."

"You haven't lit it yet," said Max, indicating his visitor's cold pipe. *This man's terrified,* thought Max; *he's not much use to anyone.*

Stallbun took out his lighter and lit the pipe. The blue smoke filtered Max's way, the sickening-sweet scent of burnt molasses assaulting his nose. He realized that if the rattled—but well-meaning—professor had indeed been followed, the damage had already been done.

"There's an informer in the group," said Max evenly.

Stallbun dropped his pipe, quickly retrieving it, stuffing it into the ashtray lying on the table between them. "Who?" He brushed the ashes off his sleeve. "General Black?"

"I don't know for sure," said Max. "I don't have a good feeling about Yves."

"The dentist chap?"

"Yes."

Max chose not to say any more. No point, he thought.

"Max." Stallbun leaned toward him, his face grave. "I may need you to hide me."

Max rose from his chair, pacing the room, thinking things through. They were moving very fast. He performed a quick calculation and decided against it. He wanted to help Stallbun but didn't know where he could hide him without getting everyone killed—including Frieda. He figured that the professor had shot off his overactive mouth or—more likely—the informant had marked him.

"Anything specific happen, Professor?"

Stallbun looked around the dwelling. "Are you sure we're alone? Where's Frieda?"

"Of course we're alone. She's giving a lecture at the University."

Stallbun's eyes narrowed. "There's a plot to kill Hitler."

Max, unimpressed by the cloak-and-dagger style and breezy divulgence, remained skeptical. *This is just idle talk again,* he thought. *The old professor's been reading too many English spy novels.*

If he ever acted, Max swore to himself again, he'd act alone.

"He's going to invade the rest of Czechoslovakia," added Stallbun. "He'll break the Munich Agreement, then it's war!"

Actually, Max silently agreed with the prediction of war, but words and thoughts alone wouldn't stop Hitler.

Stallbun made strong eye contact, his baggy eyes dripping significance. "When it's time, will you help us kill this maniac?"

Max stopped, his eyes locking onto his guest. He considered for a moment, and then decided that the visit had lasted long enough. "Good night, Professor."

Stallbun, nonplussed, stood up. "God be with you, Max. Will we see you again at the meetings?"

He ignored the question.

As Max closed the apartment door after Stallbun left, he glanced out the window, noticing that evening had come. Not quite, though.

He saw an orange glow coming from across the street. Last time he saw something like that, the Reichstag had burned down—and then more violence followed. Surely, thought Max, it must be a small fire, started in a careless homeowner's hearth.

Then he heard the shattering of glass from the sidewalk below . . .

* * *

Frieda stumbled her way through the shards of broken glass heaped upon the sidewalk along Unter Den Linden. Terrified, she strode home as fast as she could, feeling the warm liquid trickling down the side of her neck. She wiped it, and then looked at her bloodstained hand. The blood came from where that grotesque man—back at the university—had slammed her head against the floor, after he had wrestled her down.

As she ambled along the storefronts, Frieda looked into the window of one of them—a shoe shop—that hadn't been vandalized yet, one of the few. In her reflection from the light of the streetlamp, she observed her dirty face, and filthy, torn clothing, the result of her almost having been molested.

The nice young couple that had rescued her from her attacker gave Frieda the shocking news. A young Jew had shot a high-ranking Nazi official at the German Embassy in Paris. Pandemonium had broken out all over Germany, but particularly in Berlin, where most of Germany's Jewish population resided.

Joseph Goebbels called for "spontaneous demonstrations" from the "people,"—in reality, blood-curdling pogroms. The radio was already branding the Nazi retribution for the assassination as "Crystal Night," due to the thousands of shattered storefront windows, caused by the rioting vandals.

On her way back home, Frieda came upon a huge synagogue that had been converted into a Jewish nursing home. SS men had cordoned off the entrance and lined the perimeter of the structure. She stopped, joining the hundreds of spectators, mostly ordinary people, on their way home from work.

The Nazis encouraged young men to help with the chore at hand: to burn down the building and incinerate everyone in it. They doused the exterior of the building with gasoline, paying special attention to drench the doors and windows—all bolted from the outside. Then, flaming torches were tossed against the building. They exploded in flames—the dry, wooden siding serving as perfect kindling.

Screams reverberated from within the resting home, as the smoke and flames filled the air. Frieda heard the sound of breaking glass, as the inhabitants tried to flee through the locked windows. She looked around at the people watching, noticing that many bystanders jeered, but not all.

Many also looked as shocked as she was, and a few cried for the victims inside.

She ran home as fast as her weak legs would take her, feeling lucky to be alive. The mob at the university had turned on her, joining the violence against anyone who they considered an undesirable. As she ran, she caught glimpses of the surreal carnage: more mountains of broken glass; mass arrests; Jewish shops and restaurants—marked with a Star of David and insults painted on the windows—looted; and screaming masses bent on destruction.

Hostages were taken; mass beatings and murders were taking place on the sidewalk; and venerable synagogues were burning to the ground, while firemen just stood by.

She dashed away from the madness to the warmth of her home and the sustenance of Max's love.

Chapter 63

From the balcony off the apartment's living room, Max shivered at the horrific sight of Crystal Night. Scores of fires glowed in the evening darkness. He had seen nothing like it since the war—the Reichstag fire, in comparison, was a trifle.

People ran amok, smashing hundreds of shop windows and torching countless businesses. Looters dashed out of Wertheimer's Department Store, with their hands full of jewelry. SS squads roamed, formally arresting hundreds of Jews.

Max desperately wanted to aid the victims, but what could he do? The massive pogrom had spread uncontrollably, and the SA would deal with all dissenters with clubs and pistols—maybe even executions. The magnificent Berlin Synagogue, a quarter mile away, its gigantic dome and spires towering above the other buildings, burned with a fiery fury that reminded him of wartime flamethrowers.

Then his mind shot to Frieda, her safety consuming him. He dashed to the door . . .

At that moment, it opened, and there she stood—her eyes wild with fear, her face dirty, and her blouse torn.

Max rushed to her, gently guiding her to the couch. "How bad are you hurt?"

Frieda, catching her breath, muttered, "I'm all right. Just a small cut on my head."

"What the hell's going on out there? How did you tear your blouse?"

"*I* didn't tear it."

Max sat down beside his wife, putting his arm around her.

He gently stroked her hair, his voice soft. "Who did?"

Frieda shook her head, saying nothing.

"What happened?"

"You haven't heard? A young Jew shot a Nazi official in Paris, just hours ago. They're killing and burning—smashing store windows owned by Jews."

"Thank God you made it back from the university." Her state of shock alarmed him. "What happened there—at your lecture? Who hurt you?"

Frieda glared at him, her eyes reflecting incredulity, seemingly unable to fathom the bestiality of mob rule. "They stopped me from speaking, shouting me down, yelling 'Jew-bastard.' The faculty and students grabbed at me, jeering and laughing. I fought my way out of the auditorium."

Max noticed the trickle of blood behind her ear. It ran down her neck, onto her collar. He wiped it off gently with his sleeve.

"The cut's nothing."

"How did you get it?"

"I don't know—a man—"

"*What* man?"

"I don't know—" Frieda's eyes hardened. "A janitor—a horrible, dirty man. He had bothered me before. Tonight, he caught me in in the dark corridor, outside the lecture room; pulled me into an empty classroom. Then, he . . . "

Frieda, trembling, her lip quivering, burst into tears, sobbing violently. Max hugged her tight. After a few moments, she composed herself.

Max noticed that her dress had also been torn and soiled. "Your dress—he had you on the ground, didn't he?" Max released his embrace; his smoldering eyes burned through Frieda. "Did he . . . "

"No. He—*tried*. I screamed as hard as I could," Frieda explained. "By some miracle, a nice couple helped me—hearing my cries. The husband chased him away."

Max, letting out a deep breath, hung his head. "It's my fault. I should have smuggled you out of the country long ago. Germans are monsters—"

Frieda wiped the tears from her cheek. "Not all! *They* cried too, Max. They were so sorry that this happened. They wanted to walk me home, but I said no."

"Did you know them?"

"No. Just an ordinary German couple—with courage—and compassion."

Max sprung from the couch. His eyes blazed. "I'm going back there to find that scum!"

She sprung up from the couch too, shouting at him. "He's long gone, Max!"

"We'll see."

"They'll kill you, Max."

Stunned and silent—he glanced toward the window, observing the orange glow of the fires, hearing the sirens and cries in the dark.

A black film had just fallen from his eyes. He moved close to Frieda, gently taking her hand. "You're right. I need to stay alive. Something must be done. I didn't understand that then. I do now. "

He led her back to the sofa, and they sat together, close. Max peered solemnly into her eyes.

"I have access to him."

Max could sense that Frieda knew full well what he meant. She remained silent, her feverish eyes doing the talking instead.

"I *hope* to have access, anyway," continued Max, "after some fence-mending. The security's tight. But I think I can get him alone."

Frieda nodded.

"I could pick him off with a rifle, but the risk of failure's high."

Frieda nodded again.

"If I can paint him, I can get close enough to kill him, for sure—then hopefully . . . "

He saw fear in her eyes—fear for *him.* "I may not escape, I know."

"Max—"

He cut her off. "We're smuggling you out of Germany with a boxcar full of art. After delivery to Switzerland, you'll be safe. I should've done this long ago—before the baby . . . " Max's voice cracked with emotion.

"What about *you*, Max? I can't believe that you'll get away with it."

Max shook his head, his voice low. "Sometimes murder's the only answer—there's no way around it, whatever the cost. If you *do* kill, make it count."

Frieda lifted his chin and then moved closer, kissing him.

"I plan to catch up with you after you reach Switzerland." Max smiled. "I know you won't tell anyone, so I won't have to tell you to keep your big mouth shut."

She smiled back, but not a happy smile—a smile of complete understanding.

"Frieda, your part in this is critical. You'll rescue masterpieces, to save them for the world, for better times. You'll also help Sarah Roth to escape. My part's dirtier, that's all."

She grasped him by his shoulders, her stare fierce. "I know you're resolved to do this, Max. So I won't tell you *not* to do it—like a good little doctor and wife. I *will* say this. *Get* him, Max. Smash him, like the insect that he is."

Max squeezed her hand. "I'm doing it alone. I'll do it right. Adolf Hitler's going to die soon, and I'm the one who's going to murder him. I swear it."

Chapter 64

Berlin, January 1939:

"I must tell you, Bauer, your new pieces are just marvelous; the Fuhrer's overjoyed." The pudgy fingers caressed the huge diamond in the rings they sported. "I understand that your post as national curator's been restored—even at a fatter salary. It's amazing what a few words in high places can do."

Goering stood in the middle of the Aryan Exhibition, near Max's painting, *Peasants Earning Their Daily Bread*, surveying the politically rehabilitated artist's recent creations.

Max stood close to the Reich minister, noticing that Hitler's paladin had gained even more weight. His costume looked even more outlandish when compared to Max's charcoal three-piece suit.

"I want to show you something special." Max guided his guest over to his latest oil painting, a rendition of a determined Hitler—garbed in knight's armor—mounted on a decorated steed. The Fuhrer held a lance horizontally, as if he were jousting. A triangular-shaped pennant, emblazoned with a gold swastika, fluttered near the end of the medieval weapon.

Goering—studying Max's kitschy fluff with laser intensity—placed his chubby hand gently upon the artist's shoulder. "Herr Bauer, the *strength*! The imagination. You're a genius."

Max stepped away, ostensibly to adjust how the painting hung on the wall, but in reality to put distance himself and Goering. Aside from the sickening perfume, he detested being touched by this slob.

"This painting's mine, you understand?" insisted Goering. "I'll buy it—name your price, Herr Bauer. I want this for Carinhall—my country estate."

"It's yours, no charge," said Max, "with my—and my wife's—compliments."

"You're a good fellow, Max. Don't worry about Frieda. I'll see to it that she's no longer disturbed."

Max, surprised—and a little wary—that Goering knew his wife's first name, was nevertheless heartened by his promise. His protection could prevent Hock from spying on her, which would place her escape and his plan to kill Hitler in jeopardy. This man had founded the Gestapo, so he had influence. Max also recognized, however, that the mercurial minister could turn on him at any moment.

"We're grateful," said Max.

Goering, noticing that a few patrons had stopped next to them, also admiring the painting, took Max aside in confidence, lowering his voice.

"In March, when the Fuhrer's vacationing at the Eagle's Nest, that degenerate freak show ends. All the garbage inside, plus any of the other filth the Gestapo can get their hands on, will be shipped from Berlin Central Station to a work camp for incineration. Hock is handling that. I might borrow a few pieces first. They may fetch good prices abroad."

Max felt an electric pulse traverse his spine. He had been waiting for this confirmation for weeks. "I remember you telling me something like this in Vienna, about nine months ago. So, it's on for March then—for sure?"

"Yes. All that garbage we rounded up at the Vienna Art Museum will be torched too. And I must tell you, Herr Bauer, that I'm taking a few of those paintings for myself, also. You tell me what you want, and you can have some too."

"Thank you, Reich Minister. Count me in. Can you let me know the exact day it leaves the station, so I can decide which ones I want?"

"Of course, my fellow. I have another train, full of priceless oils and tapestries, going to Switzerland—about that time. The big auction in Zurich will be on. I might give you one or two of those, too. In return, any great stuff you find on your own, you tell me about them first—is that understood? By the way, after March—when the weather's better—I may be tied up with the Air Force, so I need to transport that damn art out . . . "

Max noted that the Reich minister had truncated his conversation. *Why? Is something afoot?*

Max had spent months ingratiating himself to get back into the Fuhrer's good graces. He had a good start. Now, Hitler's mother must be painted from a photograph—a delicate undertaking indeed.

* * *

"WELCOME TO WANNSEE BEACH."

The welcome sign, lit by the luminous full moon, blew back and forth in the snowy wind. Max slogged through the deserted beach with the long, cylindrical package under his arm, careful not to trip on the patches of ice and snow. He passed where he had spent that wonderful, warm afternoon at the beach, with Frieda, after they had first begun to date. How different it looked now, he thought, and how long ago it felt.

Max, dressed in his heaviest winter clothing, trudged along the icy trail to the pine forest, about a quarter mile beyond the public beach—bordering the desolate shoreline. Max arrived at a clearing and saw white, glistening pinecones lined up in the trees—the lunar rays and bright stars lighting them up like Christmas ornaments.

He unwrapped his package, removing the sawed-off fishing pole sticking out of the end, which had been used to thwart suspicion. Nocturnal ice fishing had been popular in Berlin for many years.

A rifle emerged—a 7.92 mm Mauser 98 with a telescopic sight, just like the one he had been issued during the war. He had applied strips of cardboard around the muzzle, a crude but surprisingly effective method to silence the rounds.

If assassination with his rifle—Plan B—turned out to be the method of choice to kill the Fuhrer, then calibration and practice were crucial He had also cleaned and oiled his rifle well. This had been his third such trip out to the shoreline.

Using a tree stump as a stabilizer, he stood about a hundred meters from the series of dangling pinecones. He aimed, gently squeezing the trigger. Three of five cones had been vaporized in succession. After recalibrating his site, he mowed down five more, with little effort. He hadn't lost his touch.

Pleased that the loud wind had also masked the rifle noise, he glanced at his watch. It showed half past eleven. With Victor due to arrive there at midnight, he got off a few more rounds of practice.

The train station and their homes were considered unsafe for a rendezvous, but the deserted forest was both accessible and—next to the vast lake—isolated. Max then thought about his palette knife. Plan A—the more reliable—began to take shape. Most would consider it a suicide mission, and they'd be more than half right. The invitation by Hitler to paint his portrait was the critical factor, and the one Max had to strive for. Plan B, the rifle, he recalled again, had too many variables, but . . .

* * *

"Nice shot," said Victor, "you're going to kill him with that thing?" His prudent eyes locked onto Max's, betraying a slight glint of skepticism.

Max put down the rifle. "Now you see that this isn't just talk. My method is still uncertain, but my resolve is firm." He looked around him to make sure they were alone. "Both art shipments are on for March, probably midmonth. I'll know the exact date later—hopefully with a few days' notice. "

"Still Sachsenhausen?"

"Sachsenhausen it is. The train will end up in Zurich, and so will Frieda and the art."

"All right," said Victor, as he cupped his hands, blowing little clouds of warm air through his fingers. "The schedule at the office confirms that Goering has a boxcar of paintings going to Zurich in early March. So what he told you is correct. Hock has his shipment going to the camp about the same time. If necessary, I'll delay one or the other—although it would be better if Hock's left first. Once the heist is discovered, all hell might break loose."

"What about the two SS guards?" asked Max.

"I'll put a man on it. And Sarah Roth, what about her?"

"She's on. The stowaways will be in in the boxcar crates." Max packed up his rifle, cleaning off the lens. "It's all set." He hadn't prayed since the war, but now he prayed for Frieda's safe passage.

Chapter 65

Berlin, February 1939:

"For a while, the Fuhrer thought you had betrayed him. Now he's softening, Max." The perfect white teeth flashed a coy smile. "But, mind you, I'm just a secretary, so what do I know?"

Eva Braun twirled the dark tie that hung from the wide navy-trimmed collar of her white blouse. The twinkle in her eye intimated to Max that she served her boss far beyond typing and social calendars, and that he'd be wise to filter any ambition through her. "I'm glad our leader has such a dedicated assistant," Max replied.

"I came to see you because Minister Goebbels and I crave for the Fuhrer to have his own Michelangelo. That's you. The Fuhrer reopened your studio on our recommendation. In return, I want you to do something for me."

"Anything I can."

The alluring young woman, attired in a sporty sailor's outfit, lounged in the black leather chair in Max's studio. With her shapely legs crossed, and her short skirt hitched high above her knees, this woman had a lot more to her than what met the eye.

"When you paint me," Eva said with a strange frankness, "I want you to make sure you do your best—going underneath the skin, I mean." Her chameleon eyes sparkled, like mirrored balls that simultaneously reflected fear, seduction, and hate.

It surprised Max that she had such an acute sense of quality about paintings.

As Eva talked, she studied her flawlessly manicured nails—painted gold—tossing her head sideways, running her delicate hands through her strawberry-blonde hair. "Send a message to all the women coming after me—a strong message."

"I hope I live up to your expectations."

"Herr Goebbels confided in me that you'll paint the Fuhrer's portrait for the Pyramid," she continued, her tone different, this time with a hint of harshness. "You'll paint mine first, and you'll be told where and when."

Max resolved that he'd allow Eva her head. This young woman, who previously had bamboozled him with her exaggerated sexuality and affected manner, was in fact complex and very intelligent. He could tell that she had something weighty on her mind.

"Whatever you say, Fraulein."

"My name's *Eva*," she snapped, with uncustomary edginess. Then she smiled broadly, patting her hands together, the coquettish prattle taking over. "I'm *so* pleased about your paintings, Max."

Confident that he had progressed in his goal of setting up Hitler, he decided to change the subject. To seal the deal, his sweetener—prescribed by Goebbels—would be revealed to her. "May I show you something very special?" he asked. "It's a present for Herr Hitler."

"How wonderful."

"Follow me." Max rose from his chair, guiding her over to the new creation that hung on the wall, next to his easel.

Max and Eva studied his portrait of the Fuhrer's mother, a haunting yet lovely piece that had taken him almost a month to paint. The sixteen-by-twenty-inch canvas revealed a middle-aged woman wearing a rustic, Austrian-style dress, peering out of a brightly lit window. Quite purposefully, it suggested the Madonna.

Max noted the long, silver palette knife perched upon the easel's shelf, reminding him of his target.

"This is my gift to our beloved Fuhrer," said Max solemnly, indicating the painting, with his mind really on the knife. "Please see that he receives it."

Eva's eyes stayed locked on the haunting image.

Max's mind raced. *When I get him alone, I'll drive my palette knife straight through his gullet, and then escape through the window the best I can. Surely, Hitler's guard will overlook this harmless painting utensil, so common to my impasto style.*

The luminous, distant stare of the dour subject in the painting, like the photo upon which it had been based, is what Max hoped would surely hook his prey.

Eerily, Hitler's eyes were perfect facsimiles of his mother's.

Eva ran her hand over the frame, seemingly mesmerized by the picture. "It's masterful," she said. Max noticed a strange quality in her stare, however, that he couldn't quite put his finger on.

"Max, promise me one thing."

"What's that, Eva?"

"When you paint his next portrait . . ."

"Yes?"

"Don't botch it. Do it right. Do it *thoroughly*."

"Of course, Eva. I intend to."

Max wasn't quite sure about what they had just agreed upon.

Chapter 66

Berlin, March 1939:

Max grabbed a copper frying pan hanging from a hook in the kitchen ceiling, and put in on the counter. He broke six eggs into a mixing bowl. He added mushrooms, onions, and garlic-butter to the bowl.

"Do you want sausage too?" he asked Frieda, who lounged on the couch across the living room, in front of the crackling fireplace. "I'll cut it thin, the way you like it."

"Do you need help?"

"I'm fine."

She threw down a magazine, and stared into the fire, fastening the tie on her thick, cotton robe. "I'm getting fat. Your cooking's too good."

Max poured the egg concoction into the sizzling frying pan, then covered it.

The buzzer to the apartment sounded, announcing that someone on the street desired entry at the ground level. Max wiped his hands on his overalls, then pressed the speaker button on the wall.

"Who is it?"

"Special delivery from the Reich Chancellery," responded the dour, unfamiliar voice.

Could this really be a Gestapo raid? Max wondered. But he had no choice but to let them in and await fate's decision.

"—All right. Come up."

Max pushed the entry button. After turning the fire off under the eggs, he rushed over to Frieda. The heavy, approaching footsteps on the wooden staircase sounded like thunder. He moved to the door. When a loud knock came, he slowly opened it a crack.

"Max Bauer?"

"Yes." Max could tell that the man wore some kind of uniform, but not Gestapo.

"This telegram's for you."

Max opened the door wide and took the official-looking envelope. He listened to the footsteps as the messenger descended the staircase, leaving the apartment building. He closed the door, then bolted it.

Max saw that the letter actually had originated from Adolf Hitler's office.

He dashed over to Frieda and sat down beside her, ripping open the envelope.

A faint smile of anticipation surfaced, as he read its contents out loud:

"THE FUHRER REQUESTS THE PRESENCE OF MAX BAUER AT THE EAGLE'S NEST TO COMPLETE A SPECIAL ART COMMISSION. HERR BAUER WILL LEAVE TOMORROW MORNING BY SPECIAL MOTORCAR. FUTHER INSTRUCITONS WILL FOLLOW. HEIL HITLER!"

"This is it! This is what we've been waiting for!" shouted Max. Then his animation faded, as the weight of his daunting task became more immediate.

Frieda's reaction, subdued and withdrawn, didn't surprise him. "Now you can get yourself killed."

"We've been over all this," Max replied. He took her hand, peering earnestly into her eyes. "I have an escape route into the mountains, remember? Then on to Italy via the backwoods of Austria."

"Sure."

A pang of remorse swept through Max, from a corner of his troubled mind. Hitler had succeeded in what he had really set out to do all along. The Fuhrer already had won.

He's made killers of us all—or, in my case, a killer again.

* * *

"Thanks for coming over, Victor, I needed to talk to you. Is there any chance you were followed?"

"There's always a chance."

"I'm leaving tomorrow morning for Hitler's retreat—the Eagle's Nest—near Berchtesgaden."

Victor lowered his serious eyes, seeming to get the point instantly: that Max likely would not return.

"I think I can get him," added Max confidently. He had decided not to divulge many details of his assassination plans. He sat close to Victor on the couch, speaking quietly, as Frieda washed the dishes in the kitchen. Max could smell the coal dust that coated the railroad man's uniform.

"I must tell you the news, Max. Goering is going down to the Eagle's Nest too, to organize a hunting party. That's not all. General Black informs us that Hitler's attacking the rump state of Czechoslovakia. That means war."

"That raises the stakes," said Max.

"What's most important is that Hitler and Goering may not come back to Berlin, but go on to Prague. Goering is loading the boxcars now with his precious loot while he's still in Berlin. The other train—the one with the paintings that will be burned—leaves for Sachsenhausen in four days, at three in the afternoon. I've already laid plans to divert it to Zurich—switching the two destinations—as planned. I think the timing will work out."

Max thought about how Goering had promised to inform him as to the precise date the train would leave. Not surprised that he had broken his word, he figured that the Reich minister desired more secrecy surrounding his mass larceny.

Max glanced over at Frieda, busily tidying up the kitchen. He saw no reason to involve her in this any more than he had to. Now, as the reality of their separation crashed down upon him, he felt empty and rudderless.

"Frieda and Sarah Roth will be ready to stow away," Max assured. "Take care of them, Victor."

"They'll be tucked in fine. I'm working on the details out now."

"I have to make sure I kill him *after* her train leaves. Before, she'd be in too much danger. The timing's delicate. Who knows about this?" asked Max.

"One other man at the railroad—"

"Stallbun too?"

"Not all the details. He's good man, but he's full of talk. How are you going to pull off the assassination?"

Max, a bit surprised by the intrusive question, batted it away. "I'll have Goering sit on him."

It took about ten seconds for Victor to crack a smile. It took a full minute before they stopped laughing.

* * *

"The train caper's set," said Max, "four days from now—Friday—it leaves at three in the afternoon. By then, of course, I'll be down there at Hitler's retreat, and you'll be off to Switzerland."

Frieda and Max, lying in bed, hugged each other. Tears ran down their faces.

"You're leaving here tomorrow too," he continued, "to go into hiding until your train leaves. Victor has it all arranged. You may not be safe here."

Max had accepted his fate. The pacifism, the rejection of violence, the warm cocoon of his beautiful art, his treasured life with Frieda were all gone, maybe forever.

Frieda sat up in bed, taking something out of the nightstand drawer. Max sat up too. She plopped it on the sheet between them. He opened the small box, knowing that the gift would be practical, and it was.

Max fingered the fine compass. "At least it's not a bottle of aftershave," he said.

Frieda laughed, wiping away the tears. "I'll fit nicely in your paint box or your knapsack."

"Like I told you before—don't count me out." He put the compass on the chair beside the bed. "I used to hunt in those mountains."

She smiled. He leaned over and kissed her. They kissed long and passionately.

"I love you, Frieda. I always will."

"Max, Godspeed in returning to me."

They peeled off the rest of their clothing. Max's body melted into hers. He knew that when they made love this time, it would probably be the last.

Chapter 67

The swastika pennant flapped on the hood of the black Mercedes, as it sped Max through the winding road, up to Hitler's Eagle's Nest. Max noticed that the driver, this time an affable, young SS recruit—not the intense, dark Bruno Meier—handled the huge convertible in the hairpin turns with a healthier regard for mortality.

When the gilded elevator deposited Max at the reception room, with the red marble hearth, he noted something different. Astonishingly, this time, his portrait of Hitler's mother hung over the fireplace.

The driver escorted Max, with his painting implements and luggage, to the small dining room adjacent to the kitchen, where he found a note resting on the table.

"MAX, I'LL FETCH YOU AT 1:30; BE READY TO PAINT MY PORTRAIT IN THE FUHRER'S STUDY. YOU'LL LODGE DOWN THE MOUNTAIN AT THE BERGHOF. GOOD LUCK! EVA BRAUN—SOCIAL SECRETARY TO THE FUHRER."

Max had anticipated this. Now that his painting of Hitler's mother had evidently pleased the Fuhrer, Eva's portrait would be his key to unlocking Hitler's personal space—alone. He looked at his watch—nearly noon.

He sat down at the table. A servant brought in liverwurst sandwiches and a bottle of warm beer. As he wolfed down the food, some of it spilled onto his dark suit. That reminded him of his painting clothes and gear, tucked away in his suitcase, it standing against the wall.

His smock, oils, brushes, compass, and—most importantly—his long, silver palette knife were safely inside.

* * *

"Max, where do you want to paint me? By the window? The light is perfect."

Eva stood at the large picture window in Hitler's study, the early afternoon rays outlining her firm, lithe body in silhouette through her lacy, white silk dress.

"Whatever suits you, Eva," Max answered.

As he readied his implements, his eyes searched the cramped and dim room, seeing no recent sign of Hitler or of his imminent return. The bookshelves and the modest wooden desk and chair still sat in the corner, as did the easels by the window—but this time without Hitler's painting or Max's own landscape. Through the window, he again noted the trees about five hundred meters away, with the zigzagging path.

Eva's body—alluring, desirable, seductively attired—overpowered him, shattering Max's cool, if for no other reason than Hitler—if he soon returned—might not appreciate the optics of the situation. His model hadn't surprised him with her boldness. He dropped his silver palette knife and then picked it up, placing it on the easel's shelf.

"Relax, Max, he's busy going over his architect's plans."

Now Max knew where Hitler had acquired his knack for reading people's minds. With the easel in front of him, he grasped his filbert brush and started his work, dipping the hog hairs into the yellow ochre paint.

"Full length," ordered Eva.

Eva stood in a dancer's pose—one foot forward, and the other turned sideways, her spine extended, and her excellent bottom pointed backward, rimmed by the soft light. She ran her red nails though her hair.

"Head to toe," she said firmly.

"Fraulein Braun—"

"Eva."

"*Eva.* I had in mind—"

"No. The Fuhrer wants *full*—so do I. It'll hang in his private quarters. Remember what I told you last time, about the *feel* of the portrait."

"Yes, of course."

Frieda's understanding face shot into his mind, making him feel even more alone. She probably would've told him that at least Eva appreciated subtext in a masterpiece, unlike most of the other dullards around Hitler.

"I remember," said Max. "Cassatt it is, then."

Cassatt had mastered the subtle, psychological landscapes of the women she had painted, very well. If he could achieve that, he would be more than satisfied. He applied the paint to the canvas with his knife, the long blade gleaming in the sun's rays.

The impasto zigzagged wildly on the canvas, like bolts of lightning. The bristle brushes followed up, his flat brush being his first choice. Eva's body slowly took form within the white lace, the hue of her skin glowing through the shimmering silk—like the body of Aphrodite, fossilized within a sparkling ice cube.

Eva tossed her head back, laughing—then became very serious.

"Start over, Max," she ordered.

She then untied the blue ribbons on her collar and from around her waist, allowing the sheer garment to drop to her nicely tapered ankles. She kicked it defiantly toward Max.

"There," she said, "that's better."

Max's jaw hit the floor. Not even the trenches during the war equaled the terror that gripped him. There stood Eva, her flawless body oiled and naked, in front of the window—in the Fuhrer's study!

"Max—"

"Don't talk, you'll spoil it," said Max, realizing that to tell her to put her dress back on would only ignite a row. He had to admit that as a model for a nude, Eva excelled, and he didn't really want her to spoil it.

So he relaxed and made the most out of this bizarre, potentially dangerous situation—resolving to paint his best portrait ever. He at least had the inspiration.

Max worked fast and silently, further motivated—strangely—by the sudden melody of Wagner's masterpiece—"The Valkyrie"—softly playing from an unknown source.

Max glanced over to the corner and noticed a door with what looked like a peephole. He thought he had heard some rattling behind the door. He had the feeling that someone was spying on them.

As he painted Eva's face, he did his best to convey her power—and the power behind the power—and her message to future generations of women through her determined expression: "My turn will come."

After four hours of slavishly painting, in a succession of thirty-minute poses, Max placed his masterpiece of Eva upon the easel before him.

Thank God, he thought with relief, *it's time to get the hell out of here!* He packed up his painting implements as Eva threw on her dress.

"Max," she called.

He turned toward Eva Braun, before disappearing through the door. She studied the painting, her confident smile emerging from her feverish mind. "It's perfect. It's your best painting so far. I'm certain the Fuhrer will be overjoyed. He'll be next."

As he glanced at his work, its subtle undercurrent whispered in his ear, which differed slightly from its message. It was the allure of the black widow spider.

What's this bizarre woman up to?

"I'm happy you're pleased, Eva."

She placed her hands upon her narrow hips. "If you tell anyone out there about our little secret, credit this, Max—and you'd better believe it." Eva's tone then hardened. "No one will believe you. More to the point, you'll be dead within the hour."

Chapter 68

Max hadn't quite recovered from his unsettling, and bizarre, encounter with Eva Braun. He felt that she anticipated something, but what? He also hadn't expected the Fuhrer's summons to be so quick, and so he returned to the Eagle's Nest the next day in the early afternoon. Good thing too, since the impending attack by the Wehrmacht on what remained of Czechoslovakia—with Hitler's departure to Prague—threatened the viability of his mission. This would be earlier than he had planned, but with Frieda in hiding until the train left, she had as much protection as he could afford her.

Hitler's adjutant spirited Max—with his suitcase of painting accouterments—to the study, with instructions to be prepared to paint the Fuhrer's portrait immediately. As he strode down the stone corridor with his escort—suitcase in hand—approaching the door to the Fuhrer's study, he noted the strapping SS guard.

Max wondered whether that was the person spying, through the peephole, the day before. Or had it been Hitler practicing a bizarre voyeurism? Would that incident complicate the task at hand? He shoved that imponderable aside . . .

The guard stopped Max, eyeing him carefully. His suspicious gaze frisked every inch of Max's person.

Max's thoughts focused like a laser: *The palette knife in the suitcase!*

"You may pass." The guard opened the door. Max—greatly relieved—was starting to enter, when the guard suddenly slammed it shut. "Open that luggage."

Max recalled that a few months before, there had been an attempt on Hitler's life in Munich, when he delivered a speech to the Nazi Old Guard in a crowded beer-hall. A carpenter had allegedly stuffed the interior of his podium with timed explosives. Uncannily, Hitler had left the building early—only ten minutes before the bomb had detonated. Many in the audience were killed, instead. The failed assassin, subsequently investigated and hunted down, forfeited his head.

"Please be careful of the tubes of thinner—they're very delicate," said Max as he put the suitcase on the floor and opened it for the guard.

He proceeded to pat Max down, finding nothing. He then pawed through the contents of the suitcase, plucking the palette knife—which had been wrapped in oilcloth—out of the luggage.

He held it up to Max's face. "What's this?"

"It's a palette knife; artists use them; especially ones with an impasto style—like mine."

The scowling hulk, no painter, looked skeptical.

"I'm already late!" huffed Max with exaggerated urgency. "The Fuhrer's waiting." He pointed to the door. "Let me pass, or you can explain *to him* this outrageous nonsense!"

The guard's eyes shifted, weighing his options. Max's escort took the man aside, whispering into his ear, undoubtedly, something about the Fuhrer's rage at being kept waiting.

"Ordinarily, I'd arrest you, but I'll just keep this knife." The guard placed the palette knife in the pocket of his uniform. "I'll give it back to you when you're done painting."

The guard packed up the suitcase and handed it to Max. He opened the door to Hitler's study, waving him through—minus the vital weapon.

* * *

There he stood, noted Max, looking almost the same as last time, next to the huge picture window and easels.

Again, he had dressed in the familiar mustard-colored tunic with the Nazi armband, a white dress shirt and dark tie, navy slacks, and the patent leather shoes. The strangely flickering gaze of his piercing blue eyes latched on to Max, as Hitler approached him cautiously, extending his warm, smooth hand.

He gently escorted him to the easels.

Max felt that this super-intuitive mind reader might have sensed that something was up. Or maybe what he saw through the peephole hadn't agreed with him . . .

"Put that thing down, Herr Bauer, next to the easel and the posing chair. I've been waiting for this for quite a while."

Max, nervous and without his implement of death, quickly unpacked his painting gear and prepared his famous subject. As the Fuhrer's scratchy voice droned on, Max's mind filled with scenarios to kill Hitler on the spot. Across the room, on the cluttered desk, rested what looked like a blunt letter knife and a few colored pencils.

The letter knife on the desk won't do, thought Max. *By the time I made it to the desk, Hitler would call out, and the guard would be at my throat.*

"I shall do my best, my Fuhrer."

I can push him through the window. No, that's not likely to succeed, either. After all, Hitler's no slouch physically—there'd be quite a struggle, and again, the guard would come. Besides, the fall wouldn't be high enough to kill him.

"I want you to paint me in a three-quarter perspective, from the shoulders up," demanded Hitler as he sat down on his posing chair.

"I know just what to do, my Fuhrer, trust me." Max positioned his subject, all the time his head catching fire with homicidal fever.

He could also go behind Hitler with little trouble, and get him in a chokehold, squeezing the breath out of him—and his ability to cry for help with it. But if Hitler reacted quickly—powerfully flexing his neck—Max realized that he might be unable to execute the maneuver. *I have one chance, and that's it. It has to be my best.*

"This will take several hours, so I'll paint in half hour sessions—with rest periods," he informed his infamous subject.

Max blocked in the composition. The absence of his palette knife would impede his style. He could complain about its confiscation to Hitler, but that might make him suspicious.

"Herr Bauer, Reich Minister Goering will be here soon, to organize a hunting party. You should join him."

Victor had been correct. *Now, there's an interesting development*, thought Max: *access to a rifle—and the surrounding terrain. Goering's always wanted me to shoot with him.*

At that moment, the guard opened the door, peering into the study. Seeing nothing extraordinary—he closed it.

As his brush moved with astounding dexterity and skill, the view out the window turned into a floodlight of alizarin crimson, vermillion, and Naples yellow, dappled with purple and the Prussian blue of sunset. Hitler's restless eyes shifted to the kaleidoscopic show of color. "Blood, blood, blood, and more blood; look, Herr Bauer, isn't that right? The sun will set soon."

"Yes, I see what you mean. My Fuhrer, perhaps I can also paint a landscape—including this building—before I leave?"

"Just work fast, Herr Bauer."

"Why, my Fuhrer?"

"The vibrant red out the window portends historic events." The Fuhrer's voice assumed a smoother, whispering quality. "Our enemies have forced my hand. I leave for Prague in two days—early in the morning," said Hitler. "Our Wehrmacht will destroy Germany's enemies—those pygmies! "

Max's hand slipped, marring his effort to construct the left eye. Stunned by his subject's remark, he wiped the canvas, realizing the predictions of war had been correct and the stakes had indeed skyrocketed.

Hitler will plunge Germany into a world war and drag everyone down with him—and soon.

Chapter 69

The veranda of the Eagle's Nest offered a panorama of the surrounding mountains and forests that could only be described as spectacular. On that next March morning, the sun shone bright and clear. The honeyed fragrance of the sprouting edelweiss dotted the surrounding meadows, announcing the arrival of spring.

Eva Braun—dressed in a red, two-piece bathing suit—performed giants on the parallel bars on the adjacent patio, showing off her gymnastic skills. Albert Speer, Hitler's architect, played chess nearby with the Fuhrer's favorite SS adjutant, Julius Schaub.

Herman Goering, costumed in a theatrical mountaineering outfit with a plumed alpine hat and a hunting rifle slung over his back, joked with his pals, who were outfitted less conspicuously. One of the Reich minister's hunting partners happened to be Max.

He had set up his easel and painting implements on the adjacent terrace, earlier that morning, to paint his first landscape. The Fuhrer had given Max the authority to roam the premises to find suitable vistas, during which effort Max spotted the Reich minister—master of the hunt—standing across the terrace. He approached Goering, figuring that the avid huntsman would invite him to join his annual stag shoot—an invitation that he had extended before but Max had declined.

And the Reich minister did exactly that.

Moreover, realizing that Max needed a rifle, he generously provided him with a Mauser bolt-action rifle, with a telescopic lens, much like the one Max had been issued during the war.

The huntsmen were off at ten o'clock, trailing through the pine forest that surrounded the Eagle's Nest. Max, having been lent a substantial hiking kit by the SS quartermaster, trudged along comfortably at the rear of the pack, in his hiking boots, woolen sweater and pants, and rucksack. He had stored his painting clothes near the kitchen, including his stained painting-pants, with the palette knife stuffed deep within its pocket.

The main trail, winding around in back of the Eagle's Nest, splintered into numerous, narrower offshoots, some well-tended and some overgrown and stone-cluttered. Max noted the treacherous nature of the tree-lined paths, which sometimes melded into the mountain's cliffs, with granite drops, hundreds of meters down.

At some places, the trees stood thick, offering the sportsmen full cover to shoot the unsuspecting game. These nimble but dumb creatures fed in the tiny meadows, which bordered the inner boundaries of the trails and were ideal places for hunters to pick them off.

"Watch your step," boomed Goering as he huffed and puffed up the path, "especially you, Bauer. You must live to complete the Fuhrer's landscape!"

Presently, Max found himself in familiar territory.

He recognized—albeit from a different vantage point—the loops of the trail that he had seen through the window in Hitler's study. Max confirmed that the distance from the study appeared to be about five hundred meters, the same estimate that he had noted from the inside of the window.

It would be a difficult shot, but not—by any means— impossible, even considering his limited opportunity to calibrate the scope. The shimmering, white-stone walls of the retreat, in the distance, suggested to him a fairytale castle; only in this case, it housed a murderous, paranoiac ogre, instead of a valiant prince.

"Rest here," ordered the Reich minister, taking a seat on a smooth boulder, the sweat drenching his shirt. "We'll be out here until midafternoon, so we must pace ourselves."

Max, finding a fallen tree to sit on, scoped the essential detail that drew him there in the first place: the far-off image of the Fuhrer's window, beside which the artsy tyrant painted almost every late afternoon.

Chapter 70

Hitler's window would offer a splendid target for Max's high-velocity rifle. The compass that Frieda had given him—buried within his bottles of water, chocolate bars, maps, and spare ammunition—rested in his rucksack. With the long rifle, he had everything he needed to hunt and kill Hitler, then attempt his daring escape.

Herman Goering's powerful voice shattered his reverie. "Stags—at fifty meters—grazing in the meadow . . . "

The Reich minister, his mass surprisingly nimble, ricocheted between the bloodthirsty huntsmen, his pudgy finger pointing excitedly in the hapless beasts' direction. "Hurry! When I fire, let them have it!"

The men sneaked in the direction of the meadow in which the stags grazed, their rifles ready. Goering lost himself in the handful of trees. Max dawdled at the back of the pack, carefully putting distance between himself and the last hunter.

The cracking of rifle shots pierced the air, echoing through the cliffs. Max looked up at the crest of the mountain, spying tiny ribbons of trails. They zigzagged their way up between the green blotches of trees and the clumps of umber boulders, extending to the summit and winding beyond. One trail—Max knew—led to the narrow neck of Austria in the far distance, and then on to the relative safety of Italy.

While the others blasted away at the targets, Max doubled back on the trail, finding a pile of branches near where he had previously scoped Hitler's window. He hid his rifle within the pile.

He had needed not only access to a rifle, but also the means to keep it—and use it, *alone*.

The path sprouted narrow, derivative trails in numerous directions, some leading dangerously close to the edge of the trail. This would be the perfect place for him to fake his accident. He would claim that he tripped over the edge of the trail, while tracking an overhead falcon.

Twenty meters away, he saw the perfect place.

It bordered a cliff, with the initial, short descent—at about forty-five degrees—offering a shelf at the bottom. Then, the fall changed into a near vertical drop, of about a hundred meters, down a ravine, to the thick vegetation below.

Max would have to explain the missing rifle, and this proved to be perfect. Goering, as sly as a fox, might question his story.

He also figured that Goering might want him to show where had he lost it. After all, it was a very expensive rifle, and Goering coveted every mark that he had. Therefore, Max resolved to stage his mishap carefully.

He hiked to the precipice of the initial fall, rolling down the embankment to the shelf, landing only inches from the lip of the ravine. Dirty and scuffed, he made his way back to the others, explaining his foolish accident in convincing detail.

"Bauer, you look like you wrestled a bear! That gun cost eight hundred marks. An experienced shot like you—I'm surprised!" Goering took a huge hit from his bottle of schnapps, and passed it around to the drunken hunters. While Max had been gone, the Reich minister and his men had celebrated, but without reason—few bucks had been bagged. They were terrible shots, and that was the only thing Max liked about them.

As they headed home, Goering, distracted by the telling of his hunting tales and his flask of schnapps, paid no notice to the location of Max's fall. Back at the Eagle's Nest, Max received minor treatment for his cuts. He changed back into his painting attire, including his paint-blotched slacks.

Eva Braun entered the tiny infirmary, her sparkling eyes wide with concern.

"Max, are you trying to kill yourself? I heard all about your accident—you even lost one of Herr Goering's best rifles."

He looked up at her bright face as he sat on the gurney, the nurse completing the bandaging of his elbow, and the dressing of the small cut on his forehead.

Damn, he cursed to himself, who doesn't know about this lost rifle?

Something about the tone of Eva's voice bothered him. "It's nothing," insisted Max. "In fact, I'm headed back out tomorrow to paint my landscape. The Fuhrer insists on having it done by tomorrow evening," he lied.

"I adore your painting of him. It's even better than the one you did of me. He treasures that portrait, Max. By the way, do you want me to go with you tomorrow?"

Max felt a twinge of alarm. With her along as a witness, his plan would be ruined. The situation called for firmness.

"Like hell. I can't paint with someone looking over my shoulder. Especially a beautiful woman." His smile flashed. "Besides, I need you to goad Hitler into completing his new painting, while I'm still around him to critique it. He's supposed to be traveling soon. He needs to be at his easel tomorrow afternoon—as usual—working away."

"Max, I insist on going."

"I said, no."

"You sound very determined, Max." She shot him a knowing glance, causing a little alarm bell to go off in his head. *What is she hinting at?*

"How did you know he's traveling?" asked Eva.

"He told me."

"All right, I'll stay here with the Fuhrer."

Disappointed, her bottom lip curved into a pout, but her frown had faded. Her eyes then lit up, as if confirming something in her mind. "I'll do what I can to get him to his easel. Painting relaxes him. It may help him to sleep. Now, you promise *me* something."

"Name it," said Max.

"Don't screw it up."

"I'm sorry?"

Eva's eyes lost their sparkle and took on heavy significance. "Do it fast, do it right, and do it *completely*."

Max clung to his silence, forcing his face to be as impassive as possible.

"Aim your brush well," she warned.

Max now thought he knew what the subtext of her banter the day before had been all about. The hair stood up on his neck. "I'm sure the painting will turn out . . ."

"Stop it," she retorted with a baleful stare, the hatred gushing from her eyes, like hot lava.

It took a few seconds for Max to fully realize the implications of his epiphany, as bubbles formed in his blood, their tingle rising up his spine: *She doesn't hate* me. *She hates Hitler.*

My God, she suspects my plan to assassinate him!

The message in this clever woman's eyes belied her sugary facade: loathing. Hate for the man who possessed her soul. Hate for the man who had crushed her self-esteem. Most important, hate for the man who had undoubtedly threatened her life and imprisoned her, just like he had done—according to Professor Stallbun—with his young niece and lover, Geli Raubal, who had died under suspicious circumstances eight years before.

"I'll complete my landscape," Max reassured her in a firm, solemn voice. "My paintbrush won't miss."

Chapter 71

Frieda, carrying only a large handbag, squinted up at the late afternoon sun, beaming through the huge dome of windows covering Berlin Central Station. Her dark overcoat already reeking of coal dust, she observed the passing, smoke-belching locomotives, whirling the sooty particles up into the air as they clanked over the greasy, littered tracks.

She made her way over to the small warehouse, navigating crowded gangplanks, gorged with passengers catching trains. She had been instructed to wait inside the unlocked storage-shed at precisely three o'clock in the afternoon—the most crowded time of the day—next to Train 57.

Victor had rejected the midnight hours as the rendezvous time, since trains and passengers were few, and therefore more noticeable, and the attention of the Gestapo—who expected nocturnal foul play— the most focused. Frieda glanced around nervously, bumping into scurrying commuters, making her way to the entrance of the shed, hoping that she hadn't been tailed.

She slowly opened its rusty, metal door.

Entering cautiously, she left the interior light off, creeping to the corner of the structure, allowing her vision to readjust to the meager light, filtering in through the lone, grease-covered window. The mountain of big crates gradually became more visible. Her eyes darted about as she listened, confirming no sign of the Gestapo.

The names of Expressionist painters whose work had been consigned to a fiery oblivion marked the crates: "CHAGALL"; "GROSZ"; "KIRCHNER"; "KLEE"; "LIEBERMAN"; "BAUER" . . .

Frieda, not surprised to see her husband's name on one of the boxes—for his early work, prior to Hitler's reign, had been considered quite avant-garde—slowly opened the lid to the crate labeled "BECKMAN," removing the cardboard stuffing from the top.

Listening carefully, she could hear the occupant's breathing. "It's only me, Frieda Bauer," she whispered to her fellow stowaway. "Are you all right? "

Peering down into the black hole, she witnessed Sarah Roth's eyes, exploding in terror. Sarah nodded, seemingly not daring to say a word, lest unfriendly ears be present.

"The train leaves in ten minutes," added Frieda. "It'll be a long ride. Don't budge until I tell you, not even at customs."

She replaced the cardboard, then found the crate marked "NOLDE."

Removing the lid and cardboard strips—porous enough to allow air to exchange with the vents in the containers—Frieda climbed in, pulling the cover over her. She then redistributed the strips of insulation over her head.

After several minutes of waiting, Frieda heard an animal scurrying about within the crate—scratching its wooden sides. By the smell, she knew a rat had infested her hiding place. It climbed onto her ankles, the tiny nails sharp. It then got trapped under her overcoat.

At that moment, she heard the door to the warehouse crash open, and the sound of jackboots hitting the floor—heading right toward her. Her heart pounded as the soldiers searched the facility.

She felt the furry creature nibbling at the inside of her leg. She suppressed a scream, biting her lip. She dare not budge, forcing her mind onto other things, such as Max's clear, blue eyes, his vibrant art, or her favorite patients.

She heard soldiers removing the lid on the box next to her, joking under their breath about the women they were meeting after their shift. Poking around into the container, they replaced the lid— seemingly finding nothing. The rat hadn't—thankfully—bitten into her, and finally scurried out through one of the vents.

She heard Train 57 blow its whistle, preparing for departure to Sachsenhausen—really, the safety of Switzerland. The thunderous sound of jackboots continued to stomp among the crates, ripping them open, searching them for contraband and stowaways. Luckily, the soldiers hadn't brought dogs with them.

Her hands shook. She heard laughter. A stream of liquid gushed against the side of her crate, the acrid scent of urine invading the vents of her stifling enclosure. Realizing that her container had been bypassed, she breathed easier.

Then, her behind thrust down against the container's wooden floor, as the soldiers picked up her crate, and carried it out of the warehouse. She heard a grating, metal door being pulled back, and then her crate crashed down against the metal floor, her rear, again, banging down against a hard bottom. As she heard other boxes plopping to the ground around her, she hoped one of those held Sarah Roth.

The train's whistle blew, only this time much louder. The door to her boxcar slammed shut. Her weight shifted back and forth, as the locomotive heaved, as it departed the station, pulling the boxcars full of doomed art with it.

Tears of relief streamed down Frieda's face, her emotion compounded by the uncertainty of Max's fate, and the fear for his life. The heavy realization that her husband had been left behind almost smothered her will to survive.

* * *

Victor lost himself among the tangles of track, just outside the station's famous dome. Tall boxcars and locomotives surrounded him in the late afternoon sun, giving him a modicum of cover from prying eyes. He approached the switch station for Train 57, resting parallel to the track that led to the Swiss frontier.

He stopped at the tall lever shooting up into the air, next to the large metal gearbox. Confirming that he was alone, he grabbed the long bar with both hands, yanking the lever toward him, the track shifting to a new position, pointing southwest instead of northeast.

As he wandered back over to his office by the main terminal, he thought about his deceased wife, murdered by Gestapo agents. Hatred, not just duty as a good German, forced him to do everything he could to defeat the Nazi juggernaut. He vowed that, one day, he'd murder Nazis by the bushel.

As he meandered up the staircase to his office, which overlooked the busy gangplanks, he noticed the black tunics, with red armbands, blending among the commuters. He ignored it, unlocking the door—noting that it had already been unlocked. In fact, the metal scratches suggested that it had been tampered with.

Victor retreated down the stairs.

The meaty face of SS Adjutant Grog met him—flanked by three SS toughs. Victor never saw coming the truncheon that smashed into his skull. His body tumbled to the bottom of the staircase, where another guard kicked the unconscious railroad man in the ribs.

The crunch, heard by passengers boarding the nearby train, even made Grog wince. "He's still breathing," said the SS adjutant. "Drag him out of here."

Chapter 72

"Submerge him again."

General Siegfried Hock sat at his table, in front of Big Gulp. Grog stood by him. Luther reclined, at his master's side. The dapper general glared at the SS guard, working the hoist over the cesspool.

"If he doesn't talk this time, kill him."

The prisoner's bleeding head dipped below the surface of the fetid water, stifling his deafening screams. The flurry of bubbles coming to the surface wouldn't happen for a couple of minutes yet, Hock figured.

This stubborn fellow is young and well built, and won't die easily. The general looked over—with some distaste—at his pudgy guest standing near him, the frumpy man observing the torture with—what appeared to Hock to be—detached, intellectual curiosity. His informer, Hock mulled, had—so far—been unproductive, and his bookish manner disgusted the crisp, decisive SS general.

"It would seem that this young man's lying," droned the informant with the beard, his words precise, his delivery plodding. "He knows more about Bauer than he's divulging. It must be blatantly obvious to you, Herr General."

The upside-down body of the prisoner—draped in the usual burlap sack, and bound at the ankles at the end of the dunking rope—squirmed and thrashed as it remained submerged, to the neck. Finally, Hock saw the burst of bubbles escape from his lungs, and the long body went limp.

"On the contrary, I think he knows nothing," insisted Hock. "This dandy—this *fire-breather*—wouldn't be trusted by Herr Bauer in any case."

"Raise him!" The general frowned at the ascending body, as if the prisoner had shown bad manners not to die quicker.

"I tell you, Bauer's up to something. It's probable that—"

Hock's buzzard eyes shifted to his guest, fondling the habitual white rose. "Shut up, Professor Stallbun."

The general sprung up from his chair, and walked over to the corpse hanging over the water. He studied the once-handsome face of Yves. "Long on bravery, short on brains."

Stallbun took a pipe from the pocket of his tweed coat and nervously lit a match.

"Put that filthy thing out!" shouted Hock. "No smoking in here. Do you want to make us all sick?"

Stallbun blew out the match, cramming the pipe back into his tweed coat. An SS guard entered the dungeon, and strode over to Grog, whispering something in his ear.

Luther growled.

"Herr General," exclaimed Grog, "we just got word. Train 57—the one headed for Sachsenhausen—was reported missing from Berlin Central Station this afternoon. Its radio must be broken."

Stallbun raised his hand to be recognized, like a student attending one of his college lectures. "May I, General?"

"Speak."

"It's sabotage. Bauer's wife has disappeared. Now the train, full of Bauer's favorite garbage, is gone too. He's traveled up to the Fuhrer's retreat to paint our esteemed leader's portrait. Is this all a coincidence?"

Hock walked over to Stallbun, peering down into his informant's eyes. "So, Professor, you think Bauer's an assassin. Is that it? Do you think that the Fuhrer's life is in danger?"

"I believe so," responded Stallbun, his hands shaking. He fumbled for his pipe. "He's down there to murder the Fuhrer! He's a decorated killer."

The professor, apparently recalling Hock's prohibition against smoking, shoved his pipe back into his coat. "I'll bet his wife stowed away on the missing train. It's headed for a neutral country, no doubt. It all fits. Bauer commits his crime, and his wife ends up safely in—let's say—Switzerland, where we can't punish her."

"Grog," snapped the general, "check out the border guards on our frontier with Switzerland. All railroad checkpoints too. Also, see if the train in question reached Sachsenhausen. Then, call up one of our men at the Fuhrer's retreat, and make sure everything's calm."

Grog clicked his heels. "Yes, my General." He tied Luther's leash to the table, then scurried to the door.

"Grog," added the general. The adjutant paused. "Prepare my car for a morning trip to Berchtesgaden. And fetch the prisoner Victor—the railroad man."

"Yes, my General."

Grog clicked his heels and left. Hock turned around and approached Professor Stallbun, as Luther growled in the background. The general glanced at his dog, then glared at his informant.

"Stallbun, my dog's hungry." Hock studied the round face in front of him. The little professor looked as though he would piss in his pants, he mused. "Don't worry, Herr Stallbun, Luther won't eat you. Not yet, anyway—"

"Please, Herr General. I've been loyal. I've helped you!"

Hock put his arms behind his back. He rocked slowly on the heels of his polished boots, mulling over his situation. "It's well past midnight. If you're right, Professor, we're probably too late, as far as the train is concerned."

Hock looked down at the sword hanging from his waist and then squeezed its handle. "The Fuhrer holds Max Bauer in high regard. I must therefore be sure before I take him into custody. We arrested your acquaintance, Victor. An informant at the station had given us a tip that something was afoot. Maybe Victor knows something."

"He won't talk," affirmed Stallbun.

Hock kneeled down to pet Luther. "Want to bet?"

* * *

"Now, Victor, you're going to tell me all about Bauer's plans, aren't you?" asked Hock.

Almost unconscious, the battered and bruised prisoner shook his head, his heavy breathing spraying blood droplets into the air.

The general strode over to Stallbun. The softness of his voice seemed to make him even more menacing. "Poor Victor needs a rest."

Grog returned.

"Well?" asked Hock. "What did you find out?"

"Everything's fine at the Eagle's Nest. The Fuhrer's pleased."

"What about the train and Frieda Bauer?"

"Nothing yet."

Hock's eyes narrowed. "Just as I thought. Bauer's too ambitious to step out of line. Still, I'd better go down there myself, to make sure all's well."

His eyes shifted to Stallbun. He looked at his watch. "It's two a.m. Grog here will interrogate this prisoner further, in the morning. You'll help my adjutant, Professor, because if Bauer causes any mischief at the Fuhrer's retreat, you're taking Victor's place."

Chapter 73

"Have you heard, Max? This morning, Germany invaded the rest of Czechoslovakia—Britain threatens war—and guarantees Poland," said Fraulein Braun.

The next day, Max had arrived at the Eagle's Nest in his painting clothes, just after lunchtime. As he unpacked his painting gear on the terrace, preparing for his new commission, Eva Braun delivered the news confirming Germany's aggression.

This news even strengthened Max's steely resolve. He stuffed more brushes into his pants pocket. He felt the tip of his silver palette knife, still there where he had placed it the day before.

As she performed her calisthenics, breathing in the fine mountain air, Eva's yellow, white, and black *trachtendirndl* outfit — the traditional country dress—reminded Max of his beach trip with Frieda, about two years before, not long after they had first met. Saddened, he ejected the thought from his mind, readying himself for his fateful mission.

"Is the Fuhrer painting this afternoon?"

"I think so." She lowered her voice. "But he may leave for Prague early."

Max pondered the bad news, as he adjusted the shoulder straps on his portable easel. It would just fit over his small rucksack.

"There's also talk that he may go down to the Berghof instead, to prepare for his trip," she added as she performed stretching exercises. "That must worry you, Max."

This uncertainty, harder to endure than the act of murder, gnawed at him. He had no choice but to carry on, and hope for the best.

"I'm off now, Eva."

Max looked at his watch—nearly two-thirty in the afternoon. Hitler usually painted at the window between four and five, he recalled, ample time for him to retrieve his rifle, and then position himself across from the study. He strode off toward the trail with his easel slung over his back, his hiking boots advancing in long strides. Glancing back, he saw Eva standing still, looking after him, her face grave.

"Steady with the brush," she shouted after him.

As he hiked, Eva intruded into his mind. She could have turned him in at any time. Despite her quiet madness, he realized, she had become a hero in her own right. She, among all those "important" Nazi men, had been the only one to consider the facts and then coolly draw the right conclusion. She hadn't been the worthless doormat, after all.

History will remember her brave resolve, he reflected, and that's why her portrait of a woman with purpose had been so important to her.

* * *

Klaus Grog was finally getting his chance to direct the torture of a prisoner. When the two SS guards dragged Victor into a quiet corner of the dungeon, the eager SS adjutant had known just what to do.

The loop of piano wire hanging from a meat hook, attached to the eight-foot ceiling, had been a favorite of the Gestapo for years. The guard moved the stool under the hook. Victor, barely able to remain standing, his hands still bound behind his back, bled from the trauma to his skull.

His head, swollen to nearly twice its normal size, displayed the telltale markings of his additional beatings all morning—the blows with batons, the punches and kicks, the scalding hot coffee thrown into his face. He still hadn't talked. But he was softening . . .

Grog scowled at Victor. "Get up on the stool!"

The prisoner defiantly fell to his knees. Grog nodded to the SS recruits. "Lift the gentleman onto the stool. That's good, now put the piano wire around his neck."

Grog moved closer, standing in front of Victor as he wobbled upon the stool. "Now, be a good little Communist. Tell me what Max Bauer's really up to."

Victor shook his head, saying nothing.

The sergeant kicked the stool out from under him.

The piano wire dug into Victor's neck—his powerful legs thrusting in order to support his weight, his bare feet not quite making the floor. He choked, his face turning red, then purple, his eyes bulging out through the red slits.

Grog moved very close to his victim, sensing weakness. "Raise him!" he screamed at the guards. They replaced the stool, and then hoisted Victor back onto it, the piano wire going slack.

"Tell!"

Victor sobbed. He shook convulsively.

"Tell me, or I'll hang your old hag girlfriend, Frau von Stoltz, right in front of you."

Victor let out a deep groan. "All—right."

When Victor had finished his confession, Grog tortured him again, to make him talk more.

Sure that there was noting left to tell, the SS adjutant pulled his pistol, and unloaded it into Victor's head. "Drag him away. Bring in Frau von Stoltz."

Grog walked over to the phone hanging on the wall. "Connect me with General Hock at the Fuhrer's retreat—the Eagle's Nest—hurry!"

Grog knew that he would be well rewarded for his day's work. "Hello, I must speak to General Hock immediately . . . What—he hasn't arrived yet? . . . The general should get there any minute. Make sure you have him call me as soon as he gets there—it's vital."

Grog slammed down the receiver. He smiled when he saw Frau von Stoltz arrive. He looked up at the piano wire. "Well, Frau, take off that wooden cross around your neck, and put that on." The adjutant pointed at the noose.

She looked up at it and screamed.

Grog laughed. It was almost the dinner hour, so for this aristocratic, treasonous sow—he vowed to himself—it would be a quick death.

Chapter 74

Max removed the rifle from under the pile of pine branches, right where he had stashed it the day before. He found the path, lined by large pines, that had offered the best shot through the study window. Hitler's huge picture window—now a small, yellowish rectangle in the fading sunlight—would frame the target nicely.

Max preferred standing—rather than a prone, aiming position—because it allowed freer head mobility and caused less irritation to the scar on his neck. Cover wasn't an issue, not yet anyway.

Standing behind the easel, which served as his stabilizer, he aimed the Mauser.

He adjusted his calibrations a tad—the best he could without trial shots—to accommodate for the longer distance. Peering through the telescopic lens, he redirected the muzzle in tiny gradations, the circular field of vision creeping over the study's white, exterior wall, splashed with orange by the receding sun. It came to rest on the glass of the window—colored an egg-yolk hue by the study's lamps—the details of its interior clearly illuminated.

Cursing his bad luck, Max saw that the white curtains had been drawn slightly, the view now limited to a smaller square of the target area, rather than the full width of the window. A voice in the distance, then the faint sound of footsteps on dry leaves, signaled an intruder. The sound got louder.

Max's eyes—outside the lens—searched in the sound's direction, peering through branches of scrawny trees about fifty meters away. Good news—it was only one of Goering's stewards hauling a deer, hiking back down toward the retreat.

Max resumed his scoping. As he lowered the field of vision, he found the window again, with the interior of the study—through the bright opening—made even more visible, from dusk transitioning to night.

Thank God, there was now a bright light on inside Hitler's study—but no Hitler!

Max focused on the easel standing next to the sill. On it rested a half-painted image of a young, blonde woman with no clothes on—looking very much like Eva Braun. He witnessed Eva herself pass the window, about two feet inside the glass, wearing nothing. Then she disappeared.

In reflex, Max raised his head from the lens, noticing a floodlight—attached to the side of the study's wall—suddenly activating. At this distance, the light barely penetrated his surroundings, but it was enough to reveal his position to the sentries, if they made their rounds on the retreat's terrace. Max recalled that a sniper's reflected glass and metal had doomed many a marksman during the war.

He hit the ground with his rifle. Stabilizing the rifle on a large stone, he squinted through the lens again, trying to get more relaxed and comfortable. There was still no sign of the Fuhrer and, almost as bad, no more sign of Eva Braun—since at this hour he expected the two of them to be together.

Then he saw the headlights of Hitler's Mercedes-Benz—its cover up—passing down the rear service road, from the retreat. Was it possible that his target had left early for Prague, as Eva had warned, or had moved on to the Berghof?

He glanced at his watch—almost five-thirty!

Soon, the dictator's customary painting time would have passed. He must also make the shot before he was missed back at the retreat. Plein-air landscapes were usually not painted at night.

He thought about Frieda, realizing, with great relief, that she had been well on her way to safety for hours now. He nervously checked and rechecked his rifle settings and his ammo—no problems there.

He re-sighted—nothing in the window. *Where is that bastard?*

* * *

Siegfried Hock stood on the terrace of the Eagle's Nest, enjoying the last of the blood red sunset, now only a small halo outlining the surrounding mountains. He liked how his silver sword glowed in the fading rays. Absent the holster at the side of his jet-black tunic, his trim waist—and the white strap around it—made the sword appear even more impressive.

Expecting his phone connection to Grog any second, which he had ordered put through to Berlin when informed that he was urgently needed, Hock welcomed the intrusion by the attendant. The young man carried a phone with a long extension. Holding its cradle for the general, he handed Hock the receiver.

As the general listened, the taste of the hunt—and the exhilaration of the ultimate blood sport—consumed him. He had the same feeling as when he had volunteered to fly fighter planes in Spain, plunging him into harrowing dogfights with his shiny, new Messerschmitt. He gripped the handle of his sword, squeezing it until his hand ached, as he listened to Grog's details of Victor's confession.

He placed the receiver down gently upon the receiver, glaring at his minion. "Where's the painter Max Bauer?"

The attendant pointed into the void of the purple mountains. "He's out there, painting a landscape, sir."

"At this hour?" commented Hock.

"He should be all right," offered the young man, "he knows the trails—he hunted all though there with Reich Minister Goering yesterday."

So, that's how he got his rifle past security. He must've stashed it out there during the hunt. Hock's eyes frisked the labyrinth of trails and pine forests in the distance, barely visible in the traces of dwindling light. It reminded him of his English maze-garden, back at Berlin headquarters.

Bauer's out there somewhere, aiming his rifle. This makes it even better, mused Hock.

He thought that he had pegged the wily artist from the start. He had been wrong. He had been *humiliated.* This man wasn't a misguided, but loyal, German. Nor was he a Nordic genius who only needed firm direction and order to showcase his great, Aryan talent. Rather, he was a *traitor*—degenerate scum through and through.

Worst of all, the general realized that he had lost his battle of nerves with Max Bauer, for obviously his campaign of terror and wits hadn't been enough to frighten him.

This betrayal is personal—and I'll repay his treachery, personally.

This time, I'm going to kill him.

Moreover, Hock vowed to return the humiliation and with the style of a true SS hero. Bauer's death would be vicious and without dignity—but *sporting*. Too bad there wasn't any music, he lamented.

Presently, the fastidious general quietly traversed the forested trails behind the Fuhrer's retreat, his gleaming sword ready.

Chapter 75

Max lay with his rifle perched upon the stone, his finger ready to pull the trigger. A soft, slow squeeze, and it would all be over, he thought. Still, no sign of Hitler . . .

Hock crept over the trail, making as little noise as possible, his sword drawn, ready to whack Max's head from his shoulders. The stealthy pursuits of his prisoners in the maze had served him well—quite the fortuitous training, he mused.

From a distant hill—at the same eye level as the retreat, but at a more advantageous viewpoint—Hock had quickly narrowed down the likely trails used by Max, in his quest to kill his prey. The right spot had to be directly across from the Fuhrer's study window, situated at the rear of the retreat, which faced a dark forest.

Bauer would have chosen this same perch, really the only one possible. Hitler seldom went on the veranda, he recalled, and only during the day—surrounded by guards.

Hock then noted a particular path, with decent cover and a perfect location for a headshot through the glass, which he knew, despite his urgings to the contrary, had not been installed as bulletproof. The range looked to be about five hundred meters.

He furtively made his way along that trail.

* * *

Max looked at his watch, which now read seven. It was increasingly unlikely that Hitler would show. In a few more minutes, he'd have to abandon his bivouac, stash the rifle, and then head back to the retreat, facing stern enquiries by the guards.

He pulled the cloth from his pants pocket and wiped the telescopic lens, the misty night air having coated his sight. He peered through the lens.

Damn! The light in the study had been turned off!

* * *

Hock thought he heard some rustling just ahead of him, at about thirty meters. It could be an animal, he thought, but he doubted it. He made sure his steps were extra light, his sword cocked behind his head, ready to whack his prey.

He fingered through low-hanging branches, carefully navigating the twists and turns of the treacherous path ahead of him. Then, where the forest thinned out a bit, the view of the Eagle's Nest appeared in the far distance, and the tiny window—bright yellow—offered a fair view through its glass.

That's when the general saw—in the moonlight—the outline of a man lying just off the trail—aiming a rifle behind a large stone—just before the edge of the cliff. *This must be Bauer. Yes! His rifle's perched upon the rock.*

Hock sneaked up behind him, his sword ready . . .

* * *

The evening mist had filmed Max's sight again.

He reached into his pocket, grasping his cloth, feeling the cold steel of his pallet knife next to it . . .

He glimpsed the reflection of steel beside him. The sound of ruffling leaves signaled attack. With lightning speed, his hand reflexively retrieved the knife from his pocket . . .

Spinning around, Max could just see the blade of the sword initiating its downward trajectory, straight toward his neck, whereupon he thrust the knife up diagonally, through the side of Hock's slender neck, driving the steel tip until it emerged from the general's opposite ear . . .

The sword fell to the ground as Hock stumbled backwards, grabbing his throat, wobbling in his death throes, like a top out of energy. His eyes wide with surprise, he hissed some words that included Max's mother and a biological function, then plummeted from the hundred-meter cliff, bouncing along the way along the sharp boulders.

The glow of profound victory warmed Max through and through as he realized that he had just killed the fiendish Siegfried Hock, second in evil only to the monster that he hoped to kill next.

Max spun toward his rifle and resumed his fully prone position, feeling the stickiness of the general's warm blood on his trigger finger. He sited, peering into the yellow window . . .

Someone had turned the study light back on!

Through the lens, Max saw the man clearly: toothbrush mustache; dark hair waxed to the side; medium height; Nazi armband . . .

The field of view revealed the hypnotic stare—albeit from an angle. Max pulled the trigger gently.

The glass exploded, the object behind it disappearing into a pink cloud of blood.

Just like the war, Max realized, the pink cloud.

Hitler's dead!

He sprung up from the ground, slung the rifle over his shoulder, and then charged up the trail through the forest into the nothingness of the dark Alps, churning his legs as fast as he could. Along the way, he thought about all that beautiful art, saved from the incinerators.

Long ago, it had saved *him*. Now, he believed, he—and his dear wife—had saved *it*. Each stride would bring him that much closer to Frieda and his cherished paintings.

Epilogue

Berlin, June 1945:

But Hitler hadn't been killed. It was Bruno Meier—the Fuhrer's look-alike chauffeur—whom Max had seen through the window and whom he had mistakenly assassinated instead. Since then, Berlin had been reduced to ruins by Allied bombs.

Shortly after the war's end, Frieda Bauer climbed out of the Ford army staff car, in front of a dilapidated building, riddled with bullet holes. It didn't have a roof. Tarpaulins covered the enclosure instead.

Stunned by the hundred-foot piles of brick and stone that had once been a fashionable Berlin neighborhood, Frieda's careworn brown eyes shifted from the late bloom of the few standing cherry trees lining the dark street, to the makeshift sign on the structure's facade: "RESCUED EXPRESSONIST ART EXHIBITION."

Frieda fondly remembered that Max had loved cherry tree blossoms and loved to paint them. So cold that she could see her breath, she pulled her camel-hair overcoat together and buttoned it up to her neck, her tufts of dark-blonde hair—now with a few streaks of grey—falling to her shoulders.

Major Garrett, a tall and skinny young man in a brown U.S. Army uniform—which nearly fell off his gaunt frame—jumped out of the driver's side. He scurried around the car to meet Frieda, standing on the dirty, litter-strewn sidewalk.

"You should've let me open that door, Dr. Bauer. The general wants me to take real good care of you. Shucks, this art wouldn't even be here if it weren't for you and . . . " He hung his head, "Sorry ma'am. I know they're still looking for him, and they'll find him, you bet they will."

"Don't be sorry." Frieda forced a smile. "You see, Major, Max won. That's what this place signifies. Much more. Don't you think?"

"Shall we go inside?" he asked.

Then Frieda noticed the music, which she hadn't heard in twelve years, filtering over from the exhibition. The melody from *The Three-Penny Opera*, by Bertholt Brecht and Kurt Weil—both victims of Nazis persecution—played softly.

Her eyes fixed upon the direction of the lilting song, as if in a trance. "Hear that, Major? That's the Berlin I want to remember."

He took Frieda's arm and escorted her into the exhibition of German Expressionist art—that had been saved from Nazi incinerators six years before and stored in Switzerland since.

* * *

"Do you like it, Major?"

She took off her overcoat and folded it under her arm, the portable heaters inside providing ample warmth. This stiff, Wisconsin farm boy, nice, but obviously uninterested in art, looked at the oil painting, as if sizing up one of his farm mares.

The commanding general of the U.S. Sector Occupation had assigned the major to her as a driver, and this bored escort probably would rather be off at the USO canteen, square-dancing, she surmised. Standing quietly beside her, he stared up at the image on the wall, his expression blank. Then he shook his head.

Frieda looked around at the small number of other patrons. Some had tears streaming down their cheeks. Others laughed. A few also looked bored.

Poles, Russians, Americans, Germans, French: You could tell each by their uniforms or the ragged attire. At least this time, she mused, the lighting and framing—unlike in the Degenerate Art Exhibition of 1937—enhanced the visual experience and didn't detract from it.

Then Frieda recognized the other painting. She observed it from across the room. She enjoyed the familiar, colorful form. Placing her arm under Major Garrett's, she gently guided him over to Max's favorite piece.

The young man's vapid eyes landed upon the painting. "Your husband's?"

"Yes, indeed."

They stopped in front of it, five meters away. Frieda imbibed the fluidly vibrant hues of the yellow pig and the purple straw. The wide smile of the pig enchanted her.

She examined the label affixed to the wall, next to the painting.

"*THE SMILING PIG,* BY MAX BAUER; GERMAN EXPRESSIONIST PAINTER, 1920; SAVED IN 1939 FROM NAZI DESTRUCTION."

And who knows, Frieda mulled wistfully, *maybe Max hasn't really died. Maybe he's a prisoner or unconscious in a hospital somewhere. No one really knows for sure.* She had been turning over every stone imaginable, trying to find him.

"Look, the pig's smiling," blurted the major. "Funny, but why?"

Frieda, snapping out of her reverie, caught herself, not wanting to respond abrasively. "Well, I don't know, exactly. There's the outside reality to *see,* and then there's the inner reality to *feel.*" That's how Max would have put it, she thought.

Sadness overcoming her, she walked away to view another piece.

The young man followed her. "You know, ma'am, I farm in the Midwest. I've never seen a pig smile before."

She realized that he was serious.

Frieda thought of what Hitler had once been quoted as saying—the same remark as the major had just made. "No? Well, Major, I suppose you haven't."

"I guess it's cute," he said gently. "I'm sure he's a great artist and all. He was your husband, but I'm sorry, I just don't know if I like it."

The man honestly said the way he felt. It pleased her to discover that he thought enough about Max's art to have any opinion at all. His honest face flushed pink. *This sweet man is embarrassed by his own brashness,* she realized.

She liked this plainspoken soldier from the American heartland.

"I guess the point of all this, Major Garrett, is that you don't *have* to like it."

More than any other event, this simple encounter, symbolized for Frieda, the true end of the dreadful war.

The major smiled. All was good.

Frieda fought back the growl in her stomach and looped her arm through his elbow. "But I must tell you now that I'm famished. If you escort me back to the officer's mess, I'll buy you dinner."

He saluted her, and they laughed. They left the exhibit, she finally leaving everything behind, except the determination to find Max.

www.ingramcontent.com/pod-product-compliance
Lightning Source LLC
Chambersburg PA
CBHW072205170626
46813CB00003B/801